GEMS OF FIRE

DIANE E. SAMSON

Diane E. Samson

GEMS OF FIRE Copyright © 2022 DIANE E. SAMSON

All Rights Reserved

This is a work of fiction. Names, places, characters, and events are fictitious in every regard. Any similarities to actual events and persons, living or dead, are purely coincidental. Any trademarks, service marks, product names, or named features are assumed to be the property of their respective owners, and are used only for reference. There is no implied endorsement if any of these terms are used. Except for review purposes, the reproduction of this book in whole or part, electronically or mechanically, constitutes a copyright violation.

Cover Art Designed by Cora Graphics

www.dianesamsonauthor.com

For Hannah

Chapter 1

Anna squinted as the afternoon sun burned the sod on the large oval track. Her fingers clenched the railing of her father's box as the horses flew around the last turn. A big brown colt surged just at the end and won by a neck. She released the rail and turned toward new guests gathering for the final race, the Landseer Cup.

One more race and then it was her turn. She quit gnawing on the inside of her cheek as an ache moved to her chest. The start drew closer with every thump of her heart. This race was the beginning of a new life for the Princess of Sutherland. This was where she proved her worth. She would be next to her brother, leading knights and men, not sitting around like a stupid court ornament.

Today she would silence the sneers of her father's advisor, Seamus. Even her father would see her as more than a little girl. They would take note as she rode Farley, the young stallion no man had been able to tame. Anna would not only ride him, she would win as Farley ran all those smug men into the ground. Her lips lifted into a slight smile. She drank the rest of her punch and set her glass on a servant's tray. It would be her first day of respect.

The air buzzed with the low rumble of people finding their seats. Women flapped their fans and exclaimed at the heat. Men exchanged last minute coins before the horses stepped on the track to run for the ultimate prize—the golden Landseer Cup. A rowdier crowd gathered at the rails where men downed large mugs of ale. The tangy scent of it drifted upward and turned Anna's stomach. She wished she had worn a dress that didn't cut into her waist.

Anna glanced down at the oval turf once again. Horses pranced onto the track for the next to last race with gleaming coats and flashy jockey's colors on their backs. Flags emblazoned with Sunderland's seal—a bright orange flame set against a white mountain—flapped above the riders' heads. It was almost time to go.

The man next to her interrupted Anna's thoughts.

"Anna, you have an eye for horses. Do you think Prince Lewis will win the Cup again?" asked Count Jadran. "His horses are always fast, but I was honestly hoping someone from Sunderland would win this year." He nodded back toward her father's seats. It was no secret winning this race was a conquest the king had never achieved.

"Lewis is hard to bet against," Anna said, heat rising in her cheeks. "But you never know, we might have a trick up our sleeves this year."

He raised an eyebrow. "A trick?"

"I heard at the stables there might be a last-minute entry. A desert horse, I think, but running for Sunderland." She flicked her eyes toward the stables where she had snuck Farley in before dawn. She should be on her way by now.

"Who told you that?" His voice softened.

"Some stable boys, but you know how they talk." Anna shrugged while beads of sweat trickled down her neck. Jadran was a perfect gentleman. She always liked the honest way the skin crinkled at the corner of his eyes when he smiled. She didn't mind giving him a betting tip, but she was running out of time. *Go away, Count Jadran.*

Jadran nodded, jingling gold coins in his hands.

"Your father needs a win. I hope he gets it today." He sauntered toward the betting table, and Anna exhaled her relief. She would get her father the win and pull him out of the twelve-year pit he's been in, ever since her mother died. He would be proud when Farley won. He would laugh. He would embrace her. He would send Seamus away. *Or it could make matters worse.* She shook her head and shoved the doubts down.

Her heart skipped a beat when some of the horses left their stalls. Grooms and riders scurried around them. Anna's stomach dropped. The time had come. She glanced at her father who was chatting with the royal court and flicked her fan in front of her nose. Her older brother, Stefan, the crown prince, was dashing in his dress-hunting tunic and surrounded by three young ladies eyeing for his attention.

"I need a little air," she said to no one in particular and slipped to the back of the landing while the crowd moved forward. No one seemed to notice as she crept down the stairs.

Anna fanned herself as she walked toward the stable, trying to cover her face as much as possible.

I have to at least try. The sweat dripping down her back was as much from nerves as the heat. Anna stopped by the entry office and gave the official the papers and the money to run. The man raised his eyebrows in surprise, but handed Anna her number, nine.

"The horse's name?"

Anna hesitated. Farley was well-known.

"Midnight. His name is Midnight."

"And the owner?"

"King Vilipp."

The man's eyebrows lowered. "The king?"

"It's a surprise." She held her finger to her mouth and winked. "Don't tell unless he wins."

The man frowned as Anna hurried toward Farley, waiting in his stall.

I have to be calm for his sake.

The earthy smell of horse hit her as she stepped inside the stables. Her heart pounded as she hurried to his stall. Farley thrust his long, black nose over the stall door and snorted, blowing sweet, hay-scented breath toward her.

She crept into the dingy stall, hid behind Farley's huge body and slipped out of her long, heavy dress. She scrambled into the small rider's uniform she had stolen…well, borrowed and stashed in Farley's stall. Her hands shook so much that she could barely fasten the pants and pull on the black boots. Though it probably wasn't necessary, she wrapped fabric around her small chest to look more like a boy. She braided her hair, tied it with a ribbon, pinned it into a high bun and pushed it up into her hat.

A shrill whinny made Anna jump. The other horses neared the track.

Hurry.

Anna's hands flew as she saddled and bridled Farley. She pulled the hat down low over her eyes as they stepped out of the stall and toward the track.

Farley snorted and tossed his head as they neared the other horses—and the race ahead. Only those with the fastest horses in the surrounding kingdoms dared compete for the golden cup. The prize lay in the hands of Prince Lewis of Durham, the kingdom bordering Sunderland on the northwest. His chestnut horse, Kaspar, would run again this year. Anna glanced at the officials as Lewis handed the cup over. It would soon belong to this year's winner. She could almost see her father holding the cup in triumph.

We'll win today, Father.

Most of the horses were already ahead of her on their way to the start. She stopped a stable boy to give her a leg up and adjusted the number on her back.

Anna moved Farley onto the track. He danced in place. She tightened her grip on the reins, feeling his energy pulse through them. Farley's sides were tight. He jumped at a tap of her leg.

"Easy, boy. Not yet," she said, attempting to calm the horse, but her shaking voice betrayed her. She wiped sweaty hands on her pants one at a time. The big horse broke into a springy trot and pulled on the bit. His nicker vibrated through her legs, and her calves tightened around his sides, ready for him to jump sideways or bolt. She let him move into the mass of horses and warm up. A faint wet-horse odor reached her nose. Flecks of foam were already on Farley's neck.

Farley's head shot straight up, and a quiver went through his whole body. He, too, had caught the scent of competition. He half-reared and shook his head. Anna pointed him toward the start and squeezed him into a canter.

Anna saw a gate open just to her right. A man carried a flag onto the track, leaving the gate open behind him. She could bolt right through it.

It's your last chance, a voice said to her.

No. Anna answered. *Father will see what I can do.*

Take it! No one would ever know you were here.

No! I'm going to finish. She swallowed hard, blocked out the crowd, and cantered past the gate. There was no turning back now.

Anna leaned forward onto Farley's neck, pressing her hands onto his black mane. She let him canter on, loosening up his legs. The start was half a lap away. He pulled on the bit again and Anna was forced to use a see-saw rein to slow him down.

Not yet, Farley.

His chin ducked toward his chest and his stride shortened to springy hops as he collected his energy. The start neared and Anna managed to get Farley slowed down and lined up next to the other prancing horses. Farley's pulse thudded against her calves. A red flag went up. Hundreds of eyes fell upon it.

The flag fell.

A bell rang.

The horses lunged forward. Farley's surge of power left Anna a little behind in the saddle. She grabbed his mane and pulled herself up. Farley galloped a few lengths behind the leader who was eating up ground with great strides. Tears streamed down Anna's face as the wind whipped into her eyes. The hindquarters of the gray horse in front rose and fell and were getting ever closer. She tried to slow Farley down. He shook his head. *No, boy! You'll tire out at this speed.* Finally, he relented, and the gray horse stayed about one length ahead around the first turn. Farley swerved at the crowd's roar as they flew by the stands the first time.

"Easy, Farley." Anna steadied him.

The gray horse was flying now and surged out ahead of them into the next turn. Farley lengthened his strides and caught up. Dodging flying sod, Anna tried to sit still to let Farley settle into his pace. She kept Farley right on the gray horse, who was running easily. Anna checked Farley again to save his speed for the finish. She glanced behind her. A couple horses were running a few strides back, including last year's winner, Kaspar. Anna hoped they kept their distance. She knew if one of them even slightly clipped Farley's heels, they would both go down. She squinted, shoving the terrible image of falling horses out of her mind.

Focus, Anna!

She and Farley were seconds from beginning the next turn. The horses behind her edged closer. The gray was slowing and drifted to the outside. Anna took a chance for the short trip around the inside turn and pulled Farley to the rail. Just as his head drew alongside the gray horse's hindquarters, there was a sudden rush on the outside. A brown horse moved up alongside the gray and bumped him over.

Anna's heart stopped for a moment as she yelled and tugged on her reins. There was no place for Farley to go! She instinctively leaned back, pulling hard on his mouth. She prayed Farley could slow down before he tripped over the gray's flying hooves.

Farley grunted, but responded, pulling up just as the big gray horse swung in front of them again. Now the gray was tiring fast. Anna heard a sudden flurry of hoof beats behind her as they headed down the backstretch. Farley bobbled and slowed his pace.

Kaspar pulled up beside them, and the gray continued to slow. Anna would have to wait for Kaspar to pass before she could get to the outside. Kaspar's rider seemed to understand Anna's predicament. *Trapped!* Kaspar would wait to finish passing the gray until it was too late for Farley to charge. Anna made a quick decision and again pulled on the reins for Farley to slow. The great horse protested, leaning into the bit. He seemed to want to run right over the gray horse.

"Easy, Farley!" she yelled, pulling hard. The big horse consented, shaking his head in fury. He pinned his ears flat against his head. At last, Kaspar's hindquarters cleared Farley's head, and Anna pulled Farley to the outside as they went around the final turn. Farley ran wide, and Anna tugged on her left rein to straighten him out. Kaspar was now several lengths ahead of them and gaining. The finish loomed in the distance. *Does he have time?*

"Go, boy, go!" she called. Farley lunged forward, his great strides eating up ground at a remarkable rate. He surged on. In a matter of seconds, Kaspar was right beside them. Farley paused and then shot ahead of the chestnut. At once, a black horse on the outside had his nose almost on Anna's right leg.

"Run!" she yelled.

The other rider went for his whip and edged his horse closer. He was now at Anna's shoulder. Then Farley saw him. He turned his head to the side and pinned his ears, swerving a bit. Anna tried to correct him, but he still drifted to the outside. Pulling on her left rein, Anna turned his nose back toward the finish. He stretched his neck forward and thundered on. The black horse's head disappeared. Farley was pulling away. With every stride the hoof beats behind them grew softer while the crowd roared. The next thing Anna saw was a red flag waving. They had won. Anna gasped for air as joyful tears slid down her cheeks.

"Good boy, Farley," she whispered into his neck as she patted him. Nothing mattered now. Farley had won, and everyone would know he was the fastest horse alive.

Anna slowed Farley to a canter and moved him toward the winner's stand. His heart pounded against her legs as she gripped his heaving sides. She glanced up at the box where her father was watching. Hundreds of eyes peered down on her. Anna's throat tightened. She shuddered as she saw a bustle of people talking and pointing at her, followed by a rumble of exclamation. A voice was shouting.

"Number nine! The owner of number nine!"

The owner was supposed to come down to the horse and accept the cup. No one was approaching, except a group of soldiers. Anna knew two of them, Frederick and Edwin.

Please, Father. Accept this.

"Halt!" one said as he grabbed Farley's reins. Farley half-reared. "You aren't properly entered in this race!"

Anna mumbled something as she tumbled off Farley's back. Her tired legs buckled as she hit the ground. Strong arms grabbed her on each side.

"Let me loosen his girth!" she snapped, wiggling free.

"How did you get in here?" one soldier demanded. Frederick, she thought. "What horse is this? Because it looks a lot like the princess's horse. If you've stolen him—"

"Keep him walking!" Anna thrust her finger in the soldier's face. "He's just run the race of his life!"

"You should be a little more worried about what's going to happen to you than cooling out your horse," spat Frederick. "And I'll teach you to speak to a soldier of the king that way!"

"Wait! Let me explain—"

He raised his hand to offer a blow, but the other man pulled her back out of range. Her head thudded against his chest.

"Let's just take him to the king," he said.

A crowd gathered. Edwin jostled her under her father's seat and shoved her to her knees.

"Speak, boy!" Edwin ripped off her hat and tossed it to her lap. Anna's golden hair dropped past her shoulders, the braid unraveling in a mess. A gasp escaped the crowd. The men jumped back and bowed before her.

"Princess Anna. We had no idea."

Anna stood, twisting the hat in her hands. She cringed as she heard the head race official scrambling to understand what had happened.

"Who entered this horse?" the track official boomed to the crowd. "Who is the owner of this horse?"

The king stood.

"I am." He glared at Anna.

The crowd quieted. The race official fell to one knee.

The king continued, "And I will take responsibility for this. Because the horse was not properly entered, we will give the cup to the fine horse who placed second. An excellent race, Answurth." He motioned to the big black horse's owner.

Lord Answurth retrieved the cup from the official's hand to subdued applause.

Anna wanted to close her eyes. She stole a quick glance at her stoned-faced father, who motioned for her to be taken away.

He nodded to Lord Seamus, who was whispering furiously into his ear. Stefan appeared at her side.

"Get your hands off her!" he demanded and led Anna away from the crowd.

"Well, that was quite a ride." His face sobered. "I wish I

could help you, but Father won't be light on this one." He led her to the king's carriage, soldiers in tow.

"But why?" asked Anna. "He finally won the Cup." She winced at the thought of the coming punishment.

Stefan flushed a bit and squeezed her shoulder. "I'm on your side, but his own daughter, riding in the race?"

The soldiers opened the carriage door. Anna glanced back at Farley. Bart, his groom, was leading him to the barn. "I needed to prove this, Stefan. Do you understand?"

"I suppose. I just wish you hadn't."

"I for once wanted him to see me—not Mother," Anna said.

"Well, I'm sure this stunt accomplished that. Mother never would have done anything so—"

"Stupid."

"I wasn't going to say that." He lifted his hand toward her for a moment but let it fall to his side.

"You might as well have. With his love of the races, I hoped I'd win his heart along with the cup. But now I see it's impossible." Her heart fell as she climbed into the carriage.

Stefan stepped up to the door. "Not impossible, Anna. He just wants you to be respectable, honorable. It's time."

"So he can marry me off."

"Of course not." He frowned. "Is there something else wrong?"

Anna's throat tightened. Her eyes filled with tears as she shook her head. She wanted so much to tell him everything—but her mouth refused. She managed a small smile. "Thank you, Stefan, for coming to me," she said, choking out the words.

He stepped back as the driver clucked to the horses.

Chapter 2

The carriage bounced along the winding road toward the castle as Anna considered Stefan. He'd always watched out for Anna since their mother had passed away when Anna was only four years old. She closed her eyes and still felt his young arms holding her as Mother's coffin was laid to rest.

"It'll be all right, Anna," he had whispered to her. "I'm here for you."

Stefan had been true to his word, except now he traveled with the army for months at a time. In addition, as crown prince, he trekked to every part of the kingdom, negotiating with dukes and lords, making sure the king still had their allegiance. When he returned, he spent long days participating in war strategy exercises with the generals. He would make a good king, but the best thing about him was he always took time for Anna when he could—even a moment for a wink, a smile, a quick banter.

She stared out the carriage window, losing focus as they passed the horse pastures where foals pranced, reared, and slept around their grazing mothers. One peeked under his mother's belly at the noisy carriage going by, but Anna hardly noticed.

The horses pulled the carriage through the outer gate, a small opening in the towering, thick stone wall that surrounded the castle grounds in a semi-circle from the bank of the river. A small village resided within the outer wall, where the tradesmen set up their shops and bartered with farmers. The village air was always tinged with the scent of tilled earth, hay, chickens, horses and manure.

The carriage horses startled as a young girl bolted out of a vendor's stall, squealing as a boy her age chased her with some creature in his hand. Anna glanced out at the single inn in the village. The innkeeper's wife was still there, loading up wagons of food and supplies for the festival to be held under the stars by the track later that evening. Anna thought of the singing, the food, the drinking and the dancing under the tents by the track. All would be missed. And for what? *Nothing*. She bumped her head on the back of the seat.

As they neared the castle, Anna didn't admire the manicured flower and hedge gardens where walkways brought visitors to fountains and sculptures. She preferred wildflowers instead of those pruned to perfection here. The benches and gazebos were empty. Everyone was at the track except the dutiful soldiers guarding the grounds from a small watchtower. Only a few horses remained in the great stone stables where Farley and about a hundred of the king's finest horses slept. She supposed Farley would eventually make his way back there in the evening.

The stone castle rested on the other side of the Alpin River, backing to a tall mountainside composed of white rock. Guards lowered a long bridge to allow people to enter and leave the castle. It was the only way in and easily guarded.

The carriage stopped in front of the bridge. The chains whined and squealed as the thick oak bridge lowered, protesting its enormous weight. It landed with a solid thud.

Anna knew most people in the kingdom thought of this place as paradise. To her, it was a prison. She could never escape the scorning disapproval of her father and his royal counsel. Anna dropped her eyes and stepped out of the carriage.

"Do you need any assistance, Your Highness?" asked one of the guards as she paused before the bridge. Fatigue washed through her as the river bubbled underneath.

"No, thank you."

"Princess Anna, may I be allowed to speak?"

"Of course, Frederick."

"I truly did not know it was you. Can you forgive me?"

"There's no need." She walked on, thinking of the blow he'd almost given her at the track. She glanced over her shoulder. "Don't worry about your head. It will still be attached in the morning."

Which is more than I can hope for my own. Her legs swayed as she crossed the bridge to the cold, quiet castle. She glanced to the white mountain behind it. The setting sun cast long shadows on the rock, turning the stone castle and mountain into a patchwork of grey and white, smooth and rough. If only there were a way out.

Cool, damp air surrounded her as she stepped through the door. It was a welcome relief from the heat and sweat of the track. Her dirty boots clicked on the quiet stone hall as she made her way toward her room. She paused a few steps from an open doorway as a hint of perfume greeted her. Giggling poured from the room. She raised her eyebrows, surprised the court ladies weren't all at the track. The last thing she wanted was an encounter with—

"You! Servant girl! Come in here, my hem is coming out of my dress and I must—" Arissa cut off her words as Anna stepped in the room. Arissa's perfect green eyes, rimmed with gold, widened in surprise before quickly turning to something like scorn.

"Your Highness," she said, barely dipping her head. Arissa

wasn't taller than Anna, but the way she held her chin and peered down her nose always made Anna feel smaller. She was the daughter of a great lord and was at court by her father's invitation. The king needed his allegiance.

"I'm surprised to see you here," Anna said to the room of ladies who were obviously getting ready for the feast and festival. "Most everyone has already left."

"We were hot at the track and decided to come back and change into fresh dresses," Lady Selina said as she twirled a lock of dark hair around her finger. "Father let us take the carriage."

"Is that what you wore to the race?" Arissa asked in a barely civil tone. One of the other girls lightly snorted and another giggled. Anna forced her chin up. She opened her mouth to speak, but Lady Gavriella interrupted.

"Oh, my! You rode in the Cup," she said. As lady of the famed equestrians of Durham and first cousin of Prince Lewis, she would recognize the racing leathers and dirt-smudged face. The girls' eyes traveled over her in shock. Anna curled her fingers toward her palms to hide the dirt under her nails. Lady Gavriella's eyes shone with a flicker of admiration. "My cousin, how did he fare?"

"He came in third," Anna said. "I beat them all."

"You won?" Arissa asked. "But how—

Just then a dark-haired girl of fifteen bounced into the room from the dressing area wearing a beautiful deep-blue silk dress. It fit her like a glove, and she giggled as she twirled toward the ladies. Anna was a little jealous of how she filled the top out.

"Lady Arissa, look!" she said. "I told you I could pull it off." She curtsied before the girls. She frowned at Arissa's wide-eyed stare and turned to Anna. "Oh, Your Highness." She dropped into a quick bow as her face drained of color.

It was Frances, Anna's maid, wearing the dress Anna was supposed to wear that evening. Anna's blood boiled. These ladies, especially Arissa, never missed a chance to mock and stab Anna in the back, but Frances was her maid and supposed to be on her side. Anna had thought Frances was her friend, but here she was playing dress up with the court's biggest snob and gossip, Arissa.

"I'm so sorry, Your Highness. I was trying it on to see if I fixed the top right," she whispered. "I'll bring it right down to your room."

Anna gritted her teeth. Frances's chest bulged out of the top as she bowed. She had indeed made it smaller to fit Anna's more modest bust line.

"Don't bother, Frances. You can wear it yourself, burn it, or cut it up into tiny, little bits and throw it into the river for all I care." *Or cram it down Arissa's throat.*

Anna turned on her heel and stormed out. She expected Frances to come running after her, but no footsteps came. She only heard echoes of harsh whispers and more giggles. Deep down, she knew she could go toe-to-toe with Arissa or any of the foolish girls of the court. But her heart thundered for more than tight dresses and rouge.

She stomped toward her room. *Frances could well go in my place.* If she did, Anna would seriously consider having her whipped. Someone needed to be. *It will probably be me.*

She kicked open her room's heavy door and was hit with the scent of lavender and jasmine. Mary was waiting for her with a steaming pot of the herbs over the fire. How did she always know what she needed? Mary took one look at Anna and instructed a servant girl, Lacy, to help prepare Anna a hot, scented bath. While they worked, Anna stared out the window, across the river, toward the races. She jerked her fingers through the knots in her hair. She wanted to pull it out.

"It's ready. It'll ease your tight muscles, my dear," Mary said.

"Thank you. You may go now. You, too, Lacy." She did appreciate her nurse, but she couldn't stand to look anyone in the eye right now. Frustration pulsed through her with every heartbeat. She had dreamed for months about this day. Her father ought to have been proud his daughter had ridden such a race. She should be celebrating at the day-long carnival, laughing with everyone tonight at the party, and dancing with noble men of all the surrounding kingdoms.

Who would Prince Lewis dance with tonight? Would he sulk after his horse's loss, or would his attention be on the ladies?

Maybe this would be a chance for Anna's sister, Saira, to shine. She was four years older than Anna, twenty years old this month, and recently returned from studying abroad. She was now a trained diplomat, elegant and graceful. Everything Anna wasn't. Many were hoping for a proposal soon—perhaps even tonight.

I'll probably miss it.

She'd also heard the terrible rumors whispered in the halls that Arissa had arrived months ago as a potential bride for Stefan. Surely she could trust him to shut down that nonsense.

Marriage was the only way it seemed Anna would have any value in her father's eyes. Someday she knew a wealthy lord or prince would come along, and she would need to marry for the betterment of Sunderland. Anna knew for her it would not be about love, but at least it would be a change from the confinement of Karfin. The northern prince would have at least been someone easy to live with. He was kind, noble, sociable and loved quality horses.

Thankfully, her father still believed Saira should be married first. So Anna wouldn't have to worry about any serious suitors at the party. Of course, now she wouldn't be worrying about the party at all.

Anna turned from the window. Her stunt today probably disqualified her from a future match with Lewis. She didn't care.

Anna undressed and slipped into the hot water. The light, sweet scent of lavender filled her nose and weaved its relaxing spell into her mind. Her nerves had kept her awake most of the previous night.

She closed her eyes and escaped back to the race. She could feel Farley's pounding hooves underneath her again, but far away and softer, almost as if he were flying, not running on sod. Farley won the race. The crowd roared. She scanned the crowd, searching and searching, only to find Seamus's deep brown eyes scolding her. Her chin hit her chest, and she started awake as her mouth slid under the water.

Great. So much for relaxation. I had to think of him.

The water felt tepid. She climbed out of the tub and dried by the fire. Restless, she dressed and walked through the empty castle, stopping below a portrait of her mother smiling. Adelaide. *Would she still be smiling if she were here now?* Anna studied her mother's golden hair, large, blue eyes, and creamy skin. She reached up and touched her mother's cold, silent hand resting on her lap.

One glance at the mirror told Anna she was looking more like her mother every day. As queen, her mother had been adored by commoner and nobility alike. After her death, the king passed into a deep depression, emerging, some had said, only as Anna grew in age and resemblance to her mother. Yet, every year Anna grew older, the king grew more protective. He wanted Adelaide back, but Anna could never replace her mother.

Anna withdrew her hand from the portrait and walked to the window. Without a queen the ladies of the court ran unchecked. Her mother would have never let the likes of Arissa to strut around the castle, conniving and backstabbing whomever she pleased.

A fresh breeze filled the dark castle with the scent of summer, laced with sweet white clover and blooming apple trees in the garden. Beyond that were the fields. She wished she could gallop Farley through those fields and never look back.

Anna headed back to her room through the darkening hallways. Something tugged her as she passed the doorway to the king's chapel. She stopped. The open door revealed an ornate room designed for the time when noblemen and peasants alike worshipped the Most High. The finest polished white stone covered the walls and floor. Behind the altar were three tempered glass windows, embedded with colorful gems. The arched roof sparkled with the precious stones as light from the altar flame flickered, warm and inviting. Anna's feet sank into the thick, crimson rug as she padded toward the front. Long ago, at least 200 people would crowd into this room. Now it was almost always empty.

She sat in the cushioned pew and stared at the jeweled altar, dedicated to the Most High. Centuries ago, many of the peoples around Sunderland had worshipped other gods. They sacrificed to them and begged for their protection and power. But Sunderland had always been different. Long ago, one man had decided there had to be a god above all the rest. He led his people here and built his kingdom on the white rock. On the altar burned an oil lamp—one that never had to be replenished for the Most High Himself kept it burning, so they said. Anna sometimes wondered if the priest and priestess didn't just refill the oil.

Priest Tobias shuffled in and started when he saw her.

"I'm sorry to disturb you. I can leave." Anna stood. The room was primarily for her father.

"No, please stay, child. I suppose I should have been expecting you. Sit down."

"Expecting me?"

"I've been having dreams, visions, actually." He rubbed his chin. "They may be nothing, yet here you are."

"Do they concern me?" Anna suppressed a shudder.

"Yes, and no. Difficult to discern." He shook his head and brushed his hand through the air. "But don't let an old man worry you. What troubles you, Your Highness?"

"I might as well tell you everything before you hear it from the vicious gossips." The day's events spilled from her lips while the old priest patiently listened. He raised his eyebrows.

"You have your father's courage," he said.

"Courage? Father's not courageous. He gave up living after Mother died."

"Years ago he was brave, so young, but with the strongest of character—always knew what was right—though these last years he has become a shadow of his former self. We were fighting then, fighting for our freedom to worship as we chose. If other kingdoms conquered us, we would have had to accept their gods."

Anna squinted at him.

"Over time I think your father fought for the wrong reason. The love of a woman drove him. *She* was devoted to the Most High. He was devoted to her."

"And now she's gone."

"Yes, but that doesn't mean we give up the fight."

"But we are at peace."

He got up and paced in front of the altar, touching the lamp holding the flame. It flickered. "We never give up fighting the lesser gods. The powers of evil."

"But they're not real. The other gods aren't real. Are they? They are just silly statues of stone and wood with jeweled eyes."

The flame flickered higher.

"No, Anna. They are real and want dominion."

"Well, they won't have it here. We've always worshipped the Most High."

"Have we? We are a kingdom fallen asleep. I sense evil stirring toward us, and in my dreams, you are there, Anna. It swirls about you. I fear you are in danger. Please. Be careful."

Anna got up and shook off a chill. *So much for finding comfort here.*

"I-I should return to my room."

Anna bolted out of the chapel. She was surprised to see the

sun had set. Anna wasn't used to the eerie stillness of the castle. She would be alone tonight.

She returned to her room and locked the door. Mary knocked with dinner not long after—not much more than bread, cheese and jam. All the best food had been sent to the feast. Anna nibbled at it and climbed into bed. Thoughts of Farley stretching his head out and crossing the finish line spun in her mind. She rolled over into a patch of moonlight. It seemed unusually bright. She rose to close the shutters, but instead leaned against the windowsill. A cool breeze ruffled her hair. She tucked a wayward piece behind her ear. In the distance, beyond the village, the horizon held a faint glow. The tents were lit up with lanterns. The people would dance most of the night out there. Her stomach twisted at the thought of facing her father the next day. She bit her lip and glanced at the river rippling three stories below. *Yes, much too far to jump.*

Chapter 3

Anna opened her eyes a few moments before Mary knocked. Her muscles protested as she stumbled to the door. The metal key felt cool in her hand as she pulled it from around her neck and turned the lock.

Mary bustled in with a breakfast of small biscuits, jam, boiled eggs and hot tea.

"Thank you." Anna opened her shutters to let in the sun. "Is Father awake yet?"

"I'm not sure he ever went to bed," said the plump woman. "He will see you in half an hour."

"What do you know?" She stuffed a hot biscuit into her mouth. Her stomach rumbled for more.

"Only that they returned late last night." Mary hurried out.

Anna bolted her food. She threw on a bluish dress and brushed her hair in long strokes. When it was smooth, she braided the sides back just as her mother used to do.

She hurried down the curved, crescent-shaped walkway of the castle until she stopped at the throne room doors in the center. Two sentries stood outside the door holding long spears planted into the floor. Swords with lavish, jeweled handles hung at their sides.

"I am to see my father now," she said. They tipped their heads and swung open the ten-foot dark, ornate wooden doors.

A sentry joined her and led her up the long, narrow white stone hall where her father, Vilipp, sat at a table with Seamus at his side. They were finishing breakfast. Seamus had been her father's friend from their youth. He'd helped her father navigate the politics of the crown, defended his life in battle, and stood at his side on his wedding day. Since the queen passed, the king made no decision without consulting him.

But Seamus was no friend of Anna's. She narrowed her eyes and set her jaw as his dark eyes followed her. He leaned over and hissed something in her father's ear. The king nodded.

Anna curtsied low before them. Her eyes rested on the stone floor at the king's feet.

"Hello, Anna." King Vilipp's voice was steady.

Anna stood up. "You sent for me?"

"You should know why."

"Yes."

The king rose and placed his hands on her arms. His eyes were red and his hair disheveled. Breadcrumbs clung to his beard.

"You know I would do anything for you, but I have a responsibility to raise a princess worthy of the title," he said.

Anna's face flushed.

He paused, letting go of her arms. "You must understand there are more important things in life than having fun."

Doubt curled up Anna's spine.

"There's class, dignity, and respect for others, especially in *this* family."

"May I speak?"

"No." He circled behind her. "Because you lost your mother at such a young age, I've had a soft spot in my heart for you. Some say I've spoiled you. Horses, archery, the best tutors—what must I do to please you?"

Anna's face hardened like the stone where she stood. "You have pleased me…"

"Then why do you cause me such trouble? I've been amused in the past, but this was a real…" he paused, searching for the right word, "embarrassment."

"I thought you'd be happy to win the Cup."

He frowned. "You embarrassed yourself—and me. And if you can't see that then perhaps more work will settle you down. I am scheduling a new tutor for you—"

"Who?"

"Do not interrupt the king," Seamus said as he flicked aside a toothpick. His eyes flared as Anna lowered her eyebrows at him.

"As you've obviously outgrown your need for an old nurse maid, Mary will be relieved of her duties," her father continued. "Your sister will oversee your tutoring until an appropriately strict replacement can be found. You can learn from Saira how a lady, even a princess, conducts herself. Life as you knew it is over. No riding, no shooting and gods forbid, no sparring. All that nonsense is over. Seamus will keep an extra close eye on you. He has already advised me to sell Farley or retire him as a breeding stallion."

"But he's mine!"

Seamus stood up, towering over Anna a few stairs above her. "You don't own anything, Princess!" he said with a snarl. "Whatever you think is yours can be taken away if you don't show your father the proper respect."

Even from this distance Anna could smell last night's wine on his breath. The blood drained from her face.

"We could retire Farley," said King Vilipp. "Perhaps one of his foals will win me the Cup in a few years." He stared in the direction of the racetrack.

"Father, please," Anna whispered, her eyes filling with

23

tears. "Don't take Farley away. He's still young, and perhaps someone else could ride him next year. I proved he can be ridden. Please."

"Hah! That wild beast!" Seamus sneered. Anna swallowed hard and scowled at Seamus again. Tall and handsome, he could have any woman he wanted. Her father seemed under his spell as well. While he had grown soft over the years, Seamus's body was hardened and battle-ready. He moved with the stealth of a cat, and Anna knew far too well the bear-like strength of those arms. His only flaw was the single red scar running down his left cheek. Anna glanced away. That scar was a reminder of the night everything changed. She met her father's eyes again.

"I won the Cup for you."

The king laughed. "You have your mother's beauty but unfortunately none of her restraint." He furrowed his brow. "I hope you can learn that from your sister." He grew stern once more. "You are almost of age. It's time for you to consider your duty to Sunderland."

"Which is what?"

"Just like me. I serve the people and ensure peace and prosperity."

Anna frowned. She glanced at Seamus, whose smirk accented the long scar. She turned again to the king. "May I at least turn Farley out into his pasture? He can't stay in his stall."

"No. I'll take care of Farley. Now return to your room, where you will stay under Seamus' supervision."

"Father! Please let Bart turn him out, he'll go crazy—"

"Enough! Seamus! Take her to her room!" He rubbed his forehead.

Please, not him.

Seamus' fingers gripped her arm like a vise as they hurried to her chambers. She had to almost trot to keep up with his hulking strides.

"I find myself in an interesting situation," Seamus said as he tossed her onto her bed.

"Just get out."

"I believe you are under my care, now, aren't you?" He chuckled.

Anna picked herself up and walked to the window. "You aren't my master."

He followed and put his hand on her shoulder. She spun toward him, wishing she had a weapon stronger than her fists. The knife in her drawer was too far to reach.

He lifted her chin with his finger and moved her face back and forth. "So like, and yet so unlike. Fascinating." His lips curled into a grin as he let her go and strode to the door, where he inspected the lock. "Give me the key."

"What?"

"Give it to me."

"No." Panic rose in her throat. Anna swallowed hard. She was keenly aware of the key's weight around her neck. It was heavy but hidden under her dress. Her only hope of safety. She was naked without it.

"I don't think you heard your father properly," Seamus said, a false, sweet tone edging his voice. It was sickening. "Give me the key, or I'll have this door torn apart and a new one put in its place." He held out his hand with a sneer.

Anna's hands began to sweat. She steadied her voice. "I don't care. I'm not giving you the key."

His face flushed red, and the scar turned white. His voice was soft and lethal. "So be it. Do not leave this room." He spun and slammed the door behind him.

She shuddered and sat down at her vanity with her face in her hands. How long would it be until he returned? She had bought herself a little time, but to do what? She could run to Farley and turn him out right now.

Anna jumped at a quiet knock at the door.

"Come in."

Mary bustled in.

"Child, I don't have much time. Please forgive me if I've ever done you wrong. I did try my best." She wheezed a bit from the climb up the stairs from her chambers. For the first time Anna realized how old she was. "They are releasing me from you. I'll serve in the kitchen now."

Though Anna knew this was coming she felt as though someone had sucked the air out of the room.

"I'm so sorry. You'll still visit me?" Anna asked.

"I loved you from the first like a daughter." She pulled a hairbrush from behind her back. "I want to give you this." It was gold with soft boar bristles. The handle was lined with blue and white gems. "Your mother gave it to me for you. I was saving it for a wedding present, as I knew I'd have nothing to offer you."

Anna threw her arms around her maid's neck. She had been her nanny, her comfort when her mother died. Someone who anticipated her every need.

"It's beautiful. How can I thank you—for everything?" Anna whispered.

"You needn't."

"Can you please get word to Stefan that I'm Seamus' prisoner? I wouldn't give him my key, and now he's coming back to put a new lock on my door. If Seamus comes to me at night, I'll jump into the river."

"No. It will not come to that. I'll run to Stefan right now. He won't allow Seamus to have the key. The river, please don't. It's too far down, and not deep enough. You'd die."

"There are worse things."

The lines on Mary's forehead and between her eyes stood out as she frowned. Anna shouldn't have worried her. "No, child. Don't speak that way! I will send word to Stefan. And Anna—don't forget to use your mother's brush. It will bring you luck, I think."

"Luck, I could use. Stefan will be at today's luncheon, dodging all the pretty girls."

Mary patted her arm as she bustled out the door, leaving her alone with her thoughts. A new maid eventually brought her food, but she wasn't hungry.

After a day of pacing and unsuccessfully trying to read, Anna picked up the hairbrush Mary had given her and ran it through her hair. As she did, a song, a lullaby her mother used to sing, popped into her head. It was a sad melody, but Anna somehow remembered the words.

> *Catch some sleep, my little one.*
> *Sleep well this night, my babe.*
> *May you always know you're loved,*
> *May you always find your way.*

Tears formed in her eyes as she thought of her mother.

If only she were here. None of this would have happened. She would have been her ally.

She glanced at her reflection and frowned. She studied her hair falling over her shoulders. It seemed longer. Her right hand holding the hairbrush tingled. Her heart skipped. She brushed her hair again. Nothing happened. Was she just seeing things? She shook her head to toss her hair. It was several inches longer.

She studied the hairbrush. It wasn't unusual for gems to be placed in combs, brushes and such. But what were these gems? She had thought the white to be diamonds and the bright blue, lapis. She couldn't be sure.

King Vilipp mined many gems from the mountain Karfin was built into—deep green emeralds, purple onyxes, and blood-red rubies. In the old days, other gems were mined as well. Rare bright white sapphires, beautiful purple-blue fluorite, gold citrine and many others were said to have great magical powers including luck, healing, strength and skill in battle—or even to help someone fall in love. Priests claimed they had learned to harness their powers and encouraged their use in war. Swords sparkled with strength gems, lucky arrows shot true and shields provided magical safety. Sunderland grew unstoppable. Proud. One fateful day the king's soldiers suddenly turned on each other in battle. Half the army was lost, including the king. The men had gone mad.

Priests later decided the use of so many different magical gems at once had confused their powers, making them erratic. In his grief, the king's son decreed all magical gems illegal. Anyone caught using them for any reason would be executed.

That prince would become Anna's great-grandfather. Magic had lain silent for many years in Sunderland, but it hadn't stopped the opportunistic from illegally mining the magical gems and trading them for oils, silks and other fineries the traders would bring from across the desert. Men were hanged for this crime every year.

The gems in the hairbrush sparkled in the candlelight.

Anna sang the song again, this time a little louder while she stroked her hair. She watched in astonishment as her hair grew at least six inches.

Mother wanted me to have a magic hair-growing brush?

She dropped it on the vanity as if it were hot. Images of dead men dangling from the end of a rope flashed through her mind. She would just braid her hair, and no one would notice. After all, no one would guess she'd practiced magic just to lengthen her hair. It was strange, but the least of her worries.

She lay in her bed, staring at the ceiling. She was trapped, trapped with a magic hairbrush. Now, if it could get her out of a door which would soon be locked from the outside, that would be lucky.

She heard footsteps outside her room. A quick knock.

"Princess?"

"Who's there?"

"Locksmith, Your Highness."

"Come in."

"I need you to unlock the door, or I have orders to tear it down."

"Of course." Anna unlocked it.

Renald the locksmith shuffled in with his head down.

"I have been instructed—"

"To change the lock and give Seamus the key," Anna finished for him.

He nodded.

"I'm sorry, Your Highness, but I cannot disobey."

"Do your work." Anna sat straight in her chair and watched him take her freedom away. In less than an hour, she would be a prisoner. She might as well have given Seamus the other key. She took it from her neck and threw it at her bed. It hit and bounced to the stone floor with a loud clank.

Renald glanced up at the noise.

"Your Highness, I'm sorry, but I must give the new key to Lord Seamus."

"I know."

The door clicked shut. The lock turned. It was official. Prisoner.

In a few hours Stefan knocked. He turned the handle, but it wouldn't budge. Anna ran to the door.

"Anna, it's me."

"Stefan—he's locked me in."

"Mary told me. Listen, I'll take this up with Father. He won't stand for it."

"Please hurry, Stefan. I'm afraid of Seamus."

"He is just punishing you. If he hurt you in any way, Father would have his head."

"I—Stefan, I don't think Father would believe me."

"I'm going to Father now, even if I have to drag his old hide out of bed."

"Thank you!"

Anna curled up on her bed and waited. She waited and waited, but Stefan never returned. Neither did Seamus, and for that she was thankful. She went to the window again. She tried to judge the distance down. There were rocks and stones in the shallow water just below her window. She'd have to jump pretty far to clear them. The deep part of the river was a long way from her window. She was a strong swimmer and could manage the current. If only there were a way down.

Just then she heard Farley whinny in his stall. He was prisoner as well. Her father still hadn't let him out? A prince from across the desert had given Farley to Anna as a young colt. He had been scared and wild, but she'd tamed him. Farley had always trusted her. This wasn't fair to him. He would injure himself if left in his stall for long.

There was a light tap on the door and someone slid a note underneath.

She tore the wax seal off. It was in Stefan's script.

Dearest Anna,

I do not know what has gotten into Father, but he cannot be reasoned with. He thinks we've all been too soft on you and trusts Seamus with your care. How will I live with myself knowing you are stuck there? I do not think he will harm you, for Father's sake alone. He is loyal to Father, if unfair to you. Seamus has heard of invaders on our southwestern borders. He is sending me and most of our soldiers to investigate. I believe this is unnecessary, as I've heard no such reports, but Father trusts his insight. He has kept us safe these last decades. I'm leaving as soon as I can gather enough supplies. Seamus feels it's urgent I go as soon as possible. I'll be gone many weeks, maybe months. Try not to worry, Anna. I'm sure Father will come to his senses before I return.

Always your loving brother,

Stefan

ANNA GLANCED OUT THE WINDOW, across the river. Men were packing up horses and wagons. Before the day was out, Stefan, her only ally, would be gone.

Chapter 4

Anna's eyes flew to the hairbrush. Surely it could do something besides make hair grow. She didn't know what. In desperation, she sang other songs and waited for something to happen. After hours of pure boredom, she sang the lullaby again and again and again, watching her hair grow at first by inches and then by feet. When golden hair fell in great piles on the floor, she sat on her bed and braided it. The long rope spiraled in circles and tumbled to the floor.

She jumped up with a start. The brush *had* given her luck. She opened the bottom of her desk lamp and poured the oil into a dish she slid into a drawer. She had just closed it when there was a knock at the door. Her heart surged with adrenaline. She scrambled for the knife in the table, slashed the braids off and stuffed them under her bed. She was just lying back to feign sleep when Seamus turned the key and opened the door.

"Yes?" She yawned.

"Get up." Seamus strode in with a maid trailing behind him. Anna stiffened and rose from the bed.

The maid set a tray of food and a pitcher of water right next to the hairbrush. It didn't move.

Please, don't see the brush—or the hair.

"I'm busy this evening with the army, but tomorrow morning, bright and early, you'll be up attending to your studies. Saira has great plans for you. You'll not be spoiled anymore."

The maid curtsied and started for the door when Anna stopped her.

"Wait," she said. "I need oil for my lamp. The candle is dim, and I know I'll need it for studying at night. Bring an extra lamp and oil for it as well. I can't read in the dark."

The maid nodded and rushed out, closing the door behind her.

Seamus's face brightened as he twirled the new, shiny key in the air.

"Now that is better. I'll report to your father I've seen an improvement already." His eyes traveled over her. "In a few more years, you will make a splendid woman. You might even fill out a bit." His eyebrows arched in a way that made her temper flare.

He chuckled to himself and locked the door behind him. *Click.* Anna shuddered and paced to her window. Seamus was seeing Stefan off with a great number of men and horses. Anna watched them go until the cover of trees blocked their mounts from view. Dark clouds gathered in the west as dusk loomed, casting the castle in shadows. Farley whinnied.

Anna's stomach rumbled. The food, at least, was welcome. She paced until the maid turned the key in the door. A guard stood with her.

"I've brought the oil, Your Highness."

"Thank you."

"I must return the key to Seamus. Will you be needing anything else?" The girl's voice was quiet, and her chin tucked down.

"No. I don't wish to be disturbed anymore tonight."

Anna hoped no one else would come. She tossed Stefan's letter into the fire. It wouldn't do for her to leave proof of

Stefan criticizing their father, not with the mood he'd been in lately. She pulled on her oldest dress and tied a handkerchief around her head like the maids did. Next she placed a golden chain with a shining green emerald around her neck that she could barter with if needed. She took the long rope of hair out from under her bed and poured the oil over it. The golden tresses greedily soaked up every last drop. She tied one end securely around the bottom leg of her iron bed.

She grabbed the knife, sheathed it, and strapped it to her leg under her dress. She glanced out the window. It was dusk, and no one was in sight. She tossed the hair out the window and watched it fall—not all the way down, but close enough. Maybe she could swing out and drop into the river? *And then what?* Ride after Stefan.

She took three unlit candles and pushed them into the braids so the wick was close to the hair. She'd wrapped the hair around the foot of her metal bed, across a stone floor and out a stone window. It should be safe. She took the candle on her desk and lit the three candles. She gently put the candle back into its holder and climbed onto the rope of braided hair. The silky strands were slippery, but by tucking her fingers into the braid, she was able to keep her grip and climb down. As she went, the hair seemed to stretch under her weight (or maybe the bed moved closer to the window) so she easily dropped into the river. She glanced at the hair hanging from the window and wished she could have cut it down, but smoke was already coming from the window. She had to keep moving.

She swam to the other side and crept up the bank. She smelled the horrible stench of burning hair. By everything that was good, she'd have to hurry. If she were smart, she'd ride out on a horse that was easier to handle, but she couldn't leave Farley. She crept to the stables.

Anna savored the sweet, earthy scent of hay and horses as she entered the large stone barn. She always loved the feel of the soft dirt under her feet as she rushed down the barn aisle.

The dirt stuck to her wet feet as she jogged, but she didn't care. This place was her refuge. Horses didn't judge, criticize or punish her. They didn't care if you were a princess or a stable boy. She could hear Farley pawing at his door. She increased her pace to his stall.

Bang! That had to have been a hind leg hitting the side of the stall.

When she reached his stall, he half-reared and lunged to the door. He nickered and rubbed his head against her chest—too hard. She stumbled back. He smeared her wet clothes with dust that quickly turned to muddy streaks.

"Easy, boy," she said, scratching behind his long black ears. "I didn't bring any carrots today." She ran her hands down his legs and found him in good condition. So the race hadn't done any damage. "You've been letting someone else do my work, haven't you?" He tossed his head and whirled around his stall.

By the gods, he was going to be hard to ride today. At least it would be a quick getaway.

Shouts rang out from the castle. She had to move. She bolted out the stall door to get his saddle and collided with a boy about Anna's age.

"Your Highness? So sorry." He reached a hand forward to steady her.

"Bart, shh—I'm not supposed to be here."

"Can I help, Your Highness?" He bobbed a quick bow.

"Anna. Call me Anna," she told him for the hundredth time. "Please help me tack up Farley."

"I've had strict instructions not to let you ride."

Anna bit her lip. "He can't stay in his stall." The shouts and noise from the castle were drifting to the stable. Bart brushed his dark hair out of his eyes and looked out the window.

"The castle guard is running around."

Anna's heart pounded in her ears. She grabbed Farley's

bridle and threw it on over his ears. She'd have to find a saddle in the next village over.

"I'll just turn him out, then." The lie tasted like vinegar in her mouth. Bart had always been good to her.

"I'll come with you." He clipped a rope to Farley's bit on the opposite side.

"No, there's no need—" She didn't want him to be any part of her escape.

"I won't let you go alone."

"Please, no."

Farley lunged forward, almost ripping the reins out of her hands. Bart helped her calm him down. He had a steady hand.

"He'll love to be outside this much," said Anna, trying to think of something to say as they stepped out of the barn into the twilight. She glanced toward the castle, but her room was out of view. She could still hear faint shouting. Seamus wouldn't be pleased her father chopped her door down to save her from a fire. She smiled in spite of her urgency to flee. She hoped the hair would burn up and cover her tracks, but it would of course also announce her departure. Her hands trembled.

She was almost running to keep up with Farley.

Good. The quicker the better. But how to get rid of Bart?

A pang of regret ran through her heart. She counted Bart as one of her few friends. He pulled on the rope to slow the horse down. Farley reared, ripping the reins through Anna's hands. Bart hung on as Farley landed and set to launch forward.

"Whoa!" he said, snapping his rope over Farley's nose and stepping in front of him, backing him up. *When had Bart grown up so much?* Anna wondered as he expertly handled the black beast of a horse. He seemed bigger, stronger and older. Soon he'd have giggling chamber maids fighting over him.

They reached the road. The field was still perhaps a

quarter mile away when a rider on a dark horse approached. Anna recognized the cloak right away.

"It's Seamus. Please, hide me. I don't have time to explain."

The horse stopped in front of them. Anna ducked behind Bart and Farley, who jigged in place. Anna struggled to keep her grip on the reins while she curtsied, eyes on the ground. She was thankful her head was covered.

"What are you doing with that horse?" Seamus's voice was threatening.

"I-I-I- am just turning him out, my lord. He's tearing his stall to pieces," Bart stammered.

"On whose orders?" Seamus growled at him.

"As his groom, I-I-decided on my own, my lord."

Seamus swung down from the saddle and picked Bart up by the collar with one hand. "How dare you!" He slammed him down and drew his sword. Before Anna could react, he hit Bart with the flat edge on the side of the head. Blood poured out of his ear as he fell to the ground. Seamus bent to pick him up, but Anna stepped forward.

"Leave him alone!"

Seamus started and looked at Anna for a long minute.

"How did you—" he began, and his eyes fell on her wet clothes. "You jumped!" His mouth fell open.

"Never mind that—you leave him alone. I asked him to help me turn Farley out, that's all. I couldn't listen to him kicking and screaming all night."

"Indeed? You are much worse than I thought. Look at what you've done to this stable boy." His lip curled in a sneer.

Bart was sitting up now, holding his head. "I'm not merely a stable boy, I'm a squire of a great knight," Bart spat. His eyes flashed in defiance.

"Who requested you to speak?" Bart instinctively threw up his arm as Seamus pulled back his hand for another blow. "Your knight hasn't taught you well. Why do you escort the princess without so much a stick to protect her?" Seamus laughed and wiped his sword clean on the grass. "You have much to learn, *squire*."

"Leave him alone." Anna stepped in front of Bart. Farley pulled on her arm and pawed in place.

"Very well." He glanced at Bart. "Boy, leave us!"

"Go, Bart. I'll be fine." Anna's voice trembled. Bart hesitated.

"I won't leave you."

Seamus picked him up by the front of his cloak.

"You wish to challenge me? I'll stick you through for insubordination without a second thought." In an instant the tip of his sword was touching Bart's stomach.

"Stop!" Anna pulled on Seamus's arm. It didn't budge. "Bart, please go!"

Bart grimaced and staggered to his feet. He shook his head so only Anna could see.

"Bart, turn around and get your head seen at the castle. I'll be back shortly," Anna commanded him with a stern voice. He frowned and started back.

"That was quite bold, even for you!" Anna snapped when Bart was out of earshot. "Seamus, I swear, I—"

"Don't start, Anna. I can have his throat cut any time I want if you breathe a word of this to anyone." He smirked. "You like him, don't you? You know, it's not safe for a beauty like you to be alone with young men." His eyes traveled over her wet dress, sticking to every curve of her body. "You know how they are."

"One day, you'll hang." Anna stepped back.

He laughed and leaned toward her.

"Perhaps, but I think not. Have you heard what the people were saying this morning?"

Anna glared at him.

"Of course not. You weren't at breakfast. Let me fill you in. The people seem to think a king who can't control his own daughter can't be trusted to control a kingdom. They are whispering not only in the castle, but in the village, too. You will be the ruin of your father."

"You lie!" Anna's eyes narrowed.

"This is no lie." His dark eyes gleamed. "Your behavior cost your father dearly. You will be his undoing, just like you were to your mother. She never recovered from bearing you." His words hit like a knife twisting in her gut. "You weakened her. Then she got sicker and sicker, until finally, she died." His face went slack for a split second.

Anna stood paralyzed.

"Your father has never forgiven you for it. That's why he wants you locked away. He's done with you. Even Stefan couldn't convince him otherwise."

Seamus ran his finger down her neck and onto her shoulder. Anna shivered in revulsion. He stepped behind her and pulled her to him with deliberate intent. Anna stiffened as his lips lightly touched her ear. He whispered, "But don't worry. I'll keep you safe. One day, I might even take you as my bride. No one else will want you."

Anna recoiled from his breath and slammed her elbow in his ribs. He flinched but held her in a vise grip. Farley's pacing yanked at the reins in her hands.

"Get away!" she said through gritted teeth. The sky darkened by the moment.

His hands slipped down her shoulders and his fingers circled one of her wrists, tugging her back. "Come back to your room and all will be forgiven. We'll keep this secret from your Father. I don't bite."

The hair stood on the back of Anna's neck. Her muscles froze, and her chest tightened more with every breath. She was no match for the skilled warrior. *Flee.* Farley danced sideways, ripping her out of Seamus's grasp. She ducked under his neck and pulled hard on the reins. The big horse swung his hind legs toward Seamus.

He jumped out of the way, dropped his horse's reins and

lunged for Anna, but she was already steps ahead with Farley. She pulled on the reins again, curling Farley's nose toward her as she wrapped her left hand around his mane, kicked her right leg up high and scrambled up the shifting horse. She was on! She imagined Seamus dragging her back to her room to teach her a lesson—or worse, behind the barn for a different kind of lesson.

Not today.

Seamus leapt for Farley's head, but Anna punched the horse with her heels and screamed, "Yah! Yah! Yah!"

The big horse bolted, knocking Seamus down as he crashed into him. She clutched his mane for dear life.

Anna's heart pounded with fury and fear. Seamus had crossed the line this time. His words flooded her mind as Farley ran. *My father's demise? No, he just likes to torture me. And now he's sure to tell Father I've been riding again.* She glanced back to see Seamus turn back for the castle, where he'd surely wait for her return.

Anna pulled on the reins to slow Farley from his blazing pace. Her stomach coiled at the thought of the trouble she'd be in now. She'd likely have a guard in her room forever. Saddle or no, she'd find Stefan.

Dark clouds approached. Anna managed to pull Farley down to a more controlled pace. She was shocked as he slipped into a trot.

She patted his neck.

"I knew you weren't so bad," she said.

Horse and rider both jumped as a loud crack of lightning popped overhead. The wind shifted, blowing leaves and rattling the branches of a bush nearby. Anna took a handful of mane as swirling clouds shifted the sky into a dark purple hue.

"Easy, boy," she cautioned him. A flock of blackbirds exploded out of a shrub on the edge of the road, squawking and flapping. Farley lunged forward to a gallop, shaking his head as he ran. Anna slipped back.

"No, boy, no! Whoa! Whoa!" But there was no slowing him

this time. With each peal of thunder, Farley surged forward. Her father's fields streaked by. Peasants led their plow horses in for the night. She cried for help, but no one seemed to hear. *Nor could they catch me anyway.* The first large drops of rain fell hard, pounding her face as Farley flew into them. He raced down the road, past the track and onward, his hooves sinking into the slick mud. He should have tired by now, but his pace was only slightly slowing. The dark sky opened and hurled sheets of rain into their path. Farley thundered onto a twisted trail through the woods.

The trees popped and cracked above as a gust of wind howled through their branches. All Anna could do was hang on and occasionally shout at the horse to slow. He ignored the reins, and the lead rope around Farley's nose was of no use to stop him. She considered jumping but knew she could easily break bones at this speed. It was a miracle Farley hadn't broken a leg flying around these rocks in the rain and dark. She pulled hard on the left rein and planted her right rein on his withers. He turned his head, but leaned to the right down a steep, rocky decline. Farley lurched to avoid a tree and slipped on the wet ground. Underbrush shredded Anna's dress. She dug her nails into his mane and neck. Farley stumbled as he crashed through a fallen branch. His head tugged forward again, and Anna flew off to the left side, striking her head against something hard and rough. Pain pierced her skull skull as she rolled and rolled, down, down, down. Lightning flashed. Then there was nothing but wet, sticky darkness.

Chapter 5

The jostling of the wagon woke Anna, but she couldn't yet open her eyes. Her head was swimming through something heavy and sticky. Like honey. Pulling her back under. She heard bottles clinking, a voice whispering and now louder as if right over her. What was that accent? She couldn't place it or the scent surrounding her. Spices. Perhaps cinnamon, turmeric and ginger? Her eyes wouldn't budge open, and her heart picked up its pace. Her head whirled and her stomach churned.

"Think she'll wake up today?"

"Dunno," grunted another voice. It too seemed foreign. "She's had an awful knock to the head."

"She'd better be up before we get there, or I don't know what we'll do with her."

Anna's heart raced, thudding the fog from her mind. *Who were these people? Mary had to be near.* She peeled her tongue from the roof of her mouth and wiggled her fingers.

"Mary, Mary," she whispered.

"Hush, she's tryin' to speak!"

She pried her eyes open and lifted her head a few inches. The whole place spun. Her stomach lurched, and she clamped her eyes closed to stem the nausea. "Mary!" she called, and her head fell back again into dizziness.

"Her name must be Mary," said the first voice.

Anna drifted back to sleep. When she woke again, someone was dripping water into her mouth. She opened her eyes to a dark room and carefully propped herself up on her elbows. The room spun. She was going to be sick.

"Where am I?"

"There, there," said the voice, who she found belonged to a smallish man dressed in strange, purple clothes with jewels draped around his neck. Pungent air pierced her nostrils. "Can you take some water?"

Anna peeled her tongue from the roof of her mouth. She gladly accepted a drink. Her head throbbed with each swallow.

"Where am I?" she asked again, willing the haze to leave her mind. She recalled riding Farley in the race, and then facing her father—Seamus! Maybe he had thrown her in the dungeon! The wagon's interior floated up and down, like she was on a ship in rough seas. Her stomach churned, and she laid her head back once more. She was just falling back asleep when she realized no one had answered her question.

The next day she was able to sit up and eat a little food. The men prepared a broth for her that, although bland, filled her empty, aching stomach.

"How long have I been here?" she asked.

"Three days," said the man. "Didn't know if you were going to make it."

Anna's head throbbed with every jolt of the wagon, which thankfully, soon came to a halt.

"Horses need to rest," came a voice from the front as the wagon lurched to a stop.

Anna could barely stand under the white canvas covering the rear of the wagon. She found she could walk if she focused her eyes straight ahead. She stumbled to the rear of the wagon and cringed as she took the man's hand to steady her as she climbed down into the blazing sun. *Where am I?* Nothing seemed familiar. Unease crept through her. She scanned the countryside for anything familiar, but found only dry grasses and hot, sandy soil.

Her knees shook as she climbed back in the wagon. After she was settled one of the men held a plate of food out for her. Anna grabbed his wrist.

"Where am I, and who are you?"

He snapped his hand back and set the plate next to her. He drew a long draught on a pipe and exhaled sweet-smelling smoke into the stifling wagon. His dark eyes locked on hers as he opened his mouth in a yellow grin. Surrounding the man were thick, luxurious rugs, antique glassware and bottles of spices.

Traders!

She eyed the man again. He was short, with dark hair and quick, beady eyes. He licked his lips and fumbled with his pipe. Many of Anna's favorite oils, spices and bath salts had come from the kingdoms across the desert. Sunderland got much medicine from traders as well.

The man chuckled. "We're your saviors, little pretty. We found you alone in the forest with a blow to your head. And we'll be asking the questions 'round here."

The past came flooding back to her. Of course, she had been riding Farley to get away from Seamus. She must have fallen off in the storm. She felt for her necklace. It was gone.

"And you didn't consider taking me to the village?"

The man who had been smoking the pipe approached her without answering. A thick, sweet odor hung in the air around him. "We're taking good care of you. We needed to make a delivery, and then we'll take you where you need to be."

Anna sat in stunned silence. If she revealed herself as a princess, what would these men do? Might they take her home?

"My father will reward you greatly if you take me directly home."

"C'mon, you're certainly not a noble woman, dressed like that," the other man said. "Filthy rags."

She looked at her dress, thin, dirty and torn. She did look like a peasant.

"What happened to you?"

"My horse spooked in the storm, and I must have fallen." Anna wanted to add so much more but bit her tongue. Her head still spun. "Please take me back north," Anna said. "You will be rewarded more than you can imagine." She also couldn't imagine what punishment awaited her.

The men laughed. Anna felt blood rise to her face.

"I demand you take me back. My father will have the whole army out looking for me by now. You are already in danger."

"Oh, yeah, and who's your father?" the taller of the two men sneered.

"King Vilipp. You better turn around this instant." She watched their surprised faces. They laughed harder.

"I knew you hit your head hard, but if you are a princess, then I'm a king," said one.

"No, no, I'm a liege—no, a baron—or a sultan!" mocked the other. "You are just lucky we bothered to pick you up. I don't care who you are, we have some precious cargo to deliver."

"Not more precious than I am to my family! My father would pay more than this whole wagon is worth."

The taller man struck her mouth. She fell, gasping and spitting blood on the wagon's floor. Her lip throbbed, and the wagon spun. She closed her eyes and clutched her head.

"Get away from the rug!" he said as he tossed her aside. The back of her head hit wood.

"You idiot!" the shorter man yelled. "Don't further damage the goods, or I'll teach you a lesson!" He poured water on a cloth and held it out to Anna. "In our land, women don't speak to men. No more talk."

———

SEVERAL DAYS later Anna fumed in silence as she contemplated what her father would do to these men. Or Stefan. He would kill them slowly, painfully. She cringed when she thought of Stefan. He was so far away.

The wagon rumbled on for a time while the shorter man mashed dark spices in a small bowl. They lurched to a stop.

"I want you to get cleaned up. We can't go to the city with you looking like that. We're approaching a warm spring bubbling up from underground. And see this?" He shoved her a bowl containing the black mixture. "Wash your hair with this; it will make it radiant." He gave her an oily smile.

The mention of her hair jolted Anna. The hair rope! Had it burned all the way, or would her use of magic be discovered? She closed her eyes and thought of her father. He wasn't exactly in a forgiving mood, but surely he wouldn't have his own daughter executed for using the gems.

Shaking, she climbed out of the wagon and found the warm spring. The man wasn't lying about the water being warm. It was incredible. She rubbed the spices on her hair and let them sit while she washed her body. She leaned back and rinsed her hair. Her head spun again, but not as severely as before. She saw something dark flop over her shoulder and her hand went to her hair. It was dark brown with reddish highlights. Hair dye.

"So," she said to the short man after she dressed and climbed back in the wagon. "The dye appears to have worked."

"Splendid, splendid," he said. "Women use that mixture to cover up gray hair. I didn't know if it would work for your golden hair. Now you'll blend in better."

47

"I demand to know what is going on." Anna fingered her knife through her skirt.

The short man leaned close. "Wait and see."

Anna drew her knife.

"No, I won't."

He knocked the knife from her hand with lightning speed. He grabbed her arm and bent it painfully behind her back.

"Drop to your knees."

Anna struggled, but the shooting pain through her shoulder had her knees bending to the ground.

"We'll have no more of that," he said, grinning. He shoved her into the corner. "We've got a feisty one!" he yelled at the other man as he picked up the knife. "Even so, it is a nice piece," he said as he fingered the silver handle.

"Give it back." Anna's voice was small. He would do no such thing.

"Did you steal it?"

"My brother gave it to me. There are plenty more that could be yours if you'd just return me."

"You are a decent liar. I'll give you that. This fine knife will add to the money I'll get out of you." He slipped it into his pocket. "Along with your necklace." He held it up and leered at her.

Anna's stomach pitched. She lunged to the closest bowl and emptied her stomach. They were selling her as a slave! She had to escape. One glance outside the wagon and she knew she wouldn't survive. Dry desert as far as the eye could see. She'd have to bide her time and perhaps find someone to help her, but the two barely left her alone long enough to relieve herself.

Late one afternoon, the driver called out, "Master, we are entering the city."

Anna glanced out to see a tall red wall protecting numerous mud-brick buildings with flat roofs and square towers. Larger, white buildings rose behind these, many of which were domed. A dirty river flowed around one side of the outer wall, lined by tall palms. Soon they were at its gates. The tent-filled streets teemed with camels, horses, and people, all battling their way through the dusty sand. The heat was like an oven, with little breeze in between the numerous buildings.

A market. Her head pounded as she squinted into the blistering sunshine. She must be in Tagora, the arid country to the south not on friendly terms with her homeland. The cruel lord Anwar ruled Tagora and made his home in the capital city, Kasdod. Her father had long suspected Anwar was not content with Tagora and wanted to rule the north with all its fertile fields and mines of gems.

"Pull up here." The short man pointed to a medium-sized tent filled with bottles, spices, rugs, bath salts, all kinds of jewelry and colorful fabrics. The men forced her out of the wagon onto the sweltering ground.

Anna tried one more time. She'd rather throw herself at the feet of her father than be a slave forever. "Please. My father will pay more for me even than lord Anwar could imagine," she said to the short man, bracing for the strike that never came.

"Return you?" The man laughed. Anna's stomach dropped. "No, we don't go back for another three months. Soon it will be too hot to cross the desert." He shrugged. "What would your father be able to give us, anyway? A pig?" Both men laughed. "A poor peasant doesn't even own the land he sweats on every day, how could he begin to pay the price you'll get for us here?"

Anna tucked her chin in feigned resignation. The dry wind blew her hair in all directions and flapped the wagon's canvas behind her. Before long, the man uncorked his canteen and threw his head back in a long drink. Seeing her chance, Anna bolted around the wagon. She dashed under the legs of the tired horses and scurried out the other side, scrambling for a shop just a few feet away with long sheets of fabric covering the entrance. She sprinted headlong into the arms of the driver.

She flailed and punched but found herself twisted and thrown to the ground in seconds. She tasted gritty dirt as he yanked her arms behind her back and secured them with rope. She tugged against the bonds. The other man joined him and jammed a knee in her back.

"Now look what you've done. I had you all cleaned up."

Anna struggled. "You, you *scum*! My father's the king, I tell you! You don't know what you're doing!"

"It won't be long," the man said. "My friend has already gone to find them." He pulled her to her feet and dusted her off like a prized horse. Anna cringed.

"Who?"

But the man turned away. Anna's heart pounded in her ears. Dizziness swept through her. *Maybe they do believe me. Will this truly be the demise of my father? Would they hold me for ransom?* She imagined her father crossing the desert with hundreds of men risking their lives to get her back. She didn't want to be the cause of any widow's tears. She'd caused her father too much trouble as it was.

Anna's hands grew numb as the ropes cut into her wrists. Finally a group of men approached. One motioned to her. He cut her ropes and tossed the short man a bag of coins. His eyes traveled over her, resting for a moment on her bruised head.

"She'll heal up fine," he said over his shoulder. He inspected her hands. "Soft for a peasant's yet calloused like you are used to holding a set of reins, but not heavy work, I suspect."

Anna shook her head.

"You'd make a servant in the lord's house." He led her away through the streets with the rope still tied to one of her wrists. *Perhaps this lord will have mercy on me and return me to my father.*

Anna took a deep breath, in a vain attempt to settle her nerves, but the heat mixed with the potent smell of the exotic cloth, spices, flowers, nuts and varieties of strange braided breads made her lightheaded again. Several women peeked at her behind their veils. All the women wore them as they meandered through the market carrying baskets, their children in tow. The man stopped at a stand and bought a dress and a head covering.

"It wouldn't do for you to enter the lord's service dressed like that." He motioned to the back of the tent. "Get changed."

Anna struggled with the strange clothes and tried to remember how the women were wearing them. *Don't panic. There must be a way out of this.* She finally emerged, recoiling under the man's critical scowl.

"That will do for now." He jerked her arm.

He led her on for some time, winding through the many streets until they left the busyness behind. Here, large, white buildings loomed over her. Their polished walls were decorated with ornate trim. Horseshoe-shaped doors, entryways and arches were adorned with intricate, colorful mosaics. The buildings grew larger and more opulent as they went. She stopped in her tracks at the beauty of one in particular. Blueish-green marble lined the walls around black front doors which were topped with a complicated tiled design of aqua and gold flowers, reaching up to a large golden mosaic, crowning the entire entrance. She had to crane her neck back to see the top.

The man tugged her arm. She snapped back to attention. The street was quiet as they approached a huge gate at the center of a great stone wall.

"This is our lord's house, the great Vahia palace," he said. "You will serve here."

"And who are you?"

"I am Kumud. You will report to me. I tell you what to do and when to do it."

"Please suffer one more question." Anna spoke quietly and did not meet his eyes. "Who is the lord of the palace?"

"Lord Anwar, of course," said Kumud.

Anna's heart sank. Lord Anwar. She shuddered to think of what he'd do if he discovered her identity. Her hope fell.

"No more questions. Do not speak to men unless you are spoken to. The master is not as forgiving as I am. His punishment is swift and irreversible," Kumud said. The gate creaked open and Anna stepped into another world.

Chapter 6

Perfumed air swirled around Anna and Kumud as they started up a white path which stretched to the entrance to the palace. It was flanked with tall, lush trees, landscaped bushes and flowering plants.

Anna couldn't help taking a second look when a one-handed servant walked by as they entered the palace doors.

"He was caught stealing food," said Kumud, following her gaze.

Anna walked silently behind her new master over polished marble floors. Kumud showed her to a room where all the clothes were washed. Thick, humid air scented with soap hit her in the face.

"You will work here," he said. "Our master has many guests and expects all the linens to be fresh. You will carry water from the well, heat it, wash the linens, wring them out, hang them to dry, iron them and put them away. And then you will attend to any other duties I assign."

He then led her to the servants' quarters, pointing her to an empty cot.

"This is where you sleep," he said. "The other maids will

show you where to get your meals. Begin your work. You eat at sundown." He left Anna with her mouth gaping under her veil.

An older woman bustled in and yelled something at her. Anna barely understood her thick accent, but she got the idea the woman wanted her to follow.

She led her to the workroom where women were busy washing many sheets and other clothes. Another group was neatly folding sheets and towels. The older woman pushed her toward them. Anna began folding as well, trying to watch what the other women were doing. The folded pile soon grew large and several women carried them away. Anna picked some up and asked where they were going. A woman motioned for her to follow.

They headed back toward the front of the palace where the guests stayed, walking across the back of a large room with many dining tables. Anna kept her eyes on the girl's back in front of her as they padded on. They continued down a hall where the first servant opened a large closet full of silky sheets and soft towels. Anna unloaded her sheets and returned to the washroom. She repeated this process many times until she thought her arms and back would give out.

She stole quick glances at the other women. Their ages ranged from young teens to middle-aged. Some of the women were kind, nodding and gently showing her a better way to fold. A couple were outright rude, snapping harsh, impatient words when Anna took too long to accomplish her task.

Mostly, though, they were silent. Perhaps years of labor with little hope of life ever changing contributed to their downcast eyes, fearful steps and expressionless faces. Anna couldn't know.

After a long day of laundry, Anna finally sat down to dinner, which turned out to be a rice dish seasoned with strong spices. Though ravenous, she barely choked it down. The fiery spices burned her throat. Her eyes glazed with tears as she gulped water in between bites. The other women blinked at her in surprise.

Kumud entered just as she emptied her cup of water. His narrow eyes scanned the room as he instructed them to hurry and clean the dining area. The guests were retiring. Anna had been hoping she'd hear something about bed. Instead, she followed another girl to the dining area and started picking up dishes. Her hands shook from fatigue. She carried load after load to the kitchen and began several hours of washing and drying. Most of the other women swept and mopped the floors on their hands and knees in the dining area while Anna worked in the kitchen.

One girl followed Anna to dry as she washed. Her dress was little more than cotton rags, but her deep brown eyes were kind.

"Where have you come from?" she whispered.

Anna jumped. Hardly any of the women had spoken to her all day. "I was captured far from here and sold just today," answered Anna. "What is your name?"

"Micah." She flashed a quick smile. "And yours?"

"Anna."

Micah seemed to be around Anna's age. "How long have you been here?"

The girl shrugged. "My whole life. My mother was a slave for the lord."

"Where is she now?" asked Anna as she rinsed yet another plate. They would need fresh water soon.

"I don't know," Micah answered. "She made a mistake a couple years ago, and he sold her."

"I'm sorry."

"I'm hoping he sold her." Micah's brow furrowed, and she blinked back tears.

Such fear and pain lived behind the gentle girl's eyes. "I'm sure she's fine."

"You don't know the lord. He is neither kind nor forgiving." Her eyes fell.

Anna remembered the servant who was missing a hand.

"Do you ever dream of leaving here?" Anna whispered.

"Shh—you don't want anyone to hear you say that! It's grounds for, for..." She left her words hang and shuddered. "Just don't talk like that. Anyway, all I have ever known has been within these walls. It is my delight to serve the Lord Anwar."

Anna pitied her for a moment and with a pang remembered that she, too, was trapped in this world.

When the work was finished, the tired girls walked back to their sleeping quarters. They all washed from a small water basin and then piled into their beds. Even the dirty water didn't bother Anna as long as it was on the way to rest. Fatigue silenced their tongues as sleep overtook them.

THE NEXT DAY started with a small breakfast and more work. First they had to haul water from the palace well for the day's supply so that Anna was already tired and sore before beginning her tasks: cleaning floors, watering plants, and of course, more laundry.

The palace was enormous. While Karfin spiraled up into the mountain, Anwar's palace sprawled across a flat landscape. Rooms opened up into verandas equipped with outdoor pools, shaded with palms. Around the next corner appeared a huge bath—a pool with aqua tiles, white marble columns and bathers pampered with expensive oils and scrubs. Anna had always thought Kasdod would be an ugly, dry place, but she couldn't help admiring the beauty here, though she was tiring of polishing floors.

She was thankful for Micah. As they worked together, Anna would occasionally whisper her questions about the palace.

One day their floor scrubbing brought them to a long, dark hallway. Its floors were polished blue marble. Anna began to take the bucket to the entrance of the hall, but Micah stopped her.

"No. We do not go down that hall, it is off-limits," she whispered.

Anna paused and peered down the hall. "Why, what's down there?"

"The lord's private quarters. Please, let's move on," Micah tugged at Anna. With one last look down the hall, Anna submitted to Micah's urgent voice. "His private servants clean for him."

"When do you think we'll see him?" she asked.

"You never know. Even when he's home, he does not always keep the same schedule. He's wary."

Anna's mind worked on the puzzle. The palace had a front door that led to the front gate, a rear door that led to the gardens as well as many side doors for servants delivering food and emptying wastewater. The entire complex was surrounded by a fence, and further out stood a large wall with solid iron gates. The only way of escape would be making it over the wall or through the gate or...She kept thinking. Perhaps like her father, Anwar had a private door only the lord and his few subjects knew about. There could be a secret tunnel or passageway out in case of siege or for convenience if he didn't wish to be seen.

With every scrub on the floor, Anna knew she would soon find a way to search the lord's private quarters. Just then she heard a commotion from the hall. The lord was coming, sandwiched between his guards in front and several girls in back. They were dressed in sheer, body-revealing materials. Their faces were hidden behind veils attached to sheer fabric around their heads. Their black hair descended in long folds down their backs. Anna and Micah scrambled to their feet.

Anna bowed with the other servants as the group passed

and moved to the front door. Anwar stepped into a litter supported by strong men on each side. Anna knew the hall was probably empty. Should she investigate? *If discovered, I would probably be killed,* she thought with a pang. *But I can't stay here forever.* She grimaced. Escaping would take a miracle. She followed Micah back to the stuffy laundry room.

Chapter 7

A week later, Anna and Micah heard a commotion erupt from the front gate. The two girls snuck to a window and peeked out. A man rode through the gates astride a red horse. Micah poked Anna in the ribs.

"It's Prince Alastair." She blushed. "He's gorgeous."

Anna's mouth fell open, but not because of the prince. Her eyes couldn't leave the smooth gait of his horse. He tossed his head as his master pulled him to a halt. He snorted out of huge, perfectly round nostrils. She only knew of one other horse with that head carriage, small ears, strong hindquarters, long legs. And the fire in those eyes. *He was a desert stallion, just like Farley.*

She tore her gaze from the horse as a servant appeared to take him to the stables. The prince's deep purple tunic, hemmed in gold, brushed the ground as he walked toward them. Bright, brown eyes flashed below a spotless, white turban covering his head. Servants ran to assist with his large caravan of belongings, packed on horses and camels. His own servants sprung to action as well. Anna noted two guards armed with long, curved scabbards followed in the prince's wake.

Kumud spied the girls and motioned for them to help. As Anna and Micah approached Kumud, they stepped aside to allow the man to pass. Instead of bowing her head like Micah, Anna ventured a glance. If he'd ever visited her father, he might be able to help her. His surprised, but friendly dark eyes held hers for a moment. Anna winced and dipped her chin as she felt him move away.

She had never seen him before.

She and Micah hurried through the chores Kumud had laid out for them, mainly unpacking Alastair's room. With the mountain of cases he had brought, Anna thought he must be staying for months. Anna folded white cotton and silk tunics and hung robes of purple, rich chocolate and other colors in the armoire.

"What do you know about the prince?" asked Anna as she hung a deep blue robe.

"His servants say he takes care of them as much as the other way around." Micah's face lifted and her eyes shone as she closed his trunk. "They are fortunate to serve him."

Anna's heart pulled toward the prince. *Would he help me?* She unpacked a pair of common camel leather sandals as well as shoes beaded with rubies for formal wear.

"What is such a good prince doing here?" Anna wondered out loud.

"If you must know, I am staying here to find fresh supplies as I continue my journey south."

Anna spun around and bowed before the prince. "A thousand apologies, my lord," she said to the floor. "We did not know you had returned." Anna and Micah backed to the wall to clear the entrance. Anna glanced around. The room seemed in order.

Prince Alastair waved his hand. "Don't apologize." He surveyed the room and nodded. "Superb. Thank you for your assistance." Two of his own servants walked in.

"It seems these girls have done your work for you," the prince said to his servants. "You may return to your quarters."

The girls bowed again and moved toward the door.

"Oh, just one more thing," he said, stumbling a bit as he leaned forward to catch their attention. His mouth turned up at his own clumsiness.

"Yes, my lord?" Anna raised an eyebrow and tried not to smile. Micah kept her eyes on the floor.

"You are quite forward, now aren't you?" he said to Anna. She blushed as her mind raced to figure out what she had done wrong. Micah stepped in front of her, keeping her eyes low.

"My gracious lord," she said quickly. "This girl has just arrived. Please forgive her."

He chuckled. "But I do not mind her." he gave Anna an appreciative glance. "She is obviously not from this region. And you, servant girl, what is your name?"

"Micah," she whispered.

"Micah, why don't you both stay for a moment and prepare tea. And tell me what you know of the palace."

Micah didn't move until Anna nudged her. "Has the lord never visited here before?" she asked. "I supposed you traveled extensively."

"I've been to the kingdoms of the north and all the way across the desert and seen the great wonders of the Eastern shores."

"And you don't have responsibilities to your own kingdom?" Anna asked.

"Anna!" Micah's eyes bugged out of her head, but the prince laughed.

"No, I am a lowly last-born prince. Fifth to the throne of Meni Bellal, and once my brother has a son, I'll be even less relevant."

Anna met his eyes. "I believe relevance is more about character than your position."

He raised an eyebrow. "I wish that were the case."

Anna couldn't take her eyes off those warm brown eyes.

"You are high born from the north," he declared.

"How do you know?" she whispered. She stepped back, but he closed the gap between them.

"Your boldness, your look, your speech. You'd have to be an idiot not to see it. Who is your father?"

Anna's heart hammered in her chest. She found her feet moving toward the door, but he caught her arm, then released it as if he were afraid he'd hurt her.

"I mean you no harm." His eyes were sincere. Anna swallowed the lump in her throat. He would help her. She knew it. She would throw her fate on a chance meeting of a prince.

"I was riding—

There was a quick rap at the door. The doorknob turned. Kumud.

"My lord, would you be needing—" His eyes fell on Anna. His face paled in fury.

Micah began to apologize, but he silenced her with a fierce glare.

"Please, my lord, make yourself comfortable while I remove these nuisances from your most noble presence," Kumud caught the girls by the arms. Anna winced as he dug his fingers into her skin.

Anna stole a glance at Micah. Her eyes were wide as her body shook in panic. Anna set her jaw.

The prince jumped up and grabbed Micah's other arm.

"Kumud!" he said. "The servants did nothing wrong. They were obeying my every request."

"My lord, they are not allowed in any circumstances to speak with our guests," he said matter-of-factly. "They are in direct disobedience of the lord of the palace and will be dealt with accordingly."

Tears streamed down Micah's face as she sobbed.

"Shut up!" He struck Micah across the face. She fell to the floor, whimpering. Kumud grabbed her by the hair.

"No!" said the prince. "I won't sleep a wink tonight knowing they were severely punished because of me. Let me pay you for them both—twice what they are worth."

Kumud considered for a moment.

"Take this one." He shoved Anna toward him. Alastair caught her in his arms and gently put her behind him. "We cannot afford to lose two servants at once. It will be a hardship for the others."

The prince nodded. "Punish her lightly for my sake," he said, nodding at Micah.

"No!" Anna shoved by Alastair and threw herself at Kumud's feet. "Take me instead. I was the one who spoke to him. Let her go with the prince." She trembled on the floor. What had overcome her? Kumud slowly let go of Micah's hair and studied Anna. His lips turned up in a savage grin. She shuddered. *Stupid, impulsive.* She peeked at Micah. Her punishment would not be in vain.

"It will be my pleasure to acquaint you with the discipline of Anwar's palace." He backhanded her across the face, knocking her to the floor. Her ears rang from the force. Anna kept her head down as fear jolted through her. *Do not be afraid. You are a princess of Sunderland.* "You don't know when to keep your eyes down—" He struck her on the back of the head. "—Or your mouth shut." He pulled her face toward him and squeezed her cheeks together until they bled against her teeth.

He grabbed her by the hair and jerked her out the door. She could hear shouting, but her head spun too much to know if it was from Alastair. Kumud dragged her to the servants' quarters and bound her hands with a rope. The rough fibers cut into her skin. He tossed the other end over a tall door and pulled her up tight before slamming it. Anna's face banged against the hard wood. *Do not be afraid. You are a princess of Sunderland.* Yet the fear possessed her all the same, like a living thing, entering her soul and laughing at the pain to come. Her heart pounded as she braced her forehead against the door. She could sense him pulling back.

She screamed when the whip met her back, shredding her thin dress.

"Quiet! Or I'll double your lashes, you ungrateful mutt!" She bit her lip to hold in the next scream. Blood pooled in her mouth before she realized she was biting too hard. She felt blood trickle down her back as well. Fear of the next crack of leather consumed her. Stinging. Crack! Biting. Crack! Pain. Crack!

Make it Stop.

All she could think about was the agony as the whip came down again. And again. And again. She gave into the pain, sinking into it. Panicking with each snap of the whip.

Her head fell hard against the door. Consciousness was slipping away when she heard a voice deep inside.

You are not a slave. You are Princess Anna of Sunderland. You will be free.

As her body broke, her spirit steeled itself. *I will survive.* She didn't remember at what point she swooned.

She found herself on her stomach on her cot. Her back rippled with pain as she moved. One of the older servants took mercy on her. Her gentle hands cleaned her wounds, applied a healing salve and bandaged her as best she could. She washed her face and gently stroked her hair. Anna drifted to sleep thinking of Alastair. Perhaps she could leave with him yet.

IF THE WHIPPING Anna received was considered light, as Alastair had requested, Anna had no desire to encounter a serious whipping. Twenty lashes with a leather whip were enough. In the days ahead, the scabs cracked and ran with blood as she struggled to keep up with her work as well as Micah's. The floors were never done to Kumud's liking, the mending never ended, the laundry never finished, and she had twice the water to haul. If she bled through one of her dresses from ripping open a scab while scrubbing the floor, Kumud would scold her with a sneer for that as well. She only had two dresses and they must be kept perfectly clean at all times.

In addition, she was assigned to work as a night serving girl in the tavern within the palace. It was just on the inside of the outer gates and though patrons were mostly guests in the palace, some probably were invited from the city as well. She shuddered, remembering the pawing hands she had to avoid on her first night as she brought food and drink to hungry guests.

She stepped into the steamy kitchen and slipped her serving smock over her drab dress. Her back, arms and legs screamed for rest as she moved through the dim dining hall filled with thirsty throats looking for a drink and a laugh. The smell of ale, goat stew and a rich spice she could never quite identify filled her nose.

The scabs on her back had healed some but were still tender. Her arms shook as she carried a tray of eight glasses sloshing over with ale. She steadied the tray with her other hand as she saw a movement to her right. Someone's heel kicked out right in her path. She swerved to avoid him, and the tray tipped to the floor sending ale and broken glass flying. She scrambled to clean up the broken mess and felt a man's hands on her backside. She jumped up as the hall filled with laughter at her expense.

"Hurry up there!" said one.

"Clean that up!" A man reached for her. Anna slipped backwards on the wet floor. Another man grabbed her from behind. She pulled forward to elbow him in sheer panic. But he was too strong to fight.

"She's mine." She knew that voice.

Her throat was thick with fear as Prince Alastair stepped around her and shoved the man back into his seat. Two of his guards flanked him. In her peripheral vision, she saw another man toss the broken glass on her tray and set it on an empty table. He stepped close. She almost pummeled him with her elbow as he leaned into her.

"You were captured from the north?" he asked in a whisper, as they bent down to finish cleaning up the mess.

She nodded, not meeting his gaze. She watched Alastair who now held the attention of the other patrons.

"Meet me after your shift. Behind the tavern. I'll find you." The man disappeared through the crowd before she could even answer.

Alastair turned to her. She stood and curtsied. She felt the eyes of everyone in the tavern watch him lift her chin. Her face was dirty, and she reeked of spilled ale. Anna blinked through a daze of confusion and paralyzed panic.

"No one will dare touch you now. They know I'll rip their arms off and cut them into tiny pieces." His eyes crinkled at the corners. Anna tried to smile her thanks. She flinched as his hand moved down her back. He pulled back immediately.

"What did he do to you?"

"Just a whipping." She swallowed. "Thank you for tonight," she whispered, "but please, I can't be seen with you."

He traced a finger down her cheek and dropped his hand to his side. He leaned close and whispered, "I would take you with me, but I can't steal from Anwar. I don't think Kumud is selling."

"No, I doubt he is selling." The words were like cotton in her mouth. Alastair's almond-shaped eyes and olive skin were distracting. Would she let herself be sold again? *No. Not even to him.* She had to escape.

"If I could help you, I would." There was regret in those dark eyes. He pulled her close again and kissed her cheek, close to her ear. "The men here will assume you are my mistress and leave you alone." He spoke so softly Anna could barely hear him above the noise of the tavern.

"Thank you." She pulled back slightly and batted her eyes at him, playing along for the sake of the patrons, which wasn't hard to do considering how handsome the prince was. He winked. She picked up her tray and scurried to the kitchen as best she could. Those customers were still waiting on drinks.

She paused by a mirror in the back and saw a thin, dirty, weary girl staring back. Her shoulders came to thin points at the top of her arms. She hadn't realized she'd lost so much weight. Always hungry. Always tired. A shadow of her former self. No wonder the prince had pity on her. She looked pitiful. A voice deep inside reminded her she was the daughter of King Vilipp. *I won't be a slave here forever. I won't.*

The events of the evening jumbled in Anna's mind when she finally staggered out of the tavern on trembling legs hours later. Who was the other man who had spoken to her? Was it some kind of panicked hallucination? She rubbed her hands across her eyes and even that small motion stretched the tender skin on her back. She considered dropping to her knees to rest. She leaned her head against the side of the tavern to catch her breath.

Mary had served her so faithfully for so many years. Had she been grateful? Had she treated any of her servants well enough? Her heart told her no.

When I return, I will be different.

She would return somehow. She started down the dark path. A hand grabbed her from behind and pulled her taut against a man's chest. Another hand covered her mouth. Her arms found new strength as she heaved on his arm of steel. It didn't budge. She thrust her elbow back, aiming for his ribs but he nimbly avoided the move while keeping her mouth covered.

"Quiet," he whispered in her ear as he pulled her behind the dense shrubbery lining the path. She squirmed, ripping open the scabs on her back. "Shh. I'll let you go once you promise not to scream," the man's voice said. Anna nodded.

"I'm here to help you." The man's calloused hands released her.

His voice lost its accent. It seemed familiar.

Her head throbbed in confusion.

"Take off your veil."

She did. He shifted her a bit more into the moonlight. She figured if he wanted to kill or rape her, he already would have. She had so little strength left, it would have been easy.

"You must be from the north," he said. "Your eyes, your look, your speech patterns all point to Sunderland," he said. "I cannot stand by and watch one of our girls be captured and treated this way."

"Who are you?"

He paused. "I can't tell you, but when I leave, I'm taking you with me."

Anna didn't know if her night could get any stranger. The adrenaline seeped out of her limbs and utter exhaustion returned. This man could be lying. He could be taking her anywhere, but she would be worked to literal death here. Kumud would enjoy it.

"That is, assuming you want to come," he said, his tone softer now, his eyes assessing her face.

"Can I trust you?" His face was cloaked in darkness.

"More than your desert prince. You don't want to become his exotic plaything, do you?" There was a note of defensiveness in his voice.

"I don't think he's like that."

"How would you know?"

"How do I know you're any different?" Anna asked, though her heart had already decided.

"You don't. But I've been watching you. You don't belong here. I promise to take you home, but the choice is obviously yours."

Hope kindled in Anna.

"How would I find you?" she asked.

"Don't worry. I'll find you," he said, his voice confident.

"My father would reward you for my return," she said.

"Is he a lord?"

"He's rich."

She could almost feel his smile in the darkness. She looked up, but he was gone.

Chapter 8

The day Micah left with Prince Alastair ripped Anna to the core. It had been a month since he'd come, and Anna had fallen into a rhythm of work. Her back healed, and her arms grew stronger. Kumud sometimes even gave the slaves a portion of meat a couple times a week. He never gave her any, but one of the older women would slip her a piece or two once in a while. Anna kept her head down, attended her duties and saw Micah occasionally. She continued to wait on the prince in the tavern, where she felt his curious eyes following her. She was tempted to tell him the truth. He could send word to her father. She sighed through her nose. *And probably start a war.* If the other man was true to his word, she would get out soon enough. If he was even at the palace anymore. She hadn't seen him at the tavern lately, although he was usually a regular. If he had abandoned her, she'd come up with another plan.

Finally the day of Alastair's departure arrived. Anna was allowed to help Micah pack for their trip. Micah chatted happily.

"We will be traveling south in a caravan," she said, no longer bothering to keep her voice low. Her eyes sparkled. "He says after the journey, we'll return to his house where I can be one of his personal servants."

"How lovely." Anna smiled. She was truly happy for her friend, though her stomach wrenched at the thought of her leaving with the prince. Micah was her only friend, and she felt safer with the prince in the tavern most nights.

They walked outside together. "Good-bye and good luck, Micah," she said, hugging her a bit longer than necessary. This was her last chance to tell her everything. A thought pricked her, and as she let go, she prayed for wisdom to the Most High, the god of Sunderland. The answer came almost audibly.

Wait.

"I haven't thanked you enough for saving me that day," Micah whispered.

"You needn't thank me," Anna answered.

"If there is anything I can do to help you, I will. I won't forget." Micah squeezed her hand. There it was. Anna could trust Micah with the truth in hopes she would someday help her. The words stuck in her throat.

"Good luck, Micah," Anna said as she helped her friend on a thin chestnut gelding. "I'll miss you."

Another servant attached a rope to the horse's bridle to lead him from his horse, as Micah didn't know how to ride. Micah glanced back and waved. Anna bowed as the prince crossed her path. She was right to refrain from speaking to him. He was obviously in some sort of alliance with Anwar. It wasn't worth the risk. He winked at her as he passed.

Anna walked back to the palace with one last glance over her shoulder. The horses and camels were moving out, and soon even the dust from their caravan had settled in the distance.

The palace seemed lonely without Micah, and the shifts in the tavern were exhausting. She occasionally scanned the rooms for the man who'd promised to get her out. She wasn't even sure what he looked like and wondered if she had imagined the whole thing.

The next weeks dragged on as Anna went about her duties. At least Anwar was on a journey and wouldn't return for a month. The palace was always less tense with him gone. Anna smiled even as her stomach rumbled for her small nightly rice bowl because she knew Micah was eating better. The poor girl deserved it.

She was alone one night as she folded the last sheet and scooped up a pile to put away. Kumud rushed in the room.

What could he want? Probably wants me to dye my hair again. He'd noticed the new blonde hair growing in and tried to punish her for it before she'd told him the traders had dyed her hair. Since then, he'd been providing spices to keep her hair dark.

"A rider just arrived with news that the Lord Anwar is returning early," Kumud said. "His maids are with him. Go to his private quarters and check that his bed is arranged properly."

"But, Kumud—"

"Just do it!" he yelled and raced out the door.

Anna didn't know where the lord's private quarters were. *Oh, well. This will be a chance to explore.* Anna walked through the dining area where a few guests were still reclining. She jumped when she felt a tug on her sleeve.

A dusty, dirty man pointed to his cup.

"Can you get me some water?" His eyes cut through her. He tilted his head to the side.

Anna checked for Kumud.

"I'm not allowed to speak to the guests," she said in a hurry. "But I'll see what I can do."

The man sat up straighter. Sparkling blue eyes shone out from under dark, messy hair. His voice was younger than his appearance.

"If you haven't changed your mind, bring me some water."

Anna jerked her head back to the man. Was this the same

man? She nodded and bumped straight into Kumud, who grabbed her by the back of the neck. She flinched.

"What are you doing?" His eyes bulged out of his head. "I would have you killed for talking to a guest again if I didn't need your work."

"He—he stopped me and asked for water," Anna said. "He's been on a long journey."

Kumud shoved her. "Attend to the lord's room; I'll take care of our guest!"

Anna ran out of the room. *Where are the lord's dratted private quarters, anyway? And how am I to get water to that man?* She peeked back at him. He had a colorful turban on his head, with bushy black hair sticking out the sides and almost covering his eyes. His scraggly beard would have been black, if it hadn't been for all the dust and who knows what else stuck in there. Anna swallowed. Could she trust him?

She hurried to the forbidden hallway and rushed to find the lord's room. Butterflies filled her stomach as her pulse throbbed. There were so many rooms! Some were accessed from the hall, while others could only be entered from another interior room. One had a quiet reflecting pool—a private bath for the king. She had to be getting close.

Anna opened a door to a room filled with strange statues of unnatural creatures—a lion with the head and wings of an eagle, a man-like statue with the head of a wolf and a red serpent curled around a black tree trunk. In the center of the room sat a massive wooden table. Large, dark cabinets lined the walls. The air was thicker in here, like an invisible presence tightened the air, pressing against her. Tiny hairs on the back of her neck stood on end. She moved on, peeking in doorways until she finally found a chamber with a majestic bed. *This must be it!* Anna quickly re-made the bed and fluffed the pillows. She opened the curtains to let in a little light and filled the water basins with fresh water.

As she set down the last pitcher, she heard voices in the

hall. *Oh, no, they're back already! And they're coming!* Anna dashed out into the hall and bolted for the first open door—the room with the statues. One of the cabinet doors was open. She darted for it. She'd hide until they passed and sneak back out. The voices grew louder in the hall just outside. Startled, Anna yanked the door shut behind her. Footsteps and gruff voices approached.

"Where is that northern scum?" said one.

"He'll be here, my patient lord. He's just entered the tavern," answered another voice.

"Get him at once!"

The servants scurried out, but Anna could tell by the footsteps pacing on the hard floor that the one giving the orders was still in the room. *Probably Anwar.* Anna heard the sound of the shades being drawn tight. The room darkened.

There was a courtesy knock on the door as several men stepped in the room.

"Your men must wait outside," said the first voice to the newcomer. "This is private business."

"Very well, Lord Anwar."

"And your sword stays outside as well. There are not many legends that do not reach my ears, sir. Your mastery of the sword is one of them."

"Thank you," said the voice again. Anna's blood froze. It was *his* voice. It couldn't be. She tried in vain to peer through the cracks around the door.

"Can I offer you a drink?" asked Anwar. "I understand you had a hasty journey."

"Just water, thank you. I do not have long before I'll be missed," hissed the voice. "I am supposed to be checking on the southern armies."

It was unmistakable now. *Seamus.* The fury inside Anna was only held back by the fear and knowledge that if she were heard at all, she was as good as dead. She held her breath.

"Did you bring me the gems?" Anwar asked.

"Yes, my lord."

Anna heard the sound of stones rattling out of a pouch onto the table.

"Ah, these will do nicely. Put the red jasper around your neck. It will protect you. Oh, I've never seen such hematite—this will open our minds. The spirits in this room will awaken. They will give us knowledge and power. We will see the future."

Seamus didn't answer. Anna imagined this was new ground for him.

"What are you going to do?" asked Seamus, his voice cautious.

"These statues represent powerful beings. They are the gods of old. The gems will allow us to connect to each one and glean what we can from them," he said with intensity. "They will tell us when the time is ripe to move on Sunderland. All in return for our devotion and blood. They demand blood." Anna heard the quick intake of breath as she assumed he sliced his hand—or was it Seamus's?

"Are you ready for your throne?" he asked.

"Yes," answered Seamus.

"You understand what would happen if you reneged now?"

"Of course, my lord. I have no such intentions."

"Oh—to rule the north! I can feel it already." Anwar took a deep breath. "And these gems—the wealth of the world will be mine."

Anna's pulse raced. She heard someone light a small fire. In an instant thick, sweet incense filled the air. A pink cloud of smoke crept through the edges of her hiding place. A soft red glow appeared through the cracks around the cabinet door.

The fire crackled and popped as Anwar dropped more herbs in it. Anna tried to peek out through the lock. She could barely make out the fire. It flickered like someone's hands were dancing over it. Thick, sweet, nauseating air seeped through the cabinet. Anna covered her mouth with the front of her dress, but the odor still penetrated her lungs.

Anna's head whirled as Anwar's voice transformed into a dull, slow chant. Louder and louder. She couldn't block out its ominous notes, knocking at the edge of her mind.

Evil. It wanted to shred her. Rip her. Kill her.

Anna closed her eyes but couldn't rid her mind of a presence with terrible red eyes and claws ready to tear her apart. She was fighting. And losing. She slipped to the cabinet's floor, overwhelmed with exhaustion.

Desperately, she thought of home. The priest. Her mother. Anything but here. *Rolling hills of green. Cool, swift streams, horses' hooves throwing sod in their thundering wake.* She concentrated and felt Farley under her again, galloping hard and eating up ground with huge strides. He was galloping toward Karfin—toward the chapel. She saw the lamp. The voices slowed in her head, but Anwar's voice was still chanting. A new voice sounded.

"In two moons, the scene will be set. A full moon will light the way. The city of white rock will fall. The dead will be your prey."

Anna focused on the riddle. The claws pricked her mind, and she almost cried out in pain. The evil eyes bored holes through her. The lamp, chapel and Farley vanished, and she was standing in front of the evil presence. Fully exposed, arms out. Claws reached for her throat, and Anna screamed in her mind, *No, I refuse you. I refuse you. Leave me!* She clamped her eyes shut and pulled her hair so the pain would block out the horrible voice. The claws lessened their grip on her throat, but the eyes pierced her soul.

A new voice, soft and sweet, now filled the air. The grip loosened as if listening as well.

"A bit of caution we give you now. A prisoner will run free. If the truth is told in time, your defeat is sure to be…"

The pressure was back twice as hard, like long, steel fingers gripping her throat. Anna gasped for air and clawed at her neck. She dropped to her knees. For the first time, she thought she might die. She fought the foul images in her mind and the overwhelming darkness they brought with them. She squeezed her eyes shut and remembered the chapel and the light on the altar. It flickered in the back of her mind, small and unattended. She focused on that light, drawing it out, toward her. The blackness increased its grip in desperation. Again Anna saw red evil eyes boring into hers, even with her eyes closed.

No! Leave me alone! Anna screamed in her head again. She thought of the chapel's light again and called to it in her mind. Fire and light pulsed through her. The pressure on her neck let go, and she sucked great gulps of air into her lungs. With a jolt she fell against the back of the armoire. It was gone. In the same instant, the fire in the room flashed and went out. She opened her eyes, panting, hoping against hope that no one had heard her.

"What happened?" asked Seamus.

"Something incredibly powerful interrupted our connection," Anwar said in a weary voice.

"Can you try again?"

"No. I am too drained. Hand me a bandage. The spirits feed on the energy in my blood and that in the gems." Anwar paused. "We may know enough. At the second full moon, the time will be right. What could the spirit have been saying about a prisoner?"

"I wouldn't know, my lord."

"Do you have more gems?"

"A whole chest full, my lord."

"Hmm. With these gems, I will be able to discern the meaning. If someone stands to thwart us, I will discover and eliminate them. The gods will help. We have time. How many men are following you?"

"Hundreds will follow me to the death," said Seamus. "They are ready to move when you say the time is right. After all the royal heads are gone, you'll have your way with the armies. Trust me," he chuckled. "That stupid king won't know what hit him."

"Are you, then, in agreement that I shall control all the north, with you on the throne, but answering to me?" the king asked. "You will pay your tribute in gems of power."

Anna heard Seamus make a kissing noise toward the floor. She assumed he had either kissed the lord's hand or feet. *Disgusting.* Worse was the slow panic rising in her heart. Seamus was plotting to overthrow her father. She thought of the man in the tavern. She must find him. She must warn her father.

"My king, you have the mind and will of one of the great rulers of the past. You will be my lord and be remembered forever for your greatness and glory in this kingdom and all the way to the north," Seamus said, groveling before him. Anna thought she was going to be sick. She was already dizzy from the incense.

"Then our time is set?"

"Two moons," answered Seamus.

"Two moons," said the king. "You won't regret giving me these gems. The spirits will guide us to victory. Now, refresh yourself and be on your way. We don't want you seen."

"Thank you, my king." Seamus left the room. *My king.* He should hang for uttering those words alone. Anna heard others join the king, who apparently ate a meal. He now spoke to his subjects in a language Anna couldn't understand. Would they ever leave?

After several hours of sitting in the cramped armoire, Anna's eyelids grew heavy. Fatigue took over, and she slept. The room was dark and silent when she awoke. She rubbed her neck and longed to stretch her legs. Her hand trembled as she pulled the latch on the door. Locked! *Oh no!* She wiggled the handle a little harder, making a quiet clicking noise. No luck. *Ugh!* She had to get out. Calling for help wasn't an option, and there weren't any loose boards in the back of the cabinet. She finally slid back to the floor, hot and thirsty. In desperation, she pushed hard on the handle in an attempt to break the lock. Her foot slid on the floor, bumping into the back of the armoire. She leaned into the door with all her strength.

It swung open with great force. A man grabbed her as she fell forward out of the cabinet.

"Been hiding out, sneaking around?" said a cruel voice in her ear. "Light a lantern!" he called. "We have a spy!"

"No, no, I was only locked in and I fell asleep—I didn't know where the sheets went and—"

"Silence!" he said, striking her nose. Anna recoiled, the shot of pain and dizziness overtaking her. She tasted blood.

"What is this?" asked a voice Anna shuddered to remember as the king's. He walked into the room. "My good king, we found a servant girl, locked in the wardrobe."

Anna kept her eyes on the floor.

"And how long have you been there?" He waved his hand. "It doesn't matter. Kill her." He turned back as he reached the door. Anna felt his eyes rove over her. "Wait. Muzzle her instead. Jaali will make good use of her. Lock her in the dungeon until he can be summoned." The king left.

"Do you know what muzzle means?" The burly man grabbed her by the hair. "We cut spies' tongues out so they can't tell what they know—either that or we cut their throats. You are fortunate. We'll see what Jaali will pay for you."

"Jaali loves the muzzled girls best," the other man said, snorting. His breath reeked.

The two men grabbed Anna and held her head back. She kicked and screamed as hard and as loud as she could.

"No! I didn't hear anything! Please no! Help me! Help!"

The man punched her in the stomach, and she doubled over in pain, gasping for air. "No! No! My father! My father." The words came out in a choked whisper. *Someone. Please.*

"Your father won't save you!" the man smirked, snapping her head back by her hair. He studied her for a second. "The king didn't say we couldn't have a little fun first."

"You idiot, get on with it!" the other man shouted, forcing her hands behind her back. Anna felt her chin jerk toward the ceiling. A rough, filthy hand grabbed her tongue. Anna gagged. She saw the other man holding a knife. She squeezed her eyes shut. This was it. *Please, no.* Her heart pounded so fast she thought she might collapse.

The door burst open.

Something sliced the air.

The hand lost its grip on her tongue as its owner fell to the floor. An instant later, the other man fell, clutching a knife piercing his chest. Anna would have fallen as well if a man's strong arms hadn't caught her and tossed her over his shoulder. He ran.

He tore down the stairs, taking them two at a time. Anna's sore head hit his back on every step and jolt. He plopped her on the ground, and they sprinted to the stables. Finally they reached his horse, and he threw on the saddle. "Can you ride?" He panted.

"Yes, yes," Anna choked out. She hoped he was the man who'd asked for water, but she hardly cared. Adrenaline pulsed through her body.

He mounted and pulled her up easily behind him. The horse charged out the stable door.

"Duck!" he yelled as the doorframe zipped over their heads. Anna whipped her neck around to see men with swords yelling and running in their direction. An arrow whizzed by her arm.

"Go, go!" she yelled. "They're coming!"

Chapter 9

The man glanced back and laid his reins on his horse's side. Anna locked her arms around his waist.

"Yah!" he yelled as the horse burst into a gallop toward the outer palace gate. His horse thundered through the city. "We must make it through the gates before they close at nightfall," he shouted over his shoulder. "We won't survive in the city tonight."

He steered his horse skillfully around covered tents, wagons and the few people left on the streets. Hooves pounded the ground behind them. Anna glanced back. Several guards were in pursuit with swords drawn.

"Hurry!" she yelled, digging her fingers into his cloak.

They flew through alley after alley as they worked their way to the front gate. A sharp right turn had them overturning a cart of melons and oranges as they raced by. The man cut around another corner and weaved through the narrow street, skidding to a stop at a dead-end courtyard. People ran out of their small homes to see who the intruders were.

The man cursed colorfully and spun his horse back the way they'd come.

The horse had to jump the overturned fruit cart on the way

back and swung around a corner onto the main road. At once, a guard on horseback burst out of an alley, right on their tail.

"Go!" Anna shouted as the guard drew his sword with a yell. Another horse joined the pursuit. An arrow smacked the wall behind them.

The man kicked his horse and lay over his neck, urging him faster. Anna doubled her grip on his cloak. The horse had another burst of speed as they rounded a bend and saw a straight path to the city gate. Anna peeked around his shoulder. It was still open.

"Hold for the messenger of the king!" he called, and by some miracle, the gate keepers kept the gate open.

Angry shouts followed as they flew through the gate. The horse charged on, galloping north until they were out of sight of Kasdod. The sand reflected the orange sunset on their left. Anna dared to look back.

"I think we lost them."

He slowed the horse. They both breathed a sigh of relief. He let the horse trot for twenty minutes as the sun finished its descent, and then turned abruptly toward the full moon rising in the east. The horse's hooves were quiet in the sandy soil as the man slowed to a walk. Dusk settled around them. Fatigue washed over Anna now that the immediate danger was gone. She didn't need to hang on to the man's cloak anymore, but she struggled to let go. She eased her grip from the front of his waist to his sides, aware of how close she was to his broad shoulders and strong back. Lack of sleep caught up to her, and the horse's easy gait rocked her into drowsiness. Every few minutes her forehead would sag against the man as she nodded off and then shook herself awake again.

Anna ignored her rumbling stomach as she forced her scratchy throat to swallow. *Just water and rest,* she thought miserably. After they had gone for perhaps an hour, the horse's hooves began making more noise. Grass had returned, and in another hour, tree branches swished in the breeze above her.

The horse stopped in the dark.

"Get down," he said. "I must care for my horse."

Anna swung off and steadied herself against the saddle.

"Come." He landed next to her and turned the horse toward what Anna realized with a burst of relief was a creek.

Anna dropped to her knees at the edge of the water and gulped long, deep drinks, quenching the horrible thirst that had tormented her so many hours.

When the horse finished drinking, the man led him away. Anna washed the blood off her face and felt inside her mouth. Her tongue was fully attached.

Anna jumped when the man appeared next to her. He moved like a ghost.

"Sorry. I didn't mean to frighten you," he said. "Are you hurt?"

"No, I'm fine."

"Your face was wounded."

"They punched me a few times before attempting to cut out my tongue. No permanent harm done." She stood. "I don't have the best luck."

"Maybe your luck has turned around." His voice was warm, not the kind of voice she imagined attached to a warrior or a thief.

Anna shrugged. "I wouldn't go that far."

"Come and rest." He took her hand in his. It felt solid as he led her through the dark to the makeshift camp. "I take it you heard something you shouldn't have?" he asked.

There it was. Who was this man? Someone sent to lure her into false security? Someone to take advantage of her weakness? She pulled her hand out of his grasp, unsure how to answer. She swayed on her feet.

"Never mind," he said. He unrolled his bedroll and motioned for her to take it. She gratefully fell to her knees and was asleep before her head hit the ground.

WHEN ANNA WOKE, she realized the sun must have been up many hours. She eased up and held her throbbing head in her hands. Her ribs ached with every breath. She touched her swollen lip and blood-crusted nose. The man was gone. She didn't even know his name. At least she was away from Anwar and his brutes. Anna rose and stumbled toward the creek. She again quenched her thirst and washed the sweat and remaining blood off her body. Her stomach growled. She hadn't eaten at all the day before.

Anna returned to the makeshift camp, tugging her fingers through her messy hair. The man must have slept on the hard ground as there was only one bedroll. Kind of him. She rolled it up and sat on it to wait his return.

Before long he came around the thicket, leading his horse. It took Anna a couple heartbeats to recognize him because he had shaved his beard. At second glance, Anna took in his square jaw, tanned skin and piercing crystal blue eyes peering out from thick, dark hair. He could use a haircut, but beyond that—she glanced away when she found those eyes studying her as he walked, every step confident and strong. Though his physique wasn't overly muscled, he moved with an ease that suggested wiry, lethal strength. Formidable. If he was truly on her side, she should be thankful, otherwise, she might be doomed.

"I found a clearing of some scrubby grass, where he's had some four hours of grazing." He arched an eyebrow. Was he teasing her? "Now that you're up, we can go soon."

"I'm sorry. I must have been tired." She stood and brushed herself off.

"Don't apologize." The man handed her the reins and stepped close to examine her head. His touch was soft around her wound and firm under her chin as he tilted her head to the light. "You had quite a day, yesterday, Miss. How are you feeling?" The kindness in his voice eased her fears.

"Better now that I'm away from the city." Anna didn't want to complain about her pounding head.

"You rode well," he said. "You must have ridden a lot in the past." He released her chin and stepped back.

"I merely hung on for life." She'd a death grip around him the night before. "You shaved your beard."

"I was glad to get rid of the filthy thing." He shook his head. "I can't go back there anyway."

Anna shouldn't automatically trust him, but there was something honest about his face. He didn't seem to belong in Kasdod any more than she did. "So what were you doing there?" Anna asked.

He shrugged. "I was on a mission I can no longer complete." So he was being cautious with her as well.

"Because you helped me."

"Yes, but I'm not sure I'd ever have found what I was looking for anyway. Few people talk."

"When have you eaten last?" He handed her a dry crust of bread out of his saddlebag. "It's all I had on me. Today we'll ride to a village where I'll buy everything we'll need for our journey."

"And where are we going?" Anna took a bite, the bread crumbling in her mouth.

He cut her a look. "Back home, of course," he said. "It might be a long trip because we can't cross the desert this time of year. Not on horseback. There would be too many enemies, and the heat would kill us anyway."

"Back home?"

"You are obviously from the north. I'll leave it up to you to tell me where. I'm sure you have people missing you. How did you end up in Kasdod?"

He'd guessed so much so quickly. Anna might as well tell the truth. She swallowed. "Some months ago, I fell from a horse and hit my head. Traders picked me up and sold me as a slave into Anwar's house. A couple days ago Kumud asked me to prepare Anwar's private quarters. That's where I went instead of bringing you water. Anwar returned before I was finished with his room, so I hid in a cabinet and accidentally locked myself inside. Later they found me, assumed I was a spy and were going to cut out my tongue." She shuddered. "Then you stepped in. How did you find me?"

"Good ole' Kumud was storming around. I figured out you were missing. I got lucky when I heard you scream."

Lucky. She ran her tongue along her teeth. "Thank you." Warmth moved into her face. She hated being at this man's mercy but didn't have much choice but to trust him. She could only hope his honest face held true. She tore off a tough piece of bread.

"How long will it take to get home?" she asked between bites. "Those men took me across the desert in less than two weeks, I'd say."

"I'm not certain. Maybe four, maybe six weeks, depending on the weather through the mountains. And depending on where home is." He winked. "Truth is, I've never gone that way." He wrinkled his brow.

Anna was lost in thought. Hadn't Seamus said two moons? Would that be two months or less, depending on when the next full moon came? Anna closed her eyes for a moment. *We must get there sooner.* She opened her eyes and found him studying her once again.

He didn't look away. "What's your name?"

"You haven't told me yours," she said.

His lips pressed together as he tightened his horse's girth.

"Or your horse's." Anna reached out to stroke his chestnut neck. "He was great yesterday." The horse nuzzled her.

"You can call me Jack, and this is Avery."

"Jack? A bit short, don't you think?"

He went to the other side of Avery to adjust the saddle. "Yeah, well, that's what my friends call me."

He dropped the reins and picked up the bedroll.

"What do your enemies call you?"

"I can't speak those words in front of a lady." The corner of his mouth lifted.

"Why would you call me a lady?"

He gestured to her entire person as if that explained it. "You are obviously from noble birth."

She couldn't deny it. "And you're just Jack?"

He attached the bedroll behind Avery's saddle. "If you must know, I was born John William. My older brother got to calling me Jack. It stuck." He leaned close enough that she could smell the tang of his sweat. They were almost sharing breath. "I would have sworn you were someone else when I first saw you. But it seems impossible."

"Who?"

"You look like a girl I remember from Sunderland, in King Vilipp's court. You remind me of his youngest daughter, Anna, but she had golden hair. With that veil on, I only got a good look at your eyes."

"I have golden hair," Anna whispered.

"What?" Jack frowned.

"Those mongrels dyed it black when they sold me." She bent down and showed him the new blonde growth at the roots.

He tilted his chin a little sideways. "Are you a cousin of hers then, on your mother's side perhaps?"

Anna blinked. He was familiar enough with her family to know she resembled her mother? She took a deep breath. "I am Anna." It was hard to form those words. "I haven't been home in a long time."

He pushed his hair out of his eyes and glanced at her thin frame and work-roughened hands. His puzzled gaze swept over her, inch by inch and settled on her eyes. Anna held his stare before he dropped into a quick bow, just a duck of his head.

"Your Highness," he said.

"Thank you, but please call me Anna. And don't bow."

He moved to take her hand and then changed his mind. His posture stiffened. "I pledge to get you home as soon as we can." He tossed Avery's reins over the horse's head and gestured for Anna to mount.

Anna rode Avery while Jack walked beside them, plodding along, hour after hour. Occasionally Anna dismounted to give Avery a break. The poor beast seemed tired. She knew the feeling. Despite her long night's sleep, exhaustion tugged at her. When she walked, she kept a hand on Avery. The warm, solid feel of the horse comforted her while she peppered the young man next to her with questions. His answers were careful, but as far as she could tell, truthful.

Anna found Jack had come to the castle from the Oclen kingdom when he was fourteen years old. Jack knew Stefan and Saira, but because Anna was four years younger, their paths hadn't crossed much. He'd then served on the guard at Hemmington and back at Karfin. He was living in the barracks before he was sent to apprentice in the desert, so he wouldn't have seen her much.

She'd never heard of a knight training in the desert before.

"I was working on a mission around Anwar's palace, but I abandoned it soon after I saw you in the tavern." Haunted grief flashed through his eyes and was gone.

"Why?"

"I knew you didn't belong there."

"There are probably plenty of other girls there just like me." She thought of Micah. "And many others born there that need to be freed as well."

He sighed. "I couldn't help all the slave girls, but I knew I had to help you."

She glanced at his face, honest and tainted with sadness.

"I haven't told you everything," she said.

"I figured that." One side of his mouth pulled up into that little smirk.

"Do you want to know why they were going to cut my tongue out?"

He nodded. "What did you hear?"

I hope he is who he says he is.

"Sunderland is in danger. We must warn my father."

"What?"

"I heard that there is going to be an attack on Father's kingdom in two moons—when will that be?"

"We are a few days past a full moon." Jack lowered his voice. "Who did you hear this from?"

"Lord Anwar, and you won't believe who else."

"Lord Anwar himself?" Jack picked up his pace. "That was why I've been wandering around that god-forsaken land. We knew he was building his army and would eventually strike."

"There's more. Seamus was there. He plans to betray Father." Now the words gushed out. "Seamus has been getting men on his side for a coup. He gave Anwar gems of power and said he'd take care of the castle—something about giving him all the royal heads. Then Anwar would sweep in from the south and attack us unprepared. As you know, Seamus is in charge of all Sunderland's armies. He'll make sure they aren't around that day. Two moons from now." Anna came to an abrupt stop. "And he's sent Stefan and the armies all the way to the western border."

Jack's face drained of color. "Seamus. You're certain?" He tugged Avery to a halt and faced her.

"Trust me, I'd know that voice anywhere." Anna swallowed the bitter tang in her mouth.

"But you didn't see him?"

"I heard him!" Anna said. "And that was enough. Please, believe me."

"That's quite a charge." Jack wrinkled his brow.

"I know how he was when you trained with him, kind and loyal. He's my godfather. He loved me and cared for me until…" she paused. "But he's changed. He's cruel and cunning, and… and he beat my stable boy just to spite me. He would have killed him without a second thought if I hadn't stopped it. You'd never know him."

Jack glanced at the sky. "We need to be going. Someone could be tracking us."

He swung up into the saddle.

"You're riding?" asked Anna. "You believe me?"

Jack reached for her hand and nodded. "I do. Now we need to ride hard."

Chapter 10

The urgency in Anna's heart stifled the beauty of the forest. To the steady beat of Avery's hooves, Anna told Jack about Farley, the race, the night of the thunderstorm, and how she'd ended up in Lord Anwar's house. She told him, too, what she remembered of the prophecies spoken.

"It was something about the white city falling and something else about a freed prisoner." What she remembered most was the horrible voices in her head and those wicked red eyes and claws ready to rip her to shreds. And the choking. She tightened her grip around his waist. His muscles tensed under her touch.

"A prisoner escaping? He will be on our tail." Jack nudged Avery forward. The honest horse increased his pace. "We don't know how the gems work," Jack said. "He may be able to track us."

"It was actually a blessing they dyed my hair," said Anna. "If Anwar had had any inkling of who I was, he'd have kept me for ransom, or perhaps worse."

"Open war would have begun, and many men would have died to get you back," Jack said.

"I'm afraid war is coming either way," Anna said.

———

ANNA MARVELED at how well Avery picked a trail through the overgrown forest. Jack cantered him through the clearings but couldn't go any faster than a walk through the thickets. It was after midday when the forest broke open to a small village, surrounded by farmland.

Jack slid off the horse.

"Water Avery back at that stream," he said. "Keep under cover. I'll go buy our supplies."

"Can't I just go with you?"

"If there are spies here, they'll be looking for a man and a woman together," he said. "Plus, they may recognize my horse. You stay here." He handed her a long dagger. "Just in case. I won't be long," he said, touching his finger to the end of her nose. With one last glance over his shoulder, he ducked through the trees and was gone.

Anna stood for a moment rubbing her nose before turning Avery toward the creek. While she waited, Anna led Avery to patches of grass and watched the horse greedily tear off the tender shoots. After a long time, she heard footsteps behind her. Thankfully, it was Jack, leading a smallish dark gray mare. She had a narrow chest and walked with a spring to her step. Atop her slightly arched neck sat a beautiful set of small ears, flickering this way and that. Her head was wide at the eyes, dipped in the middle before flaring out into large nostrils. Her large brown eyes were calm.

"She's pretty."

Jack handed her the reins. "Her name is Kokabi."

Anna peeked under the mare's forelock and found a splash of white. "I'll just call her Star," she said.

He laughed.

"What?"

"I think that's what Kokabi means."

Anna shrugged. "So I'm not all that original. Did you bring

anything to eat?" She stroked the horse's silken neck, marveling at the incredible horses this part of the world produced.

"Hey," he said, tossing her some bread. "I think you ate last."

Anna laughed. "But I hadn't eaten for a long time before that."

They dug into the bread, cheese and apples he had bought. After eating, they watered the horses and set their path for the day. Anna held out her apple core for Star, who gobbled it down. Avery nickered, and Jack offered his.

"You'll have these horses spoiled." The right side of his mouth always pulled up into the smile first, giving his half-smiles a lop-sided look.

"It doesn't hurt to make a friend out of them," Anna said.

Jack shook his head and gave Avery a pat. "He's been my friend a long time." He pulled something made of cloth out of a canvas bag and handed it to Anna.

"Trousers?"

"We have a long ride ahead, and here's a dagger as well. Tuck it in your belt."

Anna ducked behind Star and slipped on the trousers under her dress. They would protect her legs from blisters. She turned the dagger over in her hand before belting it to her waist. Though Jack probably viewed these things as no more than common practicality, Anna's heart warmed at his thoughtfulness. It had been a long time since anyone had offered her simple kindness.

Jack mounted Avery. "We'll be heading north now, in the open."

Anna settled into the saddle and moved her mare behind Avery. Jack alternated walking, cantering and trotting along the way. Avery had long legs that covered the ground in easy strides. While Star was smaller, she kept up without even breathing hard. At nightfall they camped near some large, tangled bushes. They ate, grazed and watered the horses before settling down for another night under the stars. The warm air cooled off just right for sleeping. Anna snorted to herself. She'd often wished for adventure, but she'd never expected this.

"Something funny?"

"No. It's just the irony that I used to want to get away from Sunderland. Now I'm trying to get back as fast as I can." Color rose to her cheeks as she realized her mistake.

"Why would you want to get away from Sunderland? Are you betrothed?"

"No, nothing like that." She sighed, and they sat in silence for a moment. Anna met Jack's thoughtful gaze and changed the subject. "Seeing all this beautiful, dangerous country kind of makes me wish I'd paid more attention to my geography lessons."

"I can't imagine you giving your tutors a hard time." He raised an eyebrow.

"I was appalling."

"That bad?"

"Father hired five—no six tutors for me. They all quit."

Jack laughed. "When you return, you'll have plenty of time to study. For now, get some rest. Tomorrow we'll cross a small section of the desert. Make sure you drink enough water because it will be hot."

"I thought we weren't going over the desert." Anna frowned.

"We're not. This is just a thin finger of sand that points to the east. It will take a day to cross, and then there will be more grassland and trees leading to the mountains. We will come to Sunderland from the east after we cross the ridge."

―――

THAT NIGHT ANNA tossed and turned in the cool night air. When she finally slipped into sleep she dreamed of a huge sand-colored snake slithering toward her. It was large enough to swallow a baby goat whole. Small horns rose from its head over its red eyes, which were marked with black stripes feathering out from the corners. It moved closer. With purpose.

Anna couldn't close her eyes. She couldn't move. She opened her mouth in a silent scream as it rose up before her, staring at her with murder in its eyes.

It's just a dream, she told herself. The words brought peace. *Just relax and it will go away.*

"Yessss. Relaxxxx. It will all be over sssoon," hissed the snake.

Just a dream. Snakes don't talk.

She was no longer afraid of the coming death. It was only a dream. Her heartbeat slowed.

The snake reared back to strike, and Anna tried to close her eyes, but her eyelids wouldn't move. As its head lurched forward a long dagger came out of nowhere and lopped it off just inches before its fangs hit her neck.

She woke up to Jack shaking her.

"By the gods, you were in a trance."

"I had a horrible dream." She propped up onto her elbows, saw the snake's head resting in her lap and let loose a piercing scream startling both horses. She leaped up and watched as the snake's body shrank from its twelve-foot length to a normal four-foot desert viper, which was horrible enough.

"What was that?" Anna asked. Her whole body trembled.

"I don't know," Jack answered. Not comforting words.

"Let's get out of here," she whispered to Jack.

"Agreed."

Jack's hands shook as he wiped the blade clean.

"Can we ride in the dark?" Anna asked.

"The moon is almost full and even if it weren't, I'm not staying here."

Jack helped saddle Star, and they packed up camp. Anna couldn't get away fast enough. Even steady Star was a little jumpy.

They mounted and rode side-by-side into the desert, and before long, the sun climbed over the long, flat horizon on their right. They were headed north. Anna felt like death—like she hadn't slept for weeks and now wasn't sure she would ever sleep again. Every time she blinked, she saw that snake—and those eyes were the same murderous eyes that had haunted her in the closet. She shivered in the cool morning breeze.

When they stopped a few hours later she was already sweating. Anna was amazed how the sand reflected the heat. She was melting. Jack managed to find a stream, but it was almost dry. The horses wasted no time in drinking from the bottom. Anna sipped from the canteen. She realized now why they couldn't cross the whole desert. They mounted again, and the horses jogged on. After some time, Anna's eyes lost focus. She was hypnotized by the constant jingle of the bridle. Hot horse, hot air, hot saddle, hot self. Jing, jing, jing went the curb chain. Sweat poured from her forehead and burned her eyes. She appreciated the white head covering Jack had given her. It seemed to reflect some heat.

When she thought she could go on no more, Jack slowed Avery to a walk. Motioning for her to dismount, he did the same and loosened the horses' girths. Anna wanted to flop onto the sand, but it would scorch her skin. It was burning her feet through her shoes. She didn't know how the horses stood it. Poor Star was breathing hard and sweating profusely. Jack let Anna have a drink from the canteen and then to her astonishment, poured a whole one out into a special leather pouch for the horses to drink. He let Avery take more than half and then poured more from the other canteen. Star consumed it as well.

"Is there any left for us?" Anna asked.

"I didn't know it would be so dry already," Jack said, frowning. "The last two watering holes were empty. We're pushing on."

Anna hadn't even realized they had passed any watering holes. The terrain was an ocean of brown sand.

The horses grunted as they remounted. Jack let them walk for about an hour, then pushed into a trot. The sun was now directly overhead. Jack stopped again and let the horses finish off the water. Anna's tongue was thick. She longed for just one swallow.

"We need to find shade," Anna said.

Jack shrugged. "There is none. We will have to make it."

At last, as the sun tipped over toward the west, Anna made out a gray shape on the horizon.

"Jack," she gasped. "What is that?"

"Trees," Jack said. "We'll be there within the hour."

Relief pulsed through her, but Anna didn't waste her strength on a reply.

True enough, in about half an hour, patches of brown grass appeared under the horses' hooves. Hard earth and rocks shot up through the sand. Jack slowed the horses to a walk. The trees overhead finally offered relief from the scorching sun. They rested there about an hour before thirst drove them on. The horses were cool now and could be allowed to drink. Too much cool water on a hot horse's stomach can kill them. She felt the dried sweat on her mare's chest as she walked beside her. She was no longer heaving for air.

"What a good girl you were today," she whispered to her weary horse. She didn't know how much longer the poor thing could make it. Just then the horses quickened their pace. Star nickered. *Trickling water!* The horses had already smelled it. Star pulled on the reins, plunging forward down the bank of a stream. Plenty of fresh, cool water bubbled up here from the earth. All four of them sank their faces into the stream. Anna took her horse's bridle off, leaving the reins around her neck. The two horses drank for a long time, pressing their lips down and drawing long, cool, delicious mouthfuls. Anna dunked her head in the water and let her hair run down her back. *A bath would be so nice.* She glanced at Jack, who had finished splashing his head with water and began filling the canteens.

"What's the plan?" Anna yawned. She could sleep for a week.

"I told you we'd make it," he said, playfully splashing her.

"Hey!" Anna cried. "You don't want to start this!" She splashed him back.

His eyes flashed, and he looked at her as if he were considering throwing her in.

Anna squinted at him and gave him a warning look, although her heartbeat increased at the thought of him touching her.

Instead, Jack quirked an eyebrow and looked over his shoulder as if assessing potential danger. He climbed out of the creek, leading Avery. "The horses need to rest," he said, stripping his horse of the saddle and packs. Anna did the same. Then they led the horses back to the creek where they drank again. Her mare got down and rolled in the stream. Anna laughed.

"You've bought me a silly little mare," she called to Jack, who laughed at her as well.

"She was more like priceless today, yes?" He winked.

Her heart swelled. She owed him.

They put halters on the horses, tied them to ground stakes and let them find what grass there was. Anna sat down beside Jack.

"You know, you will be greatly rewarded when we return," Anna said. "I am truly grateful."

He nodded.

"I know you spent a lot of money on the horse and gear," she added.

"I'm not doing this for a reward," he answered. "You must know that."

"I do." Anna bit her bottom lip. "I just, well…wanted to thank you anyway." Anna lost her words. How could she convey her appreciation? Conversation with Jack was easy. Being with him was easy. He treated her with kindness and respect, was quick to smile, yet she knew instinctively he'd fight to the death for her. Even with the fear of the coming attack on her kingdom, she was happier than she'd been in a long time. She had a purpose, and that felt good.

She lay back in the grass, exhausted, and closed her eyes. She wanted to put the feeling into words for Jack but found herself speechless. It probably didn't matter, for on some level, he probably felt the same way. She opened her eyes and found him watching her. There was care and concern mixed with grim determination in his blue eyes, so bright against his tan skin. Her cheeks pulled up into a smile as her stomach flipped. She could lose herself in those eyes. "So we rest here?"

Jack glanced up. The trees were quiet. Not a bird singing or a branch rustling. "I'd like to move on a bit. Anyone following us will come here first. It won't do to have them find us napping. Not that I can get a lot of sleep after that snake."

So it had bothered him, too.

"Do you think someone is still following us?"

Jack frowned. "Or *something*? I don't know," he said. "But I'd rather be safe."

They moved the horses to the edge of a small clearing where they could either eat or rest in the shade. Both chose to nibble and then dose, nose to rear, heads hanging down.

Anna leaned back against a tree. She closed her eyes, but all she could think about was getting her sticky, stinking body back to the stream. Jack appeared ready to drop off. *Do I wake him?*

"I'm sorry to bother you, but I'm going back to the stream to get a real bath. If you'd like to stay here." She stood. "I'll be right back." She picked up her dagger and started walking toward the stream. *I'd like to at least wash out some of these underclothes. They are soaked with sweat.* He jumped up.

"You're not going back there alone."

"Well, I'm not comfortable bathing with you standing over

me," she said with irritation rising. "Surely I can be trusted for ten minutes."

"It's not a matter of trust," Jack caught her arm. "That is the first watering hole off the desert. Someone, anyone, could see you."

"So, I'll go a little further downstream, closer to camp." She pulled away from him. "Don't worry, I'll be right back."

He stared at her. "Make it quick," he finally said.

She rolled her eyes. "Jack—you advise me on what to do every second we're together. Please leave me alone for once. I'll be fine."

He scowled as she marched off. She immediately felt bad for what she'd said. She talked to herself as she went. *It's just a quick bath. I can take care of myself for ten minutes.*

"Anna!" he called to her. "Come back for a second." Her annoyance grew worse. Perhaps the hot sun had drained all the courtesy out of her.

"What?" Anna called back in a sharp tone she was surprised to hear come out of her mouth. He ran up and tossed her a hard chunk of something. She smelled it. "Soap!" She flashed an embarrassed smile and tromped off.

Anna had intended to bathe closer to camp, but as she reached the stream, she realized the original point was the only good place for getting down the banks. She headed through the trees and down the bank to the edge of the creek. Immediately, she took off her clothes and dipped her body in. She had to lie on her stomach to not touch the bottom. She lathered up and let the small current carry the soap and dirt away. *Ah, heaven!* Anna could have stayed there all day, but remembering her promise to be quick, she climbed on a rock, dried for a moment and pulled her dirty outer covering around her. *I wish I could wash all these filthy clothes.* At least she dunked her underclothes in and swished them in the clear water.

Just then, she heard a splash behind her. She sat up straight. A small creature swam toward her. It was the size of a medium dog with a mouse-brown coat. *A beaver?* Anna jumped up when its head came out of the water. Their eyes met. Its face was like a seal's with long white teeth protruding out of its mouth. It squealed and dove under the water, splashing its large, webbed front feet.

Anna was already backing up out of the water when another one emerged—five times the size of the first. *Its mother?* Clutching her clothes to her chest, Anna scrambled up the bank and bolted toward camp.

With a leap, the thing was after her, snarling and slapping its giant webbed claws through the water as it raced behind her. It was as fast as a bear. Anna ran through the underbrush, screaming as she went. *By any god in heaven, please help.*

"Jack! Help!" was all she could manage as she crashed toward camp. Every time a branch scratched or pulled at her she was sure the creature's claws were grabbing her. "Jack!" It was catching her. She dared not turn around, but felt its weight pounding the ground after her. She dropped her clothes as she scrambled over a fallen tree—where was camp?

As she screamed again an arrow whizzed over her head. Then another, and another, and another. Anna glanced over her shoulder. The creature stumbled to a halt and shook its head. It snarled a last time and headed back to its young one wailing in the distance.

Anna leaned against a tree and gasped for breath. She wrapped her garment quickly around her as Jack appeared in front of her.

"What was that thing?" Anna said, shaken. "I've never seen anything like that—hey, how did you get here so fast?"

"I heard you calling," Jack avoided her eyes.

"And why didn't you kill it?"

"She had a young one to care for. It wasn't her fault you were splashing in her watering hole." His eyes said *I told you so* in a most irritating way.

"What?" Anna said, her face flushing. "How did you know

she had a pup or whatever you call it? You followed me?" Jack didn't answer. "You followed me, climbed a tree and watched me?"

He stared at her.

"Deny it!"

"Anna, I wasn't looking *at* you, just looking out *for* you. Big difference," Jack tried to cover a smile. "And as it turns out, you should be happy I did."

She sniffed. Her heart still hammered in her chest. "You didn't answer me—what was that thing?"

"A bunyip." He frowned. "You hear stories about them, but I never thought they existed."

Just then Anna realized she had to go back to get her underclothes. Would this day never end?

"Well, whatever it was, it wanted me for dinner," Anna said as she turned to retrace her steps. She took a few steps before fear stopped her.

Now he laughed out loud. "Where are you going?"

"I have to go back for my clothes, which I dropped as the jaws of death were pursuing me," she snapped, the embarrassment making her cross. "May I have your sword?"

"No, I'll go with you."

"Of course, why not? I suppose I can't get any more humiliated!"

Jack chuckled as he followed her, putting an arrow to the bow. "I didn't see much…" he murmured.

"What was that?" Anna snapped as she picked her clothes up off the forest floor. She only thought they were filthy before. In fact, she looked at her dirty feet and legs and wondered if the bath had been any good at all. Fatigue and frustration washed over her.

"Nothing."

When Anna caught back up to him, he held his arm out, motioning for her to go in front of him. His hand grazed her shoulder, pulling the fabric down and baring her shoulder. He opened his mouth to say something. Anna slapped his hand away with one hand and drew her knife with the other. He jumped back.

"What are you doing? I just saved your life!"

Anna pointed the tip of the knife at him.

"Don't you ever lay a hand on me again, *Jack*!"

Jack's eyes widened. Anna pressed her lips together furiously and withdrew the knife. Jack's right hand had instinctively gone to his sword. He released the handle of his blade. He walked back to camp ahead of her in stunned silence.

She followed him, heart still pounding, shocked at her own behavior. *He saved my life twice, and this is how I act?* Perhaps the heat, embarrassment and exhaustion had overwhelmed her, but she wasn't about to apologize. She went to Star and buried her head in the tired horse's soft mane. Star's ears flicked to acknowledge her presence, but she didn't move. Anna stroked her neck, rubbed down her shoulders and rump. The horse leaned into her touch and nuzzled her arm. Anna scratched Star's neck. The horse's steady, deep breathing somehow calmed Anna. She took a deep breath of her own.

That evening, after moving some miles from the watering hole, Jack sat roasting a freshly shot rabbit at a small fire. He hadn't spoken to her since the incident. She went to the saddle bags and pulled out bread and dried fruit. She didn't deserve any rabbit, but he offered anyway. They both ate in silence, watching the flames lick the last of the sticks. Jack lit a pipe. He smoked in silence for a while, and finally Anna couldn't stand the tension one second longer. She scooted next to him.

"I didn't know you smoked," she said.

"Only when I'm angry," he said through clenched teeth.

"Oh," Anna whispered. She thought of retreating to her horse but decided to try again. There was nowhere to run. Looking straight ahead, she said, "About what happened earlier. I'm sorry." Apologizing had never been her strength. He didn't respond for a moment, and she got up to leave.

"Wait," he said. "Let me try to understand what happened today. First, you foolishly go off on your own after I tell you not to, you almost get eaten by a mythical creature, from which I saved you, and then you pull a blade on me? For what?"

Anna sat in silence, a tear balancing on the edge of her eyelid. She closed her eyes, and it slid down toward her nose.

"All because you thought I was spying on you? You know what?" His voice grew louder. "I swore an oath to your father to serve him faithfully until he releases me. You are the daughter of the king. I know for a fact he'd want me to protect you with my life, which you and I both know I'd lay down for you in an instant. Seeing you without your clothes wasn't important compared to getting you back to your father in one piece! It's my honor and duty to do so!" He threw his hands in the air and waved her off, dismissing her. Anger flashed through Anna.

"Honor and duty to return me?" she repeated. "Like a lost piece of property? You know nothing about me." She stomped back to her mat.

"I know enough. You're a spoiled little princess who's always gotten her way and probably had every fine thing imaginable and yet never was satisfied. Am I close? I bet it wasn't even Seamus you overheard. Why would he do such a thing? I hope you're just not trying to repay him for giving you some well-deserved discipline!" He turned around as her mouth fell open. "I'd heard you were a handful for your father, but I never believed it. Until now."

"That's none of your business," Anna spat. "You have no idea what you are saying."

Jack grunted. "I pity your father."

"I never had any parents who cared about me," Anna's voice was intense. "Mother died before I could have any decent memories of her, and the man my father was died along with her."

Anna threw herself on her mat. *He doesn't believe me about*

Seamus. My father won't either. I'm doomed. We're doomed. She clenched her fists and fought back angry tears. Angry at Jack. Angry at herself. But mostly, she was angry at how much she needed him. She felt him lie down next to her and was angry at the part of her that was glad he was near, especially with the bunyip still out there. They didn't speak again as night fell.

Jack stirred next to her, and she moved a little closer to him. Snakes and bunyips. Her hand slipped to the dagger. She stared into the woods for hours, holding back the threatening tears.

Chapter 11

In the morning, Anna found Jack smoking by the fire. She dropped next to him.

"Still angry?" she asked, gesturing to the pipe.

He exhaled. "No. I guess I just wanted to finish it off." His jaw was set. She bit her lip. He didn't have to like her, but she wanted him to at least understand her a little. She grabbed a twig and drew circles with it in the soft earth. Her heart throbbed as she broke the silence.

"Again, I'm sorry about yesterday." Her chest was so tight she thought it might burst. "I've never told anyone—not Stefan or Mary, my nurse. But maybe you'd understand more if you heard a story." Anna closed her eyes and took a deep breath.

When she opened them, out of the corner of her eye Anna saw Jack turn toward her. She kept her gaze down, following the twig's scratches in the dirt. Her voice trembled.

"One night when I was twelve years old, there was a ball at the palace. I wasn't old enough to go, but after it had begun, I snuck into my sister's room and slipped into her smallest gown. It was still too big, but I found a servant and demanded she pin it up for me. I borrowed Saira's jewelry, did my hair the best I could and smeared her cosmetics on my face. I had a wonderful evening. It was great fun dancing with the younger soldiers in the smaller ballroom, far from the notice of Father or anyone in the court. I was just a few inches shorter than I am now, so I blended in. Until I ran into Seamus. I was leaving early, sneaking out the side door when he bumped into me. He was drunk and almost knocked me to the ground. He had a woman with him, but he still looked me up and down in a way that made me feel queasy. I thought it was because I had interrupted his moment with the woman.

"When I returned to my room Mary drew me a bath and then left. I bolted the door behind her and headed for the bathtub. Before I got in, there was a knock. Supposing it to be Mary who had left something behind, I wrapped myself in a robe, opened the door and peeked around the corner. To my surprise, it was Seamus. I tried to shut the door, explaining I wasn't dressed."

"He shoved his way into the room, despite my protests. I'll never forget him turning and slowly locking the door. He had a strange look in eyes—I can still see them gleaming down at me." Anna paused, wondering if she could keep going. Jack's firm jaw quivered. She continued. "I can still smell the wine on him." She swallowed hard to get the lump out of her throat.

"I tried to get away from him, but he grabbed me and covered my mouth. I stepped backward and tripped on something. I twisted away from him as I fell, toppling my whole dinner tray over with me. I landed on my stomach, and miraculously my hand fell on a knife from my tray. He grabbed me and rolled me over. As his face came toward mine, I cut him under his eye to just above his mouth. There was a lot of blood —all over my robe. He let me go. I can remember lying on the floor watching him look in the mirror. He was furious. He's barely even been wounded in battle, and here a little girl scarred him where everyone would see it forever. I crawled backward, slipping in his blood, holding the knife before me. And then, there was a noise, something outside that distracted him. He knocked the knife from my hand, stripped off my robe and used it to mop up the blood. Then he threw me into the tub, cleaned the rest of the blood, threatened me to tell no one and stormed out, holding my robe to his face. I think he burned it. Nurse scolded me for losing it."

Anna closed her eyes for a moment, trying to erase the humiliating memory even as she told it. "From that day on, he's hated me." Anna peeked at Jack, to see if he believed her. "He changed that day."

"That's how he got the scar?" Jack's mouth dropped open. "Not from a practice joust?"

Anna blushed and nodded. Then Jack tilted his head toward her. "Did he... hurt you?" Anna knew what he was asking.

"No, he didn't and never has. So, obviously it could have been much worse. He did tell me if I told anyone he'd take my ponies out to the mountains, cut their legs open and let the wolves finish them off."

"So you never told anyone to protect your ponies?" Jack asked.

Anna frowned. "Don't think he wouldn't have done it. I was young and scared. I couldn't understand how someone who was my godfather could suddenly do such a thing. He had been kind to me, but from then on, he was a different person. Besides, I loved those ponies."

She glanced up and found his eyes searching hers. "After that, whenever I saw him, he'd whisper some horrible thing he'd do to me if I told. He'd show up in my room or at the stables sometimes just to harass me. And I never knew if he'd try, well, try again." Anna stopped and looked at Jack directly for the first time. "You must understand how afraid I was—am of him. Everyone is afraid of Seamus." Anna got up and walked away, suddenly ashamed. *Jack doesn't care.* She crossed her arms tight to her stomach. *What was I thinking telling him this?* She heard Jack's steps behind her.

"I know people think I'm spoiled or crazy," said Anna with her back to Jack. "But the last four years I've lived in fear. Father was lost without mother. Then Seamus poisoned him against me, so that if I ever told, Father would never believe my story. I'm a threat to him in that way, I suppose. I have no mother and am only a nuisance to my father. Seamus twists the truth and turns him against me." Jack was silent. "Stefan was always on my side, but he's grown busy with the army, and is gone months at a time. And as you know, Seamus sent him away just before I left."

"What about Saira?" Jack murmured.

"She had just returned from studying abroad for four years when I was captured." Her hands shook as she brushed a loose hair out of her eyes.

Jack was speechless. Anna couldn't tell what was going on behind those steely eyes.

"I have been haunted in my own home. I've wanted to leave so many times. If it weren't for the danger my father is in, I'm not sure I would go back now that I'm free of Anwar."

Jack stepped closer.

"Your father loves you," he whispered. "You know you mean more to him than Seamus or anyone else. He'd do anything to protect you, his daughter, his own flesh and blood. You must know he has favored you from the beginning."

"I don't know that and besides, he'll never favor me now. By now he knows what I've done." She told him about the jeweled brush. "Seamus will refute my story and use my use of magic gems as a way to force Father to have me executed. He won't have a choice." Anna wouldn't look at Jack. Fresh tears rolled down her cheeks at the thought. "He'll never believe me over Seamus."

"No, he will believe you when you tell him everything. The king has the right to pardon anyone. He'd never put you to death," Jack said. "That is nonsense." Softness filled those blue eyes. His arm hovered toward her and then fell as she backed away.

"You didn't believe me before. I don't blame you. You don't know me, and I can act a little crazy sometimes. After the bath, I was angry and just reacted. You didn't deserve that. And by the way," she tried to smile, "I never thanked you for saving my life."

He moved to touch her hand, then hesitated.

"It's okay." She grinned. "I'm not afraid." She took his hand. "I'm sorry."

Jack lifted her chin with his free finger. Anna wanted to turn away, but the tip of his finger and his captivating gaze held her.

"I'm the one who is sorry, Anna. I'm sorry I questioned you. I should have never spoken to you that way. You have gone through too much at a young age," he said. "I will protect you, and I promise, when we get home, we will expose Seamus." He dropped his finger to touch his sword. "His treachery will end, and you will feel safe in your own home."

Anna dropped her chin. "I feel safe with you now." She stole a glance at him as she felt heat go to her cheeks. She was exposed before him. She tucked her hair behind an ear. She studied him—that quiet physical confidence warring with the occasional flash of sorrow and insecurity in his eyes. She was suddenly aware of how close they were. He locked eyes with her and finally gave her a lopsided grin.

She knew she should drop his hand, but she wanted to hold onto him. She had always thought if she told someone about Seamus that she'd feel nothing but shame. But not with Jack. She felt her heart slowly opening. She squeezed his hand tight before letting it fall. She frowned up at him.

"What's your story, Jack?" she asked. "How did you end up here?" Anna asked.

"That's a long story." He doused the fire with a splash from the canteen. "Let's get moving."

Chapter 12

They continued riding north under tall pines, hard maples and wide oaks as well as through underbrush that poked and tore at them along the way. After yesterday's conversation with Jack, Anna's chest was lighter—like it had cracked open and something ugly that festered within her for years was finally out. She felt cleaner somehow. Perhaps things could be set right in the palace.

What she would have given to kick Star up to a gallop. Instead, she took a deep breath and filled her lungs with fresh air. Her heart bounced with the springy gait of the mare underneath her. When they stopped for a meal, Jack motioned for her to come over. He presented her with the silver handle of his sword. "Let me see what you know."

He picked up a sturdy tree branch and snapped off the twigs springing from it.

Anna stretched the sword out before her, gauging its weight. Heavy. "I'd never be able to handle this thing. I might stick with a dagger," she said.

"Just for fun," he said, slipping a thin leather sheath over it for safety. He drew his tree branch. She laughed as he took a step toward her, gently swinging it at her shoulder. She blocked it and swung her own sword around, striking at his chest. He sidestepped out of its reach. "Oh—" He laughed. "You do know how to handle a sword, a bit."

"Stefan taught me. It was one of the many things I loved that Father did not approve of." She swung the sword again. Her skills were nothing compared to his effortless ability. She was trying hard, but she knew he was just playing. His feet and eyes danced. She whipped the sword over to strike his side, but the sword's weight threw her off balance. She let her arm fall.

"Your sword is too heavy for me." Though she'd worked hard as a slave, lack of food and rest had taken its toll on her body. She had lost so much weight. His eyes fell to her skinny shoulders. She curled them back, away from him.

"Practice with it every day. You'll grow stronger," he said.

Anna scowled. "Perhaps I'd like to rest when we stop?"

"Oh, no," he retorted. "You who ride stallions in races and fight off a great swordsman can handle this."

"I didn't fight him off," Anna mumbled as she drew the sword once again, swinging it at his ridiculous log-sword. She bit her lip at the effort.

Day after day they sparred, and Anna didn't see any improvement on her part. Her arms ached as she tumbled off Star for the last time one evening. Jack said he'd hunt for dinner, but Anna didn't care. She barely had the strength to unroll her mat. He said something to her, but she was already drifting off. *So tired, so tired*, her mind kept repeating. She didn't move as she felt rough hands cover her with a cloak and gently smooth the hair away from her face.

THE NEXT DAYS provided more riding and sparring. Anna was always hungry, and Jack kept busy shooting game for their nightly dinners. Once he took down a buck, hauled it to a village and had it dried and salted. He paid the butcher with some of the meat and returned with a little fresh fruit and bread as well. The venison solved their need for daily protein, but it didn't taste like much. Still, Anna chewed and chewed on it as they rode.

As if Anna weren't humiliated enough by her performance with the heavy sword, after a couple weeks, Jack added archery to her training. Normally she loved archery, but her arms were so exhausted, she could barely hold the string back. She was flustered by her sorry display.

"Honestly," she told Jack. "At home, I could shoot well. I just lost my strength eating two bowls of horrible rice every day." She tossed the bow to the ground. "Give me a day's break."

"You can quit whenever you want." Jack raised an eyebrow as he picked up the bow. "If that's what you want." He plucked leaves out of the string.

Anna groaned. She *wanted* to quit.

Jack curled his lips in a poor attempt to hide his grin. He put an arrow to the string and released, striking a tree some distance away.

"Here," he said, handing her the bow. "Put an arrow below mine. It's an easy distance."

Anna couldn't help but look where his arrow had landed. It *was* an easy distance.

"All right." She placed an arrow on the string and drew it back by her right ear, ignoring the protests in her arm. The bow quivered slightly. She released the arrow. *Ping.* The arrow struck the tree not six inches below Jack's arrow.

"Good." He winked. "You have some skill."

She glared at him. "I have more than *some skill*."

"I'd love to see it," he said. "See that tree beyond with all the pinecones hanging down in a bunch?"

She had to squint. *Oh no. It was far.* "Yes, but I don't know if I can manage it today with my sore arm," she said, pulling the string back. She'd never shot that far, but he didn't need to know that.

"Let me help." He stepped behind her, put his hand on top of hers and pulled the string back an inch further. Her arm trembled. She felt his strong arms around her and his warm breath just above her left ear. She aimed, tipping her bow a little higher to compensate for the distance.

"Good, now, release!" Jack said.

Off went the arrow and down came the pinecones.

"We got it!" His eyes lit up. He pulled her in for a quick one-armed hug. For a moment she forgot the fear, the urgency to go home. All she could think about was the feel of his skin on hers. She blushed, worried he could sense her throbbing heart. He held her gaze for a moment before jogging off to find the arrows. Anna pursed her lips and studied him. He moved with the quickness and stealth of a predator. She was glad he was on her side. He jumped halfway up the tree and pulled out the embedded arrow like she pulled a pin out of her hair. It was nothing to him. He inspected each arrow tip and brushed aside any debris. He caught her eye and Anna couldn't help the rush of pleasure that he flushed a little at her stare.

The next evening, they hunted. It had been a while since they'd had fresh meat. The thought of striking down an animal made Anna's knees a little weak, but she would try.

They crept along the forest floor until they scared up a large rabbit.

"Now!" whispered Jack. Her arrow landed right behind the darting rabbit. "Good try." He nodded.

They ran a little farther, again flushing the poor rabbit out of its hiding place. Before it had jumped three times Jack had pierced it with an arrow.

"How can you do that so easily?" she asked.

"Practice."

Thankfully Jack spared her the unpleasant job of cleaning

the rabbit. Anna started a fire with Jack's flint stone—another task she'd finally learned. She tried to rub the ache out of her shoulders. Sore or not, she had to admit she loved improving her skills. If a battle came to Sunderland, she would be ready.

"You must think we'll be fighting our way to Sunderland," Anna said. "I can't imagine you are training me for the battlefield."

"No. Battles are ugly, horrible places. I would never wish that for you. The memories of killing stay with you forever."

"Then why are you teaching me this?" Anna stood.

"Lots of reasons. One, something could happen to me and you'd still need to get home. Two, you tend to attract bad luck—like that strange snake. Three, you'll be a lot safer in general if you know how to defend yourself."

"I could fight in the battle then."

"No. Don't think for a second you'd last long against grown men who've trained for years."

"That's insulting," said Anna.

"I don't mean to insult you. I've known a few women in the desert who've trained their whole lives to be masters of the sword and dagger. I faced one in my training who taught me to never underestimate an opponent." He lifted his shirt to display a jagged scar across his muscled abdomen. "But if anyone tells you it's not an ugly business, they're lying."

Anna reached her hand toward his scar. Their eyes met. She closed her fingers and pulled her arm back after hovering over his skin. He pulled his shirt down.

"Was it serious?" she asked.

"Not as serious as it was for her." His face paled as his eyes drifted.

Anna sensed a terrible memory lurking. She didn't know whether to pry.

"I have scars," she blurted.

"I know."

"You've seen them then?" She searched his face.

He hesitated before nodding. "At the creek."

"Are they bad? Do they look like yours?"

She watched his Adam's apple move up and down as he swallowed. Choosing his words.

"No. This almost killed me." He gestured to his stomach. "Yours are surface wounds."

She was quiet for a minute. "Thank you for all you've done for Sunderland."

He nodded.

"Do you think scars make you stronger?" she asked.

"Scars can be a teacher, I suppose. They make you stronger if you learn from them."

"You are strong enough for both of us." Sudden emotion clouded her voice.

"You are a daughter of kings. Strength flows in Sunderland blood. We will make it." He squeezed her shoulder.

Anna nodded. "We must."

Their journey northward continued. And Jack was right. After almost two weeks, muscles were forming under her sleeves. The sword that had once seemed clumsy felt lighter every day. She sliced the air in front of her and smiled in delight.

"Come and fight." Jack held up his branch. The leather sheath on the sword met the wood in the air with a thud. As the joust began, Anna found herself swinging and spinning with more skill than she knew she had. She aimed for his legs and missed.

"Move your feet, that's it, back, then forward. Remember, it's harder to hit a moving target." He panted. "Look for an opening. It's about skill and strength, but for you, mostly speed."

She shot her blade at his ribs and struck hard.

"Hey—" Jack backed up, holding his side. He squinted at her. "Good. Point one for Anna."

"Yes!" She beamed and raised her sword. She shuffled back a couple steps, tripped over a stump and fell, barely stretching her arm out in time to break the impact. He laughed.

"Yeah, that's what I get for gloating." Anna rolled her eyes at herself.

He took a deep breath and sat down next to her. "Perhaps enough for today?"

"Not on your life!" Anna leaped up and spun her sword around, gracefully resting it under his chin. "You should know better than to lower your defenses!"

He raised his arms in mock surrender. A flick of his leg tripped her, but his arm extended just in time to break her fall. He grinned and raised his eyebrows as she jabbed him with her elbow.

They both laughed, and she flopped back into the leaves again, staring up at the puffy white clouds floating effortlessly in the bright blue sky. She closed her eyes as she caught her breath. What she would have given to have this adventure under different circumstances. But just as the thought passed through her mind, the nagging urgency of their mission returned. Her stomach flipped. Anna glanced Jack's way and found him watching her.

Her stomach flipped again for a different reason. His gaze moved to her mouth. She bit her lower lip and turned away to fight the sudden desire to feel the touch of him.

"Will we make it back in time?" She asked the question to push other thoughts from her mind.

"We need to pin our ears back."

As she let go of the sword, her hand brushed his. He took it in his palm, lightly rubbing her knuckles with his thumb. Her heart throbbed in response. She wanted to lean her head against his shoulder. It felt so good to have someone on her side.

"We'll make it," he whispered, suddenly serious.

"There's no one else I'd rather have by my side than you." She laced her fingers through his. "No one else."

The corners of his mouth twitched up. "I'm so glad I found you."

She returned his smile. "Maybe it's time I watered the horses."

Her hands felt clammy as she untied Avery. Her stomach refused to settle. Jack had pulled out a sharpening stone and was working on his sword. She led the horse to the creek. She forced herself to act normal as she returned for Star and watered her as well. She started as a flock of blackbirds croaked noisily overhead, followed conspicuously by a rabbit bounding through the brush. Odd.

"The horses are ready," she called to Jack. He motioned for her to be quiet and join him. He brought his mouth down to her ear.

"Someone is coming," he whispered.

Anna's eyes grew wide as they hurried behind some large bushes. It wasn't easy keeping the horses quiet.

"Hide here," he whispered. "I'll be back."

She watched him disappear around the corner of the brush pile. His bow was strapped to his back and long dagger out. Every muscle in her body was taut. The horses picked up on her tension and stomped their feet. She wished Jack hadn't gone alone. He was capable, of course, but she couldn't stand this waiting. After about thirty tortuous minutes, he returned.

"There is an army camping in the forest. We'll have to turn east to avoid it," he said. "Whoever was coming our way must have turned back."

Making as little noise as possible, they mounted their horses and headed east. Off and on that day, Jack would dismount and travel north for a while, returning only to tell Anna he had found more soldiers. They were gathering here. He pointed out their tracks any time they crossed them. Anna's stomach was tight, and she strained to hear any movement in the woods. They rode a few more hours and just as the trees opened into a clearing, they spotted soldiers grazing their horses. Jack backed up Avery.

"I hope we haven't been seen," he said, filling his quiver. "Take the sword, we may be in for trouble." They retreated into the woods. Anna's hand shook as she gripped the weapon.

"Stay here." Jack took a couple steps.

"Don't leave me," she whispered. "I'm safer with you anyway."

Jack's eyes cut through her like ice, but he relented. "You must be absolutely quiet."

They ground-tied the horses and then crept through the brush toward the soldiers. Jack's leather boots did not make a sound, and Anna tried hard to emulate him. She tested every step before putting her whole weight down lest she snap a twig. When she fell behind, Jack waited for her. They moved behind a large boulder and crept from rock to rock until they were dangerously close. The soldiers' conversations drifted toward them.

"I hate all this waiting around," one said. "Why can't we get on with it?"

"Because, you idiot, we're waiting for the rest to join us."

"We have plenty of men to take down that yellow-bellied king," the first replied. "We could be burning their flesh in a week." He took a drink from a flask. "King Vilipp is a weak, depressed, sick old man. From what I hear, he can't even keep a handle on his own family."

Anna's heart fluttered. That was *her* father they were talking about.

"Regardless, our superiors want to draw all their forces at once. We must wait for the rest. We'll outnumber them so much they won't have a chance."

Anna felt the blood drain from her face.

"How many more are we talking about?" the first man asked.

"At least a thousand."

"We've so many soldiers packed in these trees I can hardly breathe as it is," grumbled the first one. "Let's go back and see if they've shot any deer yet."

After the soldiers left, Jack and Anna crept back to their patient steeds. Jack thought it prudent to stay hidden and not cross the meadow until dark. The moonlight would have to be enough to guide them.

Jack and Anna unpacked the horses in the thicket and tried to get some rest. Anna couldn't close her eyes. Her senses were heightened to every movement, every sound. And her mind kept repeating the soldiers' conversation over and over. *Another thousand men. Their flesh would be burning...* The urgency in her chest made her heart feel like bursting. Her eyes found Jack's. He wasn't asleep either.

"Will we ever make it in time?" she whispered cautiously.

He shook his head. "I don't know." He motioned for her to be quiet. They ate a little and waited for the sun to set. As darkness fell, they watered the horses and let them graze at the edge of the meadow until the blackness enveloped them. Chilly air blew against Anna's face. She leaned into it, a new determination fueling her soul.

"No matter what happens to me," Anna said, "I want you to go on. Leave me if you must, but Father must be warned. I'm tempted to order you to go on without me. You'd get there quicker riding alone."

Jack stepped close to her. "We'll go together, every step of this journey." He tucked her hair behind her left ear. The darkness shielded his eyes from her, but Anna could feel them burning into her anyway. "That's not negotiable." He squeezed her hand and mounted Avery. The faithful horse was ready.

Her fingers tingled from his touch as she gripped Star's reins. Jack wouldn't leave her. She suspected he was motivated by more than just duty to her father, but she couldn't be sure. She was, however, surprised at her own conviction. If it came to it, she would give her life for her country.

Anna mounted Star and steered her next to Avery's neck. They listened intently for any noise. Hopefully the soldiers would be sleeping, and they'd pass unnoticed.

Chapter 13

All night they rode heading northeast, in the opposite direction of the castle, which lay to the north and west of the desert. With each step, Anna's stomach twisted tighter. Every time they turned north, they ran into sleeping armies. Jack had no idea how this many men had eluded the network of northern spies. Was Anwar using some sort of cloaking gem from afar, or—

"The Black Woods." Jack scowled.

"What?"

"The armies are forcing us toward the Black Woods."

"Even I have heard of that dark place. No one ventures there." Anna bit her lower lip.

They had been planning to go straight north, to the west of the Black Woods. "How long would it take to ride around the Black Woods to the east?"

"Weeks. Too long." Jack cursed under his breath.

Luckily no scout had spotted them. Anna was surprised how cold the night had become. She shivered visibly. Jack pulled up to rest.

"We can't risk a fire," he said. "But you can wear my cloak if you like." He took it off.

"No," Anna said. "I can't let you freeze."

Jack ignored her, draping the leather garment around her shoulders even as Anna shivered again. She slid off the mare and pressed her body against the horse's warmth, letting Star block the wind. Star moved her head to Anna and exhaled her sweet breath. She patted her neck and ran her fingers through her black mane.

Soon they watered the horses and moved on again. Anna gasped at the cold wind when she remounted. Still Jack pressed on until the darkness changed into a midnight blue. The cold numbed her cheeks, and her eyelids grew heavy from the mare's steady walk. Her chin bobbed to her chest more than once and Anna shook herself awake. One by one, the stars disappeared. The sky morphed into a dark gray that gradually lightened until a single golden ray appeared over the horizon. Before long, the light illuminated the mist creeping up from the ground, adding damp to the chilly air. Finally, Jack pulled Avery to a stop.

"How are you doing?" he asked. "I hate that we had to ride all night through the cold." He shivered.

Anna tumbled off Star, pain from her numb feet and legs shooting up to her hips. "I should apologize to you for wearing your cloak all night," she said. "But the important thing is getting home as quick as we can." Anna stretched her fingers that had grown cold and stiff from holding the reins.

"I should have thought to get you your own cloak. Let me check out the area," he said, handing Avery's reins to her. Reading her eyes, he added, "I'll be back shortly."

After unpacking and tying up the horses, Anna sat down against a large oak tree, with her back to the wind.

As promised, Jack soon returned and offered her dried figs and stale bread.

"How are we doing on our food supply?" Anna asked.

"We are getting a little low," Jack replied. "I was planning to stop at a village on the other side of this forest, but we'll not make it there now."

"What will we do?"

"Hunt."

"Can we risk a fire?"

"We will have to be careful. We may get to the point where we have no choice. It will take us five more days to get to the mountain pass. Then it may take a week or more to follow the river to Karfin."

Anna furrowed her brow. The knots in her empty stomach weren't accepting the scant breakfast well.

"Get some rest," Jack said, sliding his hat down over his dirty face. Anna took her hair down and let it fall around her neck, providing some small amount of warmth. As uncomfortable as she was, soon she was asleep.

When she awoke, Anna figured it must be mid-afternoon. The wind had died down, and Anna gratefully greeted the warmer air. Jack was gone. She stretched and rubbed the kinks out of her arms and shoulders. She thought of all her warm baths at home. No, perhaps it was better not to think about it. She smoothed her filthy hair as she put it back up. It was too cold for a bath, but she found a stream and washed her face and hands. She dried them on her dirty clothes and found Jack rubbing down Avery.

"How's he holding up?" Anna asked cautiously.

"They deserve a long vacation in green pastures, that's for sure." Jack gave Avery a pat. "We need to keep an eye on your mare," he said. "She's losing weight."

Indeed, she was. Anna had noticed she was pulling up the girth further than a few weeks ago. She led Star to some grass. The mare devoured it, tugging on the rope.

She let the mare eat for several hours, then loaded her up as the sun started to set. Jack was already on Avery.

"You finish with her, and I'll be right back," said Jack. "I want to look around before we start." He handed her the sword which she tied to the saddle. Anna watched him slip daggers into sheaths on either hip.

Anna finished tacking up Star and packing her few things onto her back. She stroked the mare's neck as a chill crept up her spine. Anna shook it off as the darkness enveloped her. Leaves rustled behind her and she felt the strong sense of being watched. A twig snapped on her other side and Anna looked expectantly for Jack. She mounted Star and turned her toward the noise. The horse skidded to the side and snorted. Anna pulled her back around and came face-to-face with a huge, solitary gray wolf.

He blinked and opened his mouth. His long red tongue flopped out between huge white teeth. This was no ordinary wolf. He was more than half the size of Star.

Anna froze.

Star swerved to the side while Anna fumbled for the sword.

"Easy, girl." She couldn't let her bolt and trigger his predator instinct. Jack would return and shoot it.

The temperature dropped at once and Anna's breath plumed into the night air. Anna shivered as she started to sweat. His horrible red eyes held her gaze and drilled into her mind. Anna sensed a great intelligence behind them. Black hair stood up on his neck like a mane. Anna's heart froze as she fixed a death grip on the reins. *Oh, please go away!* Her heart hammered against her chest.

Then, as if he had read her mind, he disappeared. Anna let out her breath. She slipped her sword back into the scabbard strapped to the saddle. She let Star move a few steps forward. Anna didn't want to go far and miss Jack's return. Darkness closed in around her. Its malice pricked her spine. *Where was he?* Again she heard a noise and horse and rider startled together. Now not one pair of red eyes gleamed at them, but at least ten! Star bolted through the trees, directly north toward the soldiers. With the wolves on their tail, Anna pulled her to the east, away from the armies. The snarling beasts were having no trouble keeping up as they crashed through the trees. Anna attempted to avoid tree limbs, but thickets and small branches were grabbing her, whipping her face and threatening to pull her from the saddle.

Her legs gripped Star like a vise. She couldn't fall.

To Anna's relief, the forest opened up into a large field. The mare dashed into the bright moonlight, frantic to outrun the wolves. This was nothing like riding Farley in the cup. She barely hung on as Star lurched and pitched forward. She darted to the side to avoid snapping teeth. She was running for her life in full-out panic.

The wolves were not slowing. Some were biting and snapping at the mare's hind legs. Others ran ahead of them, slowly closing them off. The horse screamed in terror and pinned her ears. Anna strained and grasped her sword. She managed to pull it out without cutting the lunging horse. She leaned back and swung it at the closest wolf. He easily dodged it and came back a moment later, trying to launch onto Star's flying hindquarters.

My, how fast she runs.

Sinking my teeth into you will be so much fun.

The voices howled and snickered in her mind. Anna's panic transferred to Star and the horse sprang forward with a new surge of speed.

Her only option was to run. Their numbers were too many to fight.

Think, Anna!

But there was no way out, and Star was tiring. Foam splashed on her shoulders and onto Anna's knees. Now the wolves were easily keeping pace alongside them, with their lips curling into snarls that Anna swore were more like sneers.

Run, run, still she tries! One voice sang out in her mind.

Run, run, until she dies! **Another answered.**
A more distant wolf howled its delight.
Muscle and flesh.
Blood and bone!
All will be crushed.
With our teeth of stone.

The wolves toyed with her. Some circled ahead, causing poor Star to dodge them or trip to the ground. She was fully winded now, roaring her exhale and still mad with fear. It was time to stop and fight, or Star would be run to death.

Using all her strength, Anna pulled Star around to face the wolves. She swung her leg over Star's neck and landed on her feet, driving her sword into the side of the closest wolf. It whimpered and fell. Star screamed as she kicked, bit and struck the attacking wolves. Her fighting instincts were strong. These desert horses were amazing. The wolves broke into two groups, one concentrating on the horse and the other on the rider. The murderous voices pushed into her skull, all jesting aside now.

We're going to rip you to shreds.

One large wolf lunged at her throat. She dodged him, as he did her sword. She heard the mare scream in pain as a wolf sank its teeth into her hindquarters and then went flying as Star put her head down and kicked it off. Her ears were flat against her head and her eyes were wild with fear.

Fight, Star. Fight!

Anna put her back to the mare and stretched out her sword. Her heart sank. There were so many wolves circling them. *Too many*.

Another wolf left the ground, lunging at the horse's throat. Anna stuck her arm out, and the beast thrust itself on her sword, which was ripped out of her hand as he fell to the ground. Star screamed and reared. Anna pulled her sword out of the wolf and stabbed the side of another one, barely dodging its snapping jaws. Star swung around and kicked it in the head. It fell dead, and Anna was grateful Star hadn't hit her.

Another wolf charged her. She swung the sword, missing its neck and jamming it into its mouth against all hope as he knocked her to the ground. His breath was hot and foul. She saw Star rear above her and strike another wolf with a foreleg. She landed a foot from Anna's head. Anna kicked at the wolf on top of her, but his jaws snarled and snapped against the sword. She braced for the killing bite, but it never came. His weight was crushing her. *Why didn't he kill her?* She pushed against him, but the wolf's massive body wouldn't move. She saw Star spin and charge off. *This one must have choked to death.* She tried to pull her sword out to no avail. Anna moved further under his body to hide from the others. Horse hooves pounded the earth. *At least Star still runs.* A trickle of blood dripped from the dead wolf's mouth. Anna closed her eyes. The others were strangely silent or had dashed after Star. *Poor, dear little Star.* She had a big heart. Cold air rushed by in a gust. An evil fear jolted through her—screaming in her mind. Then it was gone.

All was silent. Then in the distance, she heard a voice calling softly.

"Anna?"

Jack.

"I'm here!" she yelled at the top of her lungs and struggled to get out from under the wolf. She called again, "I'm here, Jack."

She heard Avery slide to a stop. Jack leaped down and pulled the dead wolf off Anna. He helped her up, pulled her to his chest in a quick hug and then held her at arm's length.

"By the gods, Anna. Are you all right?" His face was pale.

"I think so." She ached all over.

"I thought you were riding Star. When I saw her bolt, I followed and killed the wolves chasing her."

"Thank goodness," Anna said, gesturing to the one that had fallen on her. "You saved my life, *again.*"

"You did pretty well on your own."

"They would have killed Star and come back for me."

"I've never seen wolves go after a horse and rider before," he said. He let Anna hold Avery and strode off to catch Star.

"These weren't ordinary wolves," Jack said. His voice shook a little.

"No. More red eyes and as crazy as it sounds, I could hear their voices—just like in Anwar's palace."

He glanced back at her. "Evil is being drawn to you. Somehow Anwar is using these gems to hunt us. Hunt you."

"How?"

"The animals crossing our path aren't natural. I don't know how, but something unnatural is possessing them."

"Is that possible?"

"A month ago, I'd have said no every time." He frowned. "But what else could it be?"

Anna glanced at the moon, shining almost full like a giant clock ticking in the night sky. "How long do we have to get home?"

"A month at most," said Jack, sitting down and putting his head in his hands. "Every decision I've made has been wrong."

"That's not true." She put a hand on his arm.

"We run into enemy men at every turn. I almost let you get killed and look at our horse. She'll be lucky to live a week." He stood to examine her.

"Please, don't say that. She'll make it." Anna tried to calm her badly shaken horse. She stroked Star's neck while Jack ran his hands over the horse's body. "They got her in her hindquarters."

He found the wound and cursed.

"It's bad then?" She'd seen the blood pouring down Star's leg.

He gave her shoulder a small squeeze.

"You are going to have to be strong." He grabbed his cloak and threw it over the shaking horse. "Try to keep her warm."

Anna talked to her in soothing tones. The mare relaxed a bit but was limping badly. Anna stopped and rubbed her with her hands, working through her muscles.

Please, Star, don't die.

Jack started a fire and heated some water in a small pot. He cooked a cloth and drew it out of the boiling water with a stick. Steam poured into the air.

"Try to hold her still," he said to Anna. "This is going to hurt." He pressed the cloth into her wound and the mare kicked plenty close to Jack's head.

"Be careful!" Anna warned.

After the wound was cleaned, Anna walked Star until she stopped shaking. She then gave the mare some water, tied her up and sat by the fire. Jack was already there, staring into the smoldering embers.

"Unfortunately, we need to let this fire go out," he said as she watched it slowly dying. "We could easily be spotted out in this field."

"Okay." Unexplainable tears welled in her eyes and slipped down her face. Her legs felt wobbly. Jack put his arm around her, shaking her slightly.

"Hey, I'm sorry about the ranting. We're going to be okay. And no matter what, I'm not leaving you again—for any reason."

The truth was Anna couldn't have explained why she was crying even if she had tried. It had been a long couple of days. He pulled her chin up and forced her to look him in the eyes.

"You did well, Anna. You killed half the pack all on your own. This whole thing was my fault, not yours. Possessed or no, most animals I can handle. From now on, we will be safe."

"It all happened so fast." Anna wiped her face.

"You said you wanted to be in a battle," he said. "Well, that was your first."

Anna looked at the dead wolves. She felt a little sick as she remembered killing two of them with the sword. She had always thought wolves to be intelligent, noble beasts. That was probably because she'd never been on the menu before.

"I am sorry about Star," Jack nodded to the mare.

"When do you think I can ride her?" Anna asked, hoping Jack would say something different than what her heart told her would be true.

"I don't know yet what we're going to do. We may have to leave the mare behind."

"No! Not after all she's brought us through!" Anna's eyes threatened tears again. She slid to the ground. *Not Star.*

"I need to think," he said, rubbing his brow. "Why don't you clean your sword and get some rest?"

Her sword was smeared with blood and gray hair. She stared at it a moment, tasting stomach acid in her mouth. Jack leaned across her to take it.

"I'll clean it," he said. "Get some rest."

Anna took him up on the offer, laying her head on the hard ground by the dying fire. She tried to rest but kept seeing those red eyes boring into her. Her eyes snapped open. *It's not real,* she told herself. *Jack is close.* She swallowed hard and closed her eyes again. Now gleaming white teeth and hot breath lunged at her throat. She gasped and sat up quickly.

Jack was at her side in a moment.

"Are you all right?"

"Yes, just…" She was embarrassed to explain her fear to him. "When I hear you moving around, I think I'm hearing something else."

"I'm finished until morning. I'll stay with you until you sleep." He unrolled the mat, and Anna crawled on it. He sat next to her.

She took a deep breath. Eventually her fatigued body surrendered to sleep.

Before dawn, Jack gently shook her awake.

"We need to get out of here before sunrise." Anna willed her stiff, sore body to sit up. She took a sip of water.

Jack had packed up Avery with everything except Star's saddle. Anna joined him, and he handed the mare's reins to her.

"Let's go," he said.

"Where?" Anna asked.

"I've spent the whole night thinking about just that question."

Chapter 14

"First," Jack said, "we get out of this field and find some cover." He started leading Avery to the northwest. The sky in the east was just turning steely gray. Anna followed a little behind with the limping mare. "Second, we make some decisions. There doesn't seem to be a way to cut back west without running into enemy soldiers." He grimaced.

Anna drew up next to him. She sensed his tension. "We are so far east now, and with the mare hurt, I don't see how we can make it to the king in time," he muttered.

Anna's heart dropped. "Those woods up ahead." She pointed. "Are they part of the same forest we left?"

Jack shook his head. "No, that is the edge of the Black Woods." He wouldn't meet her eyes.

"The Forest of Mor." Anna shuddered. "We can't go there."

"No one who enters there ever returns, so the old superstition says." Jack's voice was quiet, his shoulders slumped.

"And why are we heading straight for it?"

"Sneaking through the forest is our only hope of getting to your father in time," he said. "It's a shortcut to the base of the mountains. We go through the mountain pass on the other side of the forest, and we'll find the river that flows in front of your castle." He stopped Avery. "It's what I must do, but I don't want to put your life at risk." He closed his eyes briefly. Those normally cheerful blue eyes now reflected great weariness.

"What do you want me to do?" Anna whispered.

"Make a terrible choice. I honestly don't know which is worse for you. Either follow me into the forest—and with any luck, home—or flee to the north and east where you could find refuge in the kingdoms there." His lips pressed together. "I would somehow find you later. I know I just told you yesterday I'd never leave you again, and here I am proposing just that." His brows pulled into a frown, and he rubbed a hand over his ashen face. He stopped and rolled his shoulders forward.

Anna blinked. She thought about wandering alone, pursued by angry beasts. There wasn't a choice.

"Of course I'll stay with you. If I must die, I'd rather it be trying to help my people," she answered. "I can't run away when they need me the most."

He squeezed her hand and nodded as if he had known that would be her decision. Devastation was in those blue eyes.

He thinks all is lost.

She frowned. He shouldn't be blaming himself. "I should have stood up to Seamus long ago, and none of this would have happened."

His face clouded. "You were too young."

"I suppose, but I should have done a lot of things differently," Anna said. "I'm going to change when I get back."

"You're not the girl I remember racing around the palace, that's for sure." He frowned again and sucked a deep breath into his lungs. "I just can't believe this evil choice is upon me."

Anguish radiated off him, and Anna longed to shoulder some of it. He was young, too. She touched his arm. He didn't flinch. Her hand trembled as she let it travel down to his hand. She laced her fingers into his.

"You are skilled and brave and have done everything

possible to keep me safe. This is the only choice now. Whatever awaits us in this forest we will face—together."

He wiped a stray hair out of her eyes and cupped his hand around her neck. He lightly brushed his thumb across her cheekbone. For a moment she thought he was going to kiss her, but instead he pulled her into a close embrace with his hand behind her head. She breathed in his scent—pine and leather mixed with wolf blood and dirt. She pulled even closer to him, sinking her face between his collar bone and chin.

"Let's go, then." He kissed her hair and released her.

They walked in silence, leading their horses as two going to their doom. Every step was heavy and slow with the mare's limping. Stealth wasn't an option. They stepped into the shelter of the first tree just as the sun peaked over the horizon. Anna peered into the gloom of tangled branches and vegetation. They rested at the entrance. A cold breeze licked Anna's neck. She shivered.

"We need to head northwest, toward the mountain," Jack said.

Anna saw the snowcapped mountain rising above them in its splendor. Even in summer these mountains were high and cold. "We won't be going over the mountain?"

"Not that one, but the smaller mountain pass we'll head through will be bad enough, I'm afraid. If we run into trouble, we both swing up on Avery and leave the mare."

Anna nodded, fear pinching her throat. Her nerves were stretched so tight her hands shook. She glanced up at the branches high overhead, which formed a tangled interweaving canopy. At first Anna struggled to find a path large enough for Star to pass easily through, but as the trees grew larger, the undergrowth thinned. The mare's ears flickered forward and back, searching for a sound. She would often stop and drop her head, and Anna had to tug her along. *How soon until Star stops for good?* After a few miles, the deciduous trees gave way to mostly pine, and now their footsteps padded on soft moss and pine needles, as little or no underbrush grew under the towering evergreens.

Anna was a little more hopeful after they had traveled for several hours with no trouble, though they had to stop often to rest Star. Anna examined the horse during their next stop. Her leg was swollen and hot. Her eyes met Jack's. They were thinking the same thing. They might have to put the mare down. Just the thought made Anna's eyes tear up. She'd been such a good horse. She stroked her silky neck. Such is the lot of the horse. Born, trained, used and discarded by humans. She knew a quick death by the sword would be better than dying of her wounds or by animals. Anna put her hand on the horse's chest, checking for a fever. She did not feel overly warm, but how could she know?

Just as they were beginning to start again something rustled. There were no leaves in this forest and no underbrush to hide in. A branch moved overhead. Star and Avery's heads shot up, and their eyes widened until she could see the whites at the edges. Anna scanned the ground and trees. She saw no deer, rabbits, birds or squirrels. She glanced at Jack. He had his bow out.

"Draw your sword," Jack whispered.

Anna stepped back to the saddle and pulled out the sword, its sharpened blade dull in the gloom. Her knuckles turned white from her tight grip. Every muscle in her body was tense. Blood pounded in her ears. *Something* was out there.

All was quiet again, so they cautiously moved forward. Anna took her next step and gasped as something fell on her. She glanced down at what hit her, and it seemed to be some kind of heavy bag. Anna held her sword in front of her as more and more fell. The horses jumped as Jack shot arrows into the trees. It was no use. The bags were falling from the sky. Anna fought the desire to run. It was too late, anyway, now small men were jumping on them from the trees. Their capes stretched out under their arms and helped them glide to the earth. Anna's stomach dropped. No wonder people thought these woods were haunted.

Jack and Anna were at one second startled and fighting and the next subdued by five, ten, fifteen, now perhaps thirty men. They tackled Jack, ripping his bow and arrows from his back and his sword from his hand. His dagger landed in the thigh of one man and the only thing stopping him from slitting another's throat was Anna's scream.

A man held her sword to her throat. Two more bound her hands.

Jack dropped his knife and the small men forced Jack to his feet with his hands bound as well. They pushed at him with primitive spears and spoke harshly in a dialect Anna barely understood. Jack started walking, calling out to her as he went.

"Are you all right, Anna?"

"Yes, I'm here," she answered, trying to be brave. Her legs were heavy as lead.

"Qui-A!" one of the men shouted at her through yellow, gaping teeth. They all had a similar appearance—pale-skinned and short, not taller than Anna, but incredibly strong. The animal skins draped around their shoulders carried a pungent odor. Their brown beards came to their chests and knotted with brown, dirty hair. They slumped as they walked, with hands almost skimming the ground.

One poked her with the blunt end of a spear, and she started moving. Some of the men led the horses behind. Anna forced herself not to think about what was going to happen to them. At least she knew why people never return from the forest. It was better than ghosts. But not a lot better.

After about twenty minutes, the men drove them up a steep, rocky, moss-covered bank. She found it difficult to keep her balance with her hands tied behind her and fell several times with her shoulder hitting the hard ground. The men pulled her up roughly each time, finally hauling her up by the back of her shirt.

She saw Jack try to stop to wait for her, but they struck him in the face. He stumbled on.

At last they arrived at a small village—or at least where these strange people seemed to live. Small huts scattered the ground, made with pine trees, needles and some kind of plaster. The men shoved Jack and Anna to the ground in front of the largest hut.

Anna trembled as she wondered what death awaited them. What kind of monster would emerge from this hut?

The door creaked open. Anna kept her eyes down. She couldn't look.

"Unbind them, for goodness sakes!"

Anna glanced up and saw a tall old man clothed in a scarlet robe.

The men slashed their ropes.

Anna rubbed her aching arms. Jack glanced her way. Immediately the tall man helped Anna to her feet and offered Jack a hand as well. "I'm quite sorry for your treatment," he said with weary eyes. "I don't know if I'll ever get through to them. They think they have the right to kill whoever walks in this forest without their permission. At least they brought you to me rather than striking you with their poison darts." Anna's face flushed as adrenaline slowly left her body. She shifted her weight.

"Why have you come here?" he asked Jack. "Surely you know the reputation of these woods."

"We are on an urgent mission, sir," Jack answered. "Wolves injured our horse, and the only way to complete our mission was to take a shortcut through this forest. Please forgive our intrusion." Jack bowed his head before the man.

The corners of the old man's eyes crinkled. "There is nothing to forgive. Come into my humble home and rest." He motioned to the hut. "I'll see that the men give your horses excellent care. These people may seem primitive, but they are extremely advanced in the art of herbs and healing. They may be able to help your horse."

Would they help them or eat them?

Jack and Anna stayed where they were for a moment and exchanged worried glances. They didn't seem to have a choice. But even now he was examining Star and motioning to the men who ran to get supplies for the horse. He nodded at Jack.

Jack put his hand on her waist and leaned toward her ear. "Keep close to me, but I don't think we have anything to fear," he whispered.

Anna wasn't so sure. Those men seemed hardly human.

Her body tensed as she ducked in the small, dark, quiet house. She blinked as her eyes adjusted to the dim light. Jack was so close he bumped into her when she stopped on the other side of the threshold. She leaned back into him. A rich, earthy pine scent filled her nose. She exhaled. The floors were wooden, but the walls were made of mud, packed in between long tree trunks. Anna touched the wall with one finger. It was surprisingly smooth.

The older man came in behind them and motioned for them to sit at the table. He returned with bread and cheese. Anna withdrew her hand from the wall.

"The people here live in these huts," said the man as he nodded to the wall. "I simply had to add a floor. I grew tired of cold, bare earth." He set the food on the table and put a pot of water over the fireplace for tea. He returned with wet cloths to wipe their hands and faces.

"I am Nicholas," he said. "I am happy to be of help to you on your journey. And you are?"

"John William." Jack hesitated for a moment. "And this is a slave girl I rescued from a harsh master over the desert. Her name is Anna."

Anna clenched her bottom lip between her teeth as she heard Jack call her a slave girl. She wanted to correct him but thought it best to trust him for the moment.

The man's bushy eyebrows went up. "A slave girl? Hmm—it was a noble deed." He looked at Anna thoughtfully. "Please, have some food, humble though it may be."

He pulled out a chair for her. Anna wondered if she were in a dream. The man didn't fit with those people outside. She took a slice of bread and a piece of soft, white cheese. He offered honey. *This is heaven,* thought Anna as she sunk her teeth into the bread. Something so simple had never tasted so good.

"How did you end up here with these people?" Jack asked, not hesitating to dig in as well.

"Good sir, I am a servant of the Most High. I felt impressed to tell others of the one true God, that they might not serve evil, especially the lesser gods," answered the man.

"So you chose these people?" Jack asked.

"No, and I probably would not have on my own. In a way, they chose me. One day, on a journey, I fell into circumstances not unlike your own. My horse had been injured. I found refuge in these trees, and by some mercy of the Most High the woodsman did not harm me."

"The woodsman?" Jack asked.

The man shrugged. "That's what I call them. I believe they are from a tribe of Caritni who entered these woods generations ago. Separate from all other society, they kept to the ancient ways of living. They hunt and gather food. They are experts with herbal medicine, as well as poison. I've introduced goats to them for milk and cheese. I've also tried to help them understand the concept of farming, but it's not going well."

"So they took you in?" Jack asked.

Anna nibbled as the conversation went on. The crust of the bread was tough, but the inside was fluffy, and the cheese was smooth. She kept quiet as she knew too well that slave girls didn't speak unless spoken to.

"Yes. Like I said, by some miracle they fed me, cared for my horse and sent me on my way. I don't know if they thought

I was perhaps a god. I promised to return some day and repay their kindness. One day I did return, and I have stayed ever since. I want to help these people understand the love of the Most High. It's what He wants me to do, here at the end of my days."

Jack tilted his head to the side and nodded to him. "I would say yours is the noble deed, sir."

"Thank you, young man. But you come to me with such a troubled heart."

Jack frowned. "Why would you say that?"

"I have the gift of discernment, my son," Nicholas said, standing and placing his hand on Jack's shoulder. The teakettle whistled, and the old priest brought cups. The warm liquid cheered Anna considerably. Something about the priest relaxed her. It wasn't ordinary tea. It was infused with something rich and a little spicy. "It's no accident you are here."

Anna couldn't contain herself. "How do you mean?" she asked.

"Whatever your errand, it must be important for you to risk these woods. And whoever you are, someone, I'd say perhaps the Most High, has protected you. No travelers make it in this far alive."

"I see," Anna said.

His kind eyes bored into hers. "Now," he continued. "You might as well tell me the truth. I have no quarrel with anyone and no one to tell your secrets to."

Jack sat in pale stillness.

Anna didn't know what to say. The priest folded his hands in his lap and dipped his chin patiently.

"Well," Anna began and glanced at Jack, who shrugged.

"First, I am not a slave girl." It felt good to say that.

"But, she was a slave in Kasdod—"

The priest held up his hand. "Let her tell the story. I'm sure I will understand the details."

Anna started at the beginning. "I am the daughter of King

Vilipp of Sunderland." She glanced at the man, who nodded and motioned for her to continue. She told him her story from racing Farley, brushing over the details of why Seamus disliked her so much. When she told him of the wolves, the priest rose and paced before the fire, rubbing his chin.

"You said they were large?"

"Yes, huge. Not half as large as my horse, but close."

"Hmm." He nodded to Jack. "And you didn't lie, either, son. She was a slave in Kasdod."

Jack lifted a shoulder.

The old priest took an ember from the fire and lit an oil lamp. Anna realized it was early evening. "You must be tired," Nicholas said. "I'll check on your horses. Why don't you stretch out before the fire?"

He left the room, returning with a thick wool blanket which he folded on the floor. Anna realized how tired she was when she saw the blanket.

"It's not much for a princess, but it's what I have to offer."

"Oh, I couldn't. I will go with you to check on Star." She stood.

"As you wish, Your Highness."

Late evening shadows waved across the path to the barn as the trees above swayed in the breeze. Anna was glad for Jack's presence and stepped close to him as they walked. She felt the eyes of those woodsmen on them. He placed his hand in the small of her back. She leaned into it.

The barn door creaked open, and the priest lit a lamp. Goats bleated as they stepped over the door onto the soft earth.

Star and Avery were together in a large stall where two woodsmen soaked Star's wound with a tea-like substance. The smell was light and potent all at once, perhaps basil or mint mixed with a deep, woody, musky smell. Star's head was down, but she flicked her ears toward Anna.

Anna pulled Star's nose to her chest. She rested her chin against the horse's forehead and whispered words of comfort.

"Can you help her?" she asked.

"These remedies are old. They work well to prevent infection, but your mare is already sick." He held the lamp closer to inspect the wound. He opened Star's mouth and pressed her gum to see if the gums remained white or refilled with blood. He then pinched her skin. It did not snap back.

"What do you think?"

"She's sick. She needs medicine, water and time to rest."

"We don't have much time," Jack said.

"I understand." The priest frowned. He placed his left hand on the top of her neck and his right on her hind end above the wound. "I will pray."

His arms stretched over the horse. The words he spoke were beautiful and sorrowful in a language Anna had never heard. They pierced her heart, and she didn't know whether to laugh at her fear or weep in gratefulness. The air swirled with confident boldness.

The woodsman fell to their knees. Star leaned into her, and Anna rested her head between her ears. Power moved through the stall, but not like the power she felt while locked in Anwar's closet. This was a rush of peace and provision, not terror.

The horse exhaled a great groan and seemed to fall asleep on her feet. The priest finished and stroked her neck.

"We will let her rest."

"Thank you," Anna whispered, her voice full of emotion. She blinked back tears. She couldn't bear to see the little horse put down. Hopefully he had saved her.

She gave Star one final stroke before they made their way back to the hut.

Anna gratefully sank onto the thick blanket by the fire. The day's events had her head spinning as she drifted off into a nap. She woke to the delicious aroma of something bubbling over the fire. She sat up and spotted Jack dozing in the chair next to the fire. The old priest was stirring a large pot.

"Hungry?" he asked.

Just the thought of something warm made Anna's stomach growl. She nodded gratefully as he poured three bowls. She gently shook Jack awake and smiled as their eyes met. He was usually the one waking her up.

After eating, Nicolas poured them fresh cups of tea and sat down across the table. "I suppose I should have been expecting you." His voice shook.

"Oh?" said Jack.

"You know, it's always easier to believe in a miracle when it is happening to someone else," he said to himself.

Anna shot Jack a puzzled look.

"I'll try to explain. I had a dream two nights ago—more like a vision."

"Go on," Jack said.

"In it, I saw a young man and a maiden come through my door, needing help. The girl carried a sword and shield with a bow slung over her back. She rode a different horse, not the little mare. It was huge, wild and black as night."

Anna felt the blood drain from her face. Jack scrunched his brow in concentration.

"And you think the girl in the vision was Anna?" Jack asked.

"Yes. I don't pretend to understand everything, but as much as an unseen hand is harassing you, I believe another is working to keep you safe. Believe in that, and you will make it home."

He rose from the table and shuffled to his small bedroom. He returned carrying a sword, shield and a bow with a set of red-gold arrows. Anna's heart quickened.

"These are the weapons I saw in my dream, Anna. You were wielding them."

He laid them on the table and stepped back. Anna glanced down and gasped.

"They're set with jewels of power? Aren't they evil?"

The priest's eyes lit up. Anna saw the cause of all those

laugh lines as his old skin pulled up into yet another smile. He sat down again.

"They were my great-grandfather's weapons, passed on from father to son for three generations. He used them in Sunderland before the edict making them illegal, and as I no longer live there, it didn't bother me to hold onto them as keepsakes." He stopped for a moment. "Now it is my turn to pass them on. I have no offspring. They were meant for you."

"But how can I take these home?"

"Don't fear them, Anna. Who made the jewels, anyway?"

Anna thought for a moment. "I suppose the Most High, if he brought everything into being," she answered.

The old priest's voice flowed with warmth. "Then why are they any different than any other substance created we take and use for our own purposes? We use the power of moving water to work our mills, we cut down beautiful trees to build our homes, and we turn the horse into a companion and beast of burden. We have the right to do so, but we need to be good managers of what is entrusted to us."

"How do you mean?"

"We can't abuse what we have been given. We leave enough trees to replenish the forests, and we don't abuse the good nature of the horses who serve us," he replied. "There are few things worse than watching a man beat a good horse. It's because it goes against the order of things—we were meant to care for creation, not destroy it."

"But people have done great harm with the gems—to themselves and each other," Anna said. She pushed back from the table. "They are dangerous if they fall into the wrong hands."

"Perhaps. But the right hands have the right to use them. The weapon itself is not evil," he said. "It is about the heart of the one who uses them. They are a tool that can be used for great good or great evil. The choice is yours."

Jack had been silent through this exchange. Anna glanced his way.

"And what do you think, Jack? If I return with these, how could Father not have me executed? I've already used the gems in the hairbrush. This would only confirm my guilt. And besides, any time I've ever done something against the rules thinking Father would understand, he never has."

"True. But this battle is more important than a horse race. These last weeks have opened my eyes to many things I'd have never thought possible," Jack said. "Of course, Nicholas is right, Anna. Any common weapon can be used for good or bad. This is something to help us—help your father in a great time of need. And, if you haven't noticed, we need all the help we can get."

Jack, always practical.

"Daughter, your reluctance to use them is the surest evidence you should," Nicholas said. The corners of his mouth pulled up. His eyes were kind and soft, but serious. "And this coming war—these men have been called here by something ominous. The Most High is giving you a chance. It's always His will to fight evil."

"Why me?" Anna asked. "Why not Jack or someone trained to use weapons?"

"Perhaps to remind the world of His existence," he whispered. "Strength through weakness."

As he said those last words, something tugged in Anna's gut, pulling her toward the table. She crossed her arms and resisted. Immediately, it subsided. They weren't beautiful pieces of armory. All but the shield looked common at first glance. The jewels deeply embedded in the hilt of the sword were small and the silver around them tarnished. She took a step forward and reached her hand toward the sword. Instantly the pull resumed, and this time she did not turn away. It called to her.

Her hand pulsed when she took the hilt of the smallish,

light sword and gently held it up to inspect it. She reached it out in front of her and felt the perfect balance. No charge of energy shot through her, yet she immediately saw the truth in the priest's words. *It was meant for me. And I'll use it well.* She stepped back and swirled it through the air. It was perfect—not heavy and cumbersome like Jack's sword. It fit her exactly right. It was peace and calm in her grip. Her eyes flicked to him, and his sparkled back. He nodded. She laid the sword on the table and took up the bow, fingering the arrows that went with it.

"Do you have string for it?"

Nicholas nodded toward the quiver. A small leather bag attached to the side of the quiver held a fine string, shimmering with gold. Her hand trembled at its touch.

"The gems of the bow make the arrows shoot true," Nicholas said. "They won't miss."

She strung the bow and laid an arrow to the string, pulling it back and sighting it. "Is the magic in the bow or the arrows?" She relaxed the bow.

"The bow. Any arrows will do." His voice was subdued.

"And the sword? What are its properties?"

"I don't know, but my great-grandfather never lost in battle. The blade is strong, I know."

The shield was more ostentatious. It was made of a light metal with a large green stone set in the middle, in the center of an engraved eagle. Anna knew it was an emerald. The eagle's wings were outstretched and lined with hundreds of small stones, red, green, white and blue, in a particular order around its body. Anna ran her finger over them. *Beautiful.*

Anna slowly picked up the shield, hooking her left arm in the sleeve. Again, there was no surge of energy or power. She set it down again and glanced at the priest who was watching her every move. She flushed.

"How can I repay you?" Her voice was soft.

"You'll take them, then?" he asked.

"Yes, but they are a treasure. I want to repay you."

He brushed her comment away with a dismissive flick of his wrist. "Just use them well."

"Will I know how?" Anna felt the hope and the burden of the weapons equally.

"When the time comes, you will know," the priest said.

Anna glanced at Jack who dipped his chin.

"Thank you. When this is over, I will return these to you."

"I look forward to your visit, but these are a gift. And your life may be too busy when you are queen."

"Queen?" asked Anna. "I am the third born in my family." Her heart skipped a beat. *Would her family die?* "Is it certain?"

His eyes narrowed. "The future always changes according to your choices. Don't hold me to it. I merely had a feeling of what you would become." His eyes rested on Jack. "Much depends on you as well, young man."

"I will do my best," Jack replied.

"Yes, I know you will." The priest had a comforting, calming air about him.

Anna had so many questions swirling in her she didn't know where to begin.

"Sir?"

"Yes, dear?"

"Can you explain how the same gems can be used for good and evil? I'm not sure I understand." Anna furrowed her brow.

"That's like asking why the rain falls on both the good and the evil," he replied. "But I will try to help."

"If I'm going to be using these weapons, I'd like to understand a bit more."

"Let's start at the beginning. In our ancient works it is written that the Most High created everything—the earth, mankind, beast and even the lesser gods. The Most High treasured man most of all and the lesser gods grew jealous and worked to deceive mankind and turn them away from him. He would reach out to people, but only a few would hear his voice.

The Most High introduced gems to people so they could have a tangible connection to him. Remember, the gems have no power in themselves, but they serve as a conduit to the Most High."

Anna nodded and the priest continued.

"Each gem stands for an attribute of the Most High—love, goodness, healing, blessing, protection, unity, peace, truth, justice and even judgment," he said. "There are many more."

"Judgment?" Anna's eyebrows shot up.

"Yes, judgment goes along with love—Sunderland, in particular, was aligned with the Most High. Centuries ago, it was tasked with judgment of the lesser gods' deception."

"What do you mean?" asked Anna.

"The lesser gods mocked the Most High and influenced mankind to use the gems for evil. Just as the gems were a conduit for good, they could also connect to the lesser gods and be used for evil. War, murder, deception, self-promotion and so forth. The lesser gods would pretend to bless the people in exchange for sacrifices—blood sacrifices."

"And would they bless the people?" Jack asked.

"Many times, yes," answered the priest, "but all for a steep cost." He frowned. "I'm surprised you know none of this. Did you not pay attention during chapel services?"

"Father banned chapel after Mother died," Anna said. "I was only four years old."

The priest's face darkened. "What?"

"Yes. I have only a faint memory of any chapel services."

Nicholas sat up straight. "It is as I feared. You've been taught nothing of the Most High."

"All I know is that his light burns in the chapel day and night without needing any fuel," Anna said.

"And what is the significance of his fire?" the priest questioned.

Anna's face flushed. "I'm not sure."

"Oh, child. There is much for you to learn."

Chapter 15

The next morning as Anna finished her tea, Nicholas brought out an ancient-looking book. Its leather cover was cracked and crumbling apart. He set it gently on the table and swatted at a plume of dust as he opened the cover.

"Jasper, sapphire, agate, emerald, onyx, ruby, chrysolite, beryl, topaz, turquoise, jacinth and amethyst," he read. "These are the twelve foundation stones." He turned the book toward her. "Read and study their meanings. Remember, they are channels of blessing from the Most High."

Anna squinted at the old, barely legible script.

> *Jasper—tracking. There are fifty types of jasper, including Leopard Skin, Bloodstone, Picture Jasper and so forth. Jasper relates to grounding a person to the earth. It is helpful for tracking, providing strength, courage and endurance. Bloodstone is the stone of selfless sacrifice. Picture Jasper allows the user to create a map to someone or someplace.*
> *Sapphire—mental focus. All sorts of sapphires aid with vision. Sapphire helps you see a way to stay on the*

right path, as well as a way of escape. Good for battle strategy. Also can help a person sense the future.

Agate—healing, especially of the soul. A translucent gemstone of almost any color, but it must have bands.

Emerald—protection, especially against evil.

Onyx—courage to fight against evil. Comes in many colorations, always with bands. At times, white onyx provides blinding heat of judgment. Black onyx is the destroyer of evil communication.

Ruby—power. Ruby should not be used with sapphire because the surge of power can cloud the mind. Main uses include defense of the defenseless, fighting evil and overcoming attack.

Chrysolite—good fortune, or luck. The user of chrysolite will experience a way out of troubled circumstances, but not unearned fortune.

Beryl—truth. Pure beryl is colorless and will expose falsehood and deception.

Topaz—virtue. The wearer will value virtue, be filled with compassion and wisdom toward others.

Turquoise—healing, especially of battle wounds. Many consider it a protector as well.

Jacinth—wisdom. The user of jacinth will be able to better hear the voice of the Most High and have discernment.

Amethyst—purity. The wearer will have purity of thought and action. Will have a desire to do what is right.

Anna finished reading about the twelve gems and glanced to the priest. "This is complicated," she said, thumbing through more pages. "And long. It would take constant vigilance to use the gems correctly."

He nodded. "I believe the problems with the gems came when the people become complacent. They cared more for the gems than the one who created the gems. Evil is always standing at the door to take advantage."

"So, it wasn't the gems that caused the Sunderland army to attack each other all those years ago?"

"It wasn't the gems." He frowned. "The men weren't using them for the right reasons."

Anna's eyes fell on her new weapons. She picked up the sword, pulled it from its sheath and set it on the table. "What gems are these?"

The priest rubbed his face. "I'm sorry, I was just a child when the gems were banned. Many gems come in similar colors, so it's difficult to tell."

"But someone would know?" Anna ran her fingers across the gems.

"Yes, but perhaps not in Sunderland."

She nodded. "Are you sure they are safe?"

"Of course not." He scoffed. "They are the right gems for battle, or they wouldn't be in these weapons." He leaned forward and touched her arm. "But I'm sure they are meant for you at this time. Don't trust in the sword or the gems, trust in the Most High. He is the protector of Sunderland."

"And his fire?" Anna asked. "What does it mean?" She studied his blue-gray eyes and thought of the lanterns on the altar.

"His fire is warmth, life and light to our path, but also exposes the darkest evil. It burns it with the most intense heat to cleanse and purify."

Anna nodded, though she was just beginning to understand. She put the sword away.

"Would you like to come with me to check on my mare?" She nodded toward the door. "I'd like to see what Jack's up to."

They found Star much improved. The herbs were a miracle, but Anna knew she needed at least a couple more days rest. Though Anna and Jack were anxious to keep moving, something about the softness of the wind through the trees above and the quiet manner of the priest put their minds at ease while their bodies rested. The holy man worked and moved with a quiet strength that was contagious. Anna slept soundly for the first time in weeks.

Anna visited Star several times a day and each time found her stronger. The woodsmen had packed her wound with several kinds of herbs, brewed in warm water. The medicine drew out the deadly infection. The horses were fed with hay kept for the goats and some corn, for which Anna was especially grateful. Their four-legged partners needed every bite to prepare them for the rest of the journey.

Anna asked the priest how to repay them.

"If we return, will they recognize us?" she asked. She had no desire to be stung with poison darts.

"Yes. I'll show you how to offer them honor before you leave," he said. "They are learning."

The little mare's big brown eyes were brighter as Anna approached the third morning. Her ears, which a few days before had been hanging limp to the side, were perking up. Anna passed the time stroking her neck, feeding her and thinking of the remaining steps on the journey. They needed to hurry.

Finally, on the fourth day since arriving with arms bound, the pair departed with healthy horses, full stomachs and renewed spirits. Nicholas also supplied them with several days' worth of bread, cheese and loads of the healing herbs to use on Star each night as they traveled. The whole village came out to see their departure. Anna and Jack bowed before the head woodsman, offering their palms up in a gesture of thanks and peace. The chief placed a drop of oil on each of their palms.

"It means you will be remembered and honored," the priest said.

Anna stood, gestured to Star and then crossed her heart with her arms. The chief nodded and bowed his head.

Anna wished the best for the priest and deeply appreciated what the woodsman had done for Star, but she was anxious to be home.

Her new sword hung on her hip and the shield lay across her back. She tied the bow and quiver to Star's saddle, within easy reach. They had packed most of their other supplies on poor Avery to lighten the load on Star as much as possible. The priest had given her a goatskin cloak as well. She relished its warmth around her shoulders.

They headed northwest out of the forest at a slow pace until it opened up at the bottom of a mountain path. The path curved through trees and rocks as it ascended the mountain. Jack took a deep breath and clucked to Avery.

All day they climbed, with the air getting thinner and colder with every step. Soon the horses' breath was spouting out of their nostrils like smoke, enveloping their riders' knees and then disappearing. Anna's fingers were numb from holding the reins. She pulled the mare directly behind Avery so she'd just follow along while she loosened her grip on the reins and buried her fingers into the black mane, soaking up what little warmth she could.

Looking ahead, Anna saw they were climbing above the tree line. Though it was sunny, a sharp wind blew down from snow-capped peaks as they paused on the top of the pass. It bit into Anna's skin. Her entire body shuddered with cold as she wondered if the old legends of a giant snow beast were real.

Jack pulled to stop. "Let's rest." He dismounted.

Anna did the same, and in spite of the voice inside telling her to hurry home, she drank in the scene. The bright green grass fed her spirit, and she wondered at its short life before the snowfall would begin again too soon. Cold mountain spring water filled numerous brooks and streams along the way, all gurgling merrily down the mountain. In the distance below, Anna heard what she thought was the distant roar of a larger river, filling with runoff from the smaller streams. From the mountain, she saw the valley below, rolling green grass spotted with trees, villages and farmland. Jack pointed to where they were headed, a castle, known as Hemmington, a couple days' ride ahead. Anna couldn't quite make it out on the horizon.

"Will Lady Avigail receive us?" Anna asked.

"Of course." His lips set into a thin line.

Anna frowned. "What is it?"

"Nothing," Jack jerked his chin toward the horses. "Let's let the horses eat a little."

They shared a late lunch and began the trek down the other side, which wasn't as easy as going up. The terrain was steep and the rocks slippery for the horses. Several times they dismounted and led their horses through the toughest parts, so the horses could balance themselves without a rider. Anna just prayed Star wouldn't lose her balance and fall on her, but the brave horse was as sure-footed as ever. After a couple hours, they stopped, rested and then went on.

Sooner than they wanted, the shadows grew long. The sun sank behind the closest mountain. Dusk closed in around them, bringing with it a band of clouds dripping a cold, fine, misty rain. In an hour, the mountain was wet, and the sun gone. The slick surfaces slowed their progress to a crawl. The cold, damp air ate into Anna's clothes. Her cheeks felt raw and numb while the cold sank into her bones. They had hoped to be at the bottom by now. Jack continued to lead them down, down, down, and finally reached a place flat enough to set up a little camp.

Anna's clothes grew wet, even with the goatskin cloak. The priest must have known she'd need it. Her teeth chattered. Jack attempted to build a small fire, but all the wood was too damp to catch. Deep chills shook Anna's body as the cold mountain air cascaded down on them. She shivered uncontrollably.

"I'm sorry you're cold," Jack said, concern flooding his eyes and voice.

Anna shook her head. "I just got chilled, and I can't fight off this damp." She rubbed her arms as another deep shiver pulsed through her.

"Come here," he said. "You haven't eaten much today." The cold bread Jack gave her felt good going down, but Anna couldn't help longing for the hot stew of the previous nights with the priest.

Still Anna shivered. Jack felt her forehead and made her drink more water, which only chilled her more.

"I hope you don't have a fever." His mouth tightened.

"No. I'm just wet and cold." Her breath spread in the heavy air before them. Jack secured the horses and then rolled out both mats under some brush where they could get a little shelter from the cold mist.

"We'll have to camp here. It's the best I can do."

Anna climbed on one of the mats and to her surprise, found Jack unbuttoning his large cloak.

"No. You need to keep warm, too," she said, her breath forming a white fog.

"I think we're both going to freeze tonight if we don't work together," he said. She noticed he was shaking, too. "We are too wet with this cold mist and the temperature is dropping."

He motioned for her to come over, and finally she did, crawling over to his mat. Anna forgot about the cold for a moment as she took his outstretched hand. Her stomach tossed a little as she scooted in front of him, putting her back to his chest. She was glad he couldn't see her face flush. Jack pulled the cloak over both of them tightly, wrapping his arms around her. Keeping her safe. She could get used to that feeling. Anna was surprised at how warm he was, and in a few minutes, she stopped shaking.

Anna couldn't think of what to say and decided against speaking. Jack, too, was silent. She adjusted her position once and glanced back at him to see if he was asleep. No, eyes open, staring into the drizzle. The darkness and the penetrating mist closed in around them, and Anna could no longer even see the tethered horses.

Now that she was warmer, her eyes grew heavy. She shifted to her other side and laid her head on his chest. After a time, she felt his breathing slow and his cheek slumped against the top of her head. Though fatigued, sleep didn't come easily with visions of red-eyed wolves and bared teeth filling her mind every time her eyes closed. Finally, the gentle movement of Jack's rising and falling chest lulled her to sleep.

Anna opened her eyes to dim light illuminating a silver sheet of ice covering everything. Jack's cloak was slick with it. She wiggled, cracking the ice on the thick cloth. His arms quickly released her.

"Awake?" he asked.

She sat up too quickly and bumped into his chin. She scrambled to her feet, blushing. *I slept in his arms all night?*

"Sorry! I forgot where I was—"

Jack's deep blue eyes danced. "Did you stay warm enough?" he asked cheerfully. Anna's blush deepened.

"Yes. Did you?"

"Of course." The corners of his mouth curved up into a lopsided grin.

Anna couldn't meet his eyes. *Stop it, Anna!* Goosebumps popped up on her arms and legs. She clutched her arms to her core in an attempt to warm them against the sudden burst of cold. She snuck a glance at Jack. He was watching her with an amused expression. *He doesn't seem to feel awkward.* She took a step toward the pack and slipped on the slanted rock. She threw her arms out to the side for balance and slowly scooted back to the bedroll.

"There's a thin glaze of ice," she said.

"I noticed," he said. "Which is why I'm not saddling the horses." Jack glanced at the sky. "The sun is coming out. It will melt soon."

Anna shivered and rubbed her arms as a sharp breeze bit into her. She couldn't help looking back at the cloak. Perhaps she had gotten up too early.

He gestured to her. "Come here, if you'd like." Back to those arms. He was as dirty and stinky as she was, but there was no other place she'd rather be. She wished she could clean up.

Anna hesitated until a gust of icy wind hit her in the face. She scooted right back under the cloak with him.

"It's still so cold," she said as she leaned into him. His arms wrapped around her back, pulling her near as he tucked in the cloak to block the wind. She was conscious of how close every part of her body was to his. She trembled, but this time, it wasn't from the cold.

"I'm sorry we have to wait it out. I can't risk the horses slipping and breaking a leg."

"While we pass the time, why don't you tell me more of your story?" Anna asked.

He was silent so long she thought he wasn't going to respond. His chest rumbled as he began.

"When my father was killed and I came to offer my services to King Vilipp, he sent me to train as a knight. It was a kindness I didn't deserve. During my training, I excelled in certain areas, stealth, opponent awareness, and the ability to handle a blade quickly and quietly in close quarters. I wasn't tall or built, but I was quick and accurate. I wasn't overly handsome as to attract notice. I could slip through crowds easily."

Anna grunted. He was not common looking. Not to her.

"Seamus himself trained me on my sword and dagger work. Then your father's captain sent me to the desert to finish my training with a master."

"So you are a spy?"

"On my better days." He paused. Anna lifted her head to look at him, but he wouldn't meet her eyes. His brow furrowed. "I've done things I'm not proud of, but always for Sunderland. For the king."

Her heartbeat increased. He probably knew ten ways to kill her in a matter of seconds. *He's an assassin.* He must have sensed her stiffen and pulled her a little closer.

"I'd never hurt you." His voice cracked. "I'll use everything I know to keep you safe."

Anna leaned into his chest as he continued.

"Could you have refused?"

"I was ambitious, and I didn't fully understand what I was getting into," he said. "It was an honor to be selected for this training, and I thought these skills would pay off in the future."

"What happened to your master?"

"I'd been part of an operation spying on that paranoid tyrant Anwar, but he must have known who we were. My master was shot dead in a crowd with an arrow to his back. I buried him in the desert, as I told you before."

"I'm sorry."

"It was tough. I suspected one of Anwar's cronies, so I disguised myself and poked around Anwar's court. So much happened so quickly, but I didn't want to return to Sunderland without answers for your father. That's when I found you."

"I'm sorry Father did this to you," Anna said. She couldn't believe her father would turn a young boy into an assassin. But Seamus would.

"As it turns out, it was a good thing he did. I was here to find you."

Anna's pulse increased again as her face flushed. She would have had her tongue cut out and sold someplace even worse if it hadn't been for Jack. "Thank you," she whispered and leaned her forehead into the quiet strength of his chest.

"Any time," he said. His cheek rested at the top of her head.

She dozed off wondering what his lips would feel like on hers.

———

THE ICE finally melted around midday, and Anna had to admit she was a little sorry to see it go. While the hours weren't exactly restful, she knew some barrier between Jack and her had just broken open. As soon as she was up and going, feeding the horses and packing up, she was more than ready to get to Hemmington.

"So," she asked as she tore a chunk of bread off a loaf. "Are you getting excited we're so close to home? I can't wait for a hot meal."

"Yes, but—"

"What?" asked Anna.

"Things are going to change when we get back. There will be talk of war, and we'll assume more formal roles." He seemed stiff.

Anna narrowed her eyes at him. "You know I don't care about formality. And I'll expect to see you, of course. I—I don't have many friends at home." Anna's voice dropped off. Confusion crept into her stomach. Had she gotten too close? While she would brave another cold night to be in those arms again, perhaps Jack felt just the opposite. He was silent. "One of my only friends is a stable boy. He's got a great heart. I hope I didn't get him into too much trouble."

"What's his name?"

"Bart. He's the one Seamus injured that day."

"Did he ever say he was a squire?"

She laughed. "He's always talking about being the squire of a great knight. Of course, no one has ever seen this knight. I'm not sure he exists."

Jack's eyes danced. "Oh, he exists all right." He tapped his chest.

Anna raised her eyebrows. "You?"

"I was working with him, then unfortunately had to leave. Bart couldn't know where I'd gone."

"You were so young to have a squire," she said.

"He was an eager peasant whose father was crippled in an accident. He needed money to care for his family," Jack said.

Anna felt her cheeks heat in shame. Had she even once asked about Bart's family?

"That was kind of you," she said.

Jack shrugged.

"I'm worried to face Seamus," Anna blurted. "I'm going to need you with me."

"Of course." His forehead wrinkled. "I will do whatever I can to be of service." He took a deep breath and his shoulders straightened.

She looked at him sideways as her stomach fluttered. *What was with the stilted speech?* "I hope Father believes me." She'd need Jack with her when she faced her father. And not in a formal way. As a friend and as whatever it was they were becoming. She swallowed a lump in her throat.

"He will," said Jack.

"I'm not sure," Anna said. "I'm just a silly, rebellious girl to him. He probably thinks I ran away. Who knows what Seamus has told him by now?"

Worry lines creased Jack's forehead as Anna continued.

"My main usefulness to him is to arrange my marriage to some lord he wants to buy peace with." Anna paused. "Sometimes I envy the village girls. At least they get to marry for love."

Jack snorted. "And they all envy you. Every man in your kingdom would love a chance for your hand."

"Is that something I chose?" Anna's words rushed out. "I always hoped somehow that I'd get to choose someone I actually wanted to spend my life with." She realized she'd said too much and looked away. "Not that it will ever happen."

Jack cringed and cleared his throat. "It's time to go."

Anna's cheeks burned as she noticed the slippery rocks were just damp.

They walked beside the horses as they continued descending the mountain. As the conditions improved, they mounted, and Anna found herself gripping the mare too tight as she wanted to urge her on faster.

"How far do you think it is now?" she asked.

Jack shook his head. "We're about an hour closer than the last time you asked."

"Yes, well, thanks." She made a face and kicked Star up to a trot ahead of Jack so she wouldn't have to look at him. He moved Avery next to her.

The next day they traveled through hills and valleys, always down, until they dropped over a ridge and entered Sunderland. Tall grasses interlaced with wildflowers tickled Star's belly as she swished through the fields. Anna even picked a few and wove them through Star's mane. Jack just shook his head at her.

"I have plenty more for Avery," Anna teased.

"Don't even think about it." Jack scowled.

Anna laughed. Anna soaked up the sun as they rode along a babbling brook. The horses seemed to cheer up as well. They had as much grass as they wanted all night and greedily gorged themselves during their rest stops. Star was recovering nicely. Jack took some weight off Avery and packed up Star again.

"She's carrying a much lighter rider, anyway," he said as he tied the mats and water containers to her saddle. But even with the added weight, her ears were up, and her step was light. Everyone's spirits seemed to rise except Jack's. As they neared the castle, Anna noticed he was keeping a distance from her. His shoulders slumped, and he hardly returned Anna's attempts at conversation. So they rode mostly in silence, trotting and cantering for many hours each day. One night as the sun set around them, they rode up a particularly steep incline. Anna gasped as they reached the top.

There it was—Hemmington. A quarter of the size of Karfin with a regiment of one hundred men, Hemmington governed the eastern side of the kingdom. Set in front of the river, it had a small moat dug around the base that allowed fresh water to surround it. Its stone towers rose up against a dusty blue sky. The day's last rays flooded its gates with warm evening light. Anna glanced at Jack's troubled face.

"It's so beautiful. Come on!" Anna said as she nudged Star down the hill. She reached the bottom and looked behind her. Jack and Avery were still as stone, staring down at the castle. Anna waited for him to follow. Finally, he walked Avery down the slope.

"When we get there, I think it would be wise to conceal your identity."

"What on earth for?" said Anna. "When they find out who I am, we'll have a feast tonight."

"No! We need to know it's safe first. Don't speak until I check things out. Perhaps the enemy is already here."

Anna hadn't thought about that. The beautiful castle grounds were full of flower gardens, hedges and all sorts of fruit trees, busy ripening their bounty. It certainly didn't appear as if any battle had been fought here. But Jack was usually right. She would have to conceal her joy.

"Whatever you say." Anna slipped on the dreaded head covering and veil. "How's this look?" she asked.

Jack only nodded.

Chapter 16

They walked their horses through the outer wall and up the lane leading to the castle. Anna could hardly contain herself. Though she'd never spent significant time here, Hemmington still felt like home. These were her people. Several guards stood watch at the bridge. They immediately recognized Jack.

"You are most welcome, good sir." A guard bowed. "I will send word of your arrival to the lady of the castle."

Jack dismounted and nodded. "Thank you, and please see to it our horses are well cared for. Especially the mare, she's been injured."

"Of course," said the man. Anna dismounted and handed him the reins, as he summoned a young man to take the horses to the stables. Jack packed their weapons into a bag he slung over his back.

Anna stood just behind Jack with her head down so she wouldn't be so recognizable. The men opened the large wooden door. She followed Jack through and waited behind him in the large foyer. Soon they heard footsteps echoing from the curved staircase above. In a few moments, a woman appeared and floated down the stairs in front of them. She had deep brown hair highlighted with silver swirled up on her head, with locks cascading onto her shoulders. Her skin was creamy white. She was looking at Jack with soft brown eyes.

"At last," she said, striding forward. She kissed him on both cheeks and then stepped back to look him over. "You seem weary and not well-fed. We'll fix that." Her face glowed in an odd way. "And who is this behind you?"

Anna was surprised to see Jack lean forward and embrace this fine lady, whispering for at least a minute in her ear. Her eyes flicked to her once in understanding. Jack stepped aside and Anna moved forward. She liked this woman immediately. Her face was full of kindness and grace.

"This is a slave girl I saved from a horrible master," Jack said plainly enough for all those gathering around to hear. "She is to be treated with utmost respect."

Anna curtsied before Lady Avigail. "Of course," the lady replied. "Follow me," she said to Jack. "Let's get you cleaned up."

Immediately a servant approached Anna and said he'd show her the servants' quarters.

"No, she will have a room upstairs," Avigail said. She whispered many instructions to the servant who gave Anna a confused glance and hurried away.

"I'll show you to your rooms," said Avigail. "I'm so happy you're here." Warmth radiated from this woman.

They followed her up the stairs and wound through the castle. Anna glanced at the wall in the long hallway, covered with portraits of her family. She tucked her chin down to hide her sudden amusement. Just months ago she would have thought it funny to be disguised in her own homeland. A pang of homesickness hit her stomach. She was ready to be home and be Princess Anna again, but she'd never be the same princess.

Avigail led them to a beautiful room with two windows and ancient tapestries covering the walls.

To her surprise, Avigail addressed her by name. "Anna, this will be your room. I'll have water brought in for washing and a bath after dinner." She touched her arm. "I'm so glad you've returned."

Anna thanked her and walked to the window after they left, hoping to catch a sunset. All that remained of the sun was a tiny sliver on the horizon. Anna sensed the darkness closing in around the castle. A servant came in with water and lit several candles.

"Dinner will be ready shortly," she said.

Anna washed her hands and face in the basin. She found a comb by the mirror and tried to run it through her tangled mess of hair. It was no use, and she pulled it back into a knot. Anna kicked off her shoes and flopped on the beautiful feather bed, encased with sheer fabric that could be pulled closed, much like her bed at home. Before long, Anna heard a tap at the door. She opened it to find Jack.

"I'll escort you to dinner," he said sticking his arm out for her to hold.

Anna laughed. "I thought I was supposed to be a slave girl."

"I still have to keep you out of trouble." Jack stopped her as she moved toward the door. "Don't forget your veil," he said. "There will be some knights I don't know at this dinner."

"Ugh! How am I supposed to eat behind this thing?" She crossed the room to peek in the mirror. "Is it necessary?"

"Humor me."

Anna rolled her eyes and positioned the veil over her nose.

"You know this is crazy, right?"

Jack led her to a great hall with a table that could have seated thirty guests. The walls were lined with portraits, paintings and rich tapestries. Anna's shoes clicked conspicuously on the hard stone floor as she walked. When they entered the room, Lady Avigail rose to greet them and show them to their seats. She sat at the head of the table with Jack on her right. Anna sat to her left.

There were a few others seated with them at dinner, but Anna didn't pay much attention to them. Some looked like traveling knights, others perhaps lords and nobles of other lands. Anna was so absorbed in the delicious food, she barely noticed the conversation and ignored the large man seated next to her. She devoured the pheasant, potatoes, green beans and bread, trying not to be rude. Fresh apple pies were for dessert, served with cream. Anna couldn't wait.

But she quickly forgot about the pie as conversation from the other end of the table drifted toward them.

"Yes," an older man was saying. "We just heard the one who brings her in alive will have her hand in marriage—even a commoner." He chuckled. "Knights all over the countryside are turning over every stone to find her. Word is traveling fast. Everywhere I go men great and small are desperately searching for the little princess."

"I'll certainly begin at the break of day," said a man with a red beard. "I'd ride through a blazing sun and a blizzard for a chance to be a prince," he said with a laugh. "Oh, and the little princess wouldn't be a bad catch either." He elbowed the man next to him.

Another man lowered his voice and whispered something Anna could not hear, but all the men at that end of the table threw their heads back and whooped in laughter.

Someone called down the table and addressed Jack. "Sir John, you haven't seen any lost girls on your travels, have you?"

Anna stopped eating with her fork in midair. She slowly put it down, trying to diffuse any attention her way. She felt her cheeks flame and was thankful for the veil after all.

Jack took a long swig of ale. "Unfortunately, not. This is the first I've heard of it." He was a skilled liar.

"Well, I don't suppose the little mouse would have scampered that far anyway," the man went on. "You know, they are saying she ran away! Now why would she do that?"

"She didn't run away," one knight said emphatically. "Someone stole her. Her horse came back the next day *unsaddled* with no sign of her. If she were to run away, she'd have saddled that horse and taken supplies."

"I heard a rope was hanging out her window," said a brown-eyed knight. "Someone scaled the wall and took her from her room."

"Then why would her horse be out?"

"It doesn't add up. It seems she just vanished," another man said.

Anna shifted in her seat. Apple pie or no, she had to get out of there. *What if one of these awful men recognizes me?* She rose and curtsied briefly to Avigail. The lady's eyes briefly rested on hers before glancing away. The conversation was getting so lively, Anna was able to slip away without notice. Back to her room, she ripped off the veil and sunk into the bed. *That was close!* Anger pulsed through Anna. *How dare they—noblemen, too—talk about me that way?* Anna couldn't imagine her father forcing her to marry one of them. But of course, he was a man of his word. Once again, Jack was right. She needed to remain disguised until she was before her father. *Will I ever feel safe in my own country?* There would be no trumpets announcing her return. She pulled out the jeweled sword and ran her fingers over it. She couldn't use it against her father's own men. A knock at the door interrupted her thoughts. She tucked the sword away before opening the heavy wooden door to a servant, who bustled in and lit a fire in the fireplace.

"My Lady Avigail requested a bathtub be brought to your room. It is on its way, along with enough steaming water to fill an ocean," he said, scowling. He sniffed. "Not that we won't be happy to be rid of that stench."

"Bless her!" she said to the man, who turned on his heel and left in a huff. Anna hardly noticed. A bath! Moments later, four men walked through her door carrying a large tub. They were followed by servant girls each carrying steaming pots of water. They gave her soap, bath salts and soft towels. Woman servants brought in several dresses, slippers, boots and other changes of clothes. Anna ran her hands over the beautiful fabrics after the servants hung them in the wardrobe. She was beginning to feel like a princess again.

One by one they filed out until one girl whispered, "The lady told me to give you this oil. Soak your hair in it and wash it out three times." The girl's eyes traveled to her hair before she stepped out, closing the door behind her.

Anna couldn't believe the kindness of Lady Avigail. She quickly stripped off her filthy garments and sank into the hot water. It was just right. She relaxed, breathing in the flowery, spiced scents rising from the steaming water. Then, she dunked her head, washed her hair and rubbed the hair treatment through it. She let it soak and rinsed it out. Yes, her hair was lighter. She put more on and let it soak longer. The thick, black color lightened some, but now her hair was the color of mud. *Well, there are worse things.*

The water grew cold too quickly, and Anna stepped out of the tub. Her skin was soft and smelled wonderful. She wrapped herself in a towel and inspected the new clothes. Anna was thankful to see a nightgown among the dresses. She chose the simplest one to wear in the morning. The two other dresses were elegant, but she wasn't sure she'd pass as a slave girl any longer. She crossed to the vanity in front of the mirror and braided her damp hair. She couldn't believe her reflection. Her face was drawn across prominent cheekbones. Her skin was tanned more than it had ever been, and a few freckles dotted her nose. No matter how different she looked, it was wonderful to be clean.

She threw her old servant's clothes into the tub water, scrubbed them clean and spread them out by the fire. Anna glanced out the window and saw the moon was up. *Less than a month until the attack. We should be home in time to warn Father.* A clock chimed a steady ten strokes somewhere in the distance. Anna headed for the bed.

Soft as the bed was, Anna couldn't sleep. The man's words at dinner kept badgering her mind. She finally had to consider the one point overwhelming her thoughts. *Would her father offer her hand to Jack? And what would Jack do?* She thought of him—strong, kind, excellent character. He'd risked his life for her without even knowing who she was.

Her heart warmed. She could think of worse fates than being married to Jack, unless, of course, he didn't want to be married to her. Anna's thoughts rushed through the last week's memories. At every turn Jack had set his face to get her home to the king and survive until they could deliver the warning of war. He said he'd stand by her in facing Seamus, but perhaps only because it was necessary to save her people.

A new doubt rose in her heart. Her insides twisted, and she rolled over. Her father certainly wouldn't force them to marry, yet she knew he would stand by his decree. She rolled over again and tried to get comfortable, but it was no use. Now she was thirsty. Though much water had been brought to her room that night, it had all gone in the tub. The pitcher next to her bed was empty. The longer she lay there the more she thought about getting a drink. Then it became all she could think about.

Anna got up, pulled on the simple dress from her wardrobe, grabbed the pitcher and went on a search for water. *I can't go far until I either find a servant or the kitchen.* She looked both ways out her door but saw no one. She crept down the hall and took the stairs toward the dining room. Surely there would be someone there cleaning up after dinner. When she arrived, the table was cleared and there was no sign of servants. She started back down the hall, looking for stairs leading to the kitchen below. She heard soft voices and crept closer to the sound. Anna found herself outside the door to a small, finely furnished room with a nice fire crackling. She was about to enter when a voice stopped her.

"Well, do you love her?" asked someone she thought was Lady Avigail. The voice that answered was a man's, but Anna couldn't make out what he said. Anna thought it was more like a grunt.

"I know I don't like the thought of being without her," he said.

Jack.

"She might be young and impulsive now, but she won't always be. This age is one of the most tumultuous of a girl's life. Her true character will rise to the surface. In any case, you must leave first thing in the morning."

"Come with us. For your safety."

"We are well fortified here," Avigail replied. "It sounds as if Karfin will be the focus."

"Yes, but they could strike here and move onto Karfin."

Anna crept away from the door. She didn't want to eavesdrop, but before she got too far, she heard footsteps and then a clear reply, "I'm glad you understand. When we deal with all this mess, I promise to stay for a couple weeks."

Jack was coming. Anna retreated down the hall. In her haste, she struck the pitcher against a large vase with a loud *clank*! It tipped precariously, and Anna grabbed it before it crashed to the floor. Anna pretended to be studying a portrait, though it was dark in the hallway.

Jack looked out the door. "Anna?" he called. "Is that you?"

"Oh, yes, Jack, hello. I was just looking for a place to fill my water pitcher."

He stared at her with his mouth open. He stopped midstride as his eyes traveled over her. He chuckled to himself and shook his head a little. "You look, well, different."

She blushed and said, "I need to thank Lady Avigail for the wonderful bath. I thought I'd never feel clean again." She looked him over as well. Clean-shaven, fresh clothes. He cleaned up well.

He was still staring.

"So, do you know where the kitchen is?" she asked tentatively.

He narrowed his eyes. "How long have you been out here?"

"Just a moment. I looked in the dining room, but I didn't see any servants, so I walked down this way." Her words rushed out. Jack wasn't convinced.

Lady Avigail appeared at the door. "John William," she said. "Why don't you fill up the pitcher and let me get acquainted with the princess?" Her eye met Anna's. "Come in, Your Highness."

One glance at Jack and Anna knew he had told Avigail everything.

"Thank you," she whispered to Avigail. "You have certainly given me royal treatment today. This castle feels so much like home, yet I can't quite relax until I'm there, I think."

"Ah," said Avigail. "Couldn't sleep?"

Anna shook her head.

"Well, come sit by the fire," she said, smiling.

Anna sat in a plush chair. Her stomach danced with butterflies at the thought of Jack coming back. He had been right—everything was so formal now. She bit the inside of her lip as her thoughts flew to what she'd overheard.

Jack entered the room shortly with a pitcher and a glorious apple pie with whipped cream piled in the middle. He poured a glass for Anna, set the pitcher down on a small table and stuck a fork in the middle of the pie.

"Seriously John? No plates?" scolded Avigail.

He winked at Anna. "I couldn't carry plates as well."

"How did you know I loved apple pie?" asked Anna.

"Who doesn't?" He raised an eyebrow. "Enjoy. I ate a whole one myself and now I'm off to bed. Anna, don't stay up too late, we'll leave early in the morning, and I know how you like to sleep." His eyes twinkled.

Anna's cheeks flushed. "Only when I'm exhausted."

His smile broadened. "I was only teasing." He laughed. Then his eyes met Avigail's. He leaned over and kissed her on the cheek. "I will knock on your door in the morning," he whispered.

Avigail's smile never quite reached her eyes.

Anna broke the silence. "This place seems so familiar to me, but I don't recall if I've ever been here before."

"Oh, you have," said Avigail. "You came with your mother as a child. We were friends." She picked up the pie and set it in Anna's lap. "Help yourself."

Anna thanked her and dug in. "You knew my mother?" Anna asked with her mouth full. "For how long?"

"Do you not know my story?" Avigail frowned. "John did not tell you?"

"No, my lady."

"Six years ago, I lost my good husband and all my family except for one son who escaped with me when our kingdom was overrun." Her lips lifted but her eyes were full of sorrow. "Your father was gracious to us and offered us this place to live in exile. It was more than generous. We have land and servants here." She got up and peered out into the darkness.

Anna's mind flew. "King Alvar of Oclen was your husband?"

"Of course."

"I-I'm sorry. I didn't realize." *And the one son was—*

"Do you not know who you ride with?" Avigail frowned.

Anna's breath caught for a split second. *Of course. If she is Jack's mother, then he lost his father and brothers in the coup of Oclen. All assassinated while the youngest prince escaped with his mother. Oh, Jack.*

"He didn't tell me," Anna said, groaning. She pulled her hand to her scalp. "Now it makes sense. I do remember him. I'm so sorry for what he must have gone through."

"Your mother and I were friends when I was still queen of Oclen. We would visit Sunderland and sometimes meet here as it was closer for us."

"And I came with her?"

"You were just a baby."

"But was she sick after she had me? I've been told I somehow caused her to be weak, that she never recovered from delivering me." Anna leaned toward the older woman. She knew so little about her mother.

"Oh, no, child," said Avigail. "You did nothing to cause her illness. Your mother simply caught a fever when you were about a year old. She almost died then. That's what weakened her, not nursing you. The next time she got sick, it was just too much for her." Avigail's eyes glistened.

Anna was lost in thought.

"She was my dear friend, and she loved her little girl so much." Avigail took her hands. "Don't ever think otherwise."

Anna forced her voice to function. "What was my mother like?"

"Her beauty ran deep. She was good, honest, kind, loyal and always thought of others before herself. She felt the role of the queen should be to care for the people. She'd ride out sometimes and bring food and medicine to poor families with sick children."

Anna drank in this description.

"Does your sister ever speak of your mother?" Avigail asked. "She was old enough to remember her."

"Saira?" Anna asked. "No, perfect Saira hardly speaks to me. She'd only just returned from studying in Hedricksburg when I was captured." She chuckled. "She's supposed to be my new tutor."

"Give her a chance to be your friend. You might be surprised how much you have in common."

"Perhaps," Anna answered. "Did Mother ride well?"

"Ride? Yes, she loved horses—any living creature, actually.

Some called her an angel. I think her heart was bigger than all of us. It was a blow when we lost her." Her eyes misted once more. "But we had you." She tipped her chin at Anna. "Her little angel."

"I'm no angel." Anna dropped her gaze for a moment.

Avigail tilted her head to the side, like she'd seen Jack do so many times.

"You've probably heard what an embarrassment I've been to my father," Anna said. "How I have my mother's looks, but none of her dignity."

"Look at me."

Anna forced her eyes to meet the older woman's.

"So much was expected of you. So many people wanted her back that they couldn't wait for the little girl to grow up. Of course you can't live up to the memory of your mother. No one can. But you have abilities she never had."

"It's when I'm being myself Father is most disappointed in me."

"Then so be it. But you can't live by striving to be someone you're not." Avigail's eyes gleamed.

Anna was silent for a moment. "I know I must go back, but suddenly I'm afraid," she whispered. "I'm afraid no one will believe me, that I won't make it in time or that I've somehow ruined my father, that—oh, I'll never live up to what he wants from me."

"That can't be," Avigail shook her head, looking at her with kindness she didn't deserve.

"I never do anything that pleases him." She thought of Seamus. *Traitor.* "My father thinks more highly of the treacherous snake who's trying to bring him down than me," Anna said. "What if I can't convince him his right-hand counsel is scheming against him?"

"He will listen. He must miss you terribly."

Anna's muscles relaxed, and her nerves unwound at

Avigail's words. The woman drew Anna with quiet assurance. She wished she could stay longer than one night.

"And you have John William to help you." Avigail interrupted her thoughts. "I'm sure he won't leave you alone."

"I wouldn't have made it here without him."

Avigail shook her head. "He carries a heavy burden of shame. "He's always felt he could have done more to help his father the day he died." Avigail sighed. "But he was just a boy."

And what happened to him in the desert didn't help.

Anna nodded, lost in thought.

"I rarely see him, but I'm hoping he's found a reason to stay closer from now on." Her eyebrows twitched up. "I don't mean to pry, but what do you think of him?"

Anna's stomach clenched. "I thought I was just getting to know him," she said. "But now I'm not sure I know him at all." She swallowed. "I certainly don't want him feeling obligated to me as far as my father's edict is concerned." Anna's voice shook. She should have realized who he was. She wanted to help him the way he'd helped her.

"You two will figure it out." Avigail's eyes crinkled in the corners. Strength flowed from this woman. She had known love. And grief.

"I'm so thankful he saved my life. More will be saved if we get to Father in time."

"You will make it," said Avigail. "Stay close to Jack on the way back. You wouldn't want to be recognized and captured by another knight."

"We won't let that happen." Anna was a little unsure of what Avigail wanted her to say. She met the older woman's gaze. She knew Avigail would approve of a marriage with her son, if it came to that. She set the half-finished pie on a side table and stood up.

"I suppose I need to get some rest."

"Don't forget your water," said Avigail, handing her the pitcher. "Can you find your room in the dark?"

"I believe so, thank you," said Anna.

Avigail hugged her warmly. She smelled of rose-scented soap and lavender tea.

"Take care. I have so enjoyed seeing you again—all grown up," she said. "Be strong and say a prayer to the Most High. Your mother did."

Anna nodded. "For what it's worth, I owe everything to your son. I couldn't have been in better hands."

Tears welled in Avigail's eyes. "I know the feeling."

Chapter 17

As promised, Jack woke her early. The candles had burned out, and there wasn't yet a hint of sunrise. He lit an oil lamp.

"Jack," groaned Anna. "It's the middle of the night. Go away." The bed was too soft and warm. Anna rolled over and covered her head.

Jack laughed. "Get on up, Anna, or…"

"Or what?" she moaned.

"Or I'll have to drag you out myself," he said, giving her shoulder a little shake. His hand rested on her shoulder a moment longer than necessary. Her heart skipped a beat as his fingers traveled to her neck and tickled under her hair.

"Just a few more minutes." She swatted his hand away.

"Or perhaps I'll pour this water you wanted so badly all—over—you!" He swung the pitcher above her head, letting a few drops splash on her hair.

"Okay, okay, I'm up," Anna quickly jumped out of bed and fell into Jack. He caught her, accidentally splashing water down her back. She shrieked and punched him.

"Oh—sorry." He laughed.

"That's cold!"

"I'm going to miss this." He stepped back to avoid a second punch.

"What?"

"Seeing you so disheveled in the morning. From now on, it will be prim and proper princess."

Anna paused. She would miss this too. His steady heartbeat, his warm, deep breaths. Something bubbled up inside her every time she thought of him. She needed him to get home, to face Seamus and her father, but Jack...? Her arms tingled for him to hold her again. Even for a moment. She shook off the thought.

"Just get out so I can dress." Jack left, and she took a step toward the bed. Her feet were freezing on the stone floor.

"Don't even think about getting back in bed," he called through the door. "Oh, and Lady Avigail gave me this if you want to wear it." His arm reached in and tossed a beautiful hat with a pointed top and white silk veil on the floor.

Anna grabbed it and crossed the floor to the wardrobe. The hat was a nice touch—better than that horrible veil she'd been wearing, but not so concealing. She chose a pretty light wool dress, trimmed in silk. She pulled it over her head and turned to the mirror. Even in the dim light, she could see it was beautiful. The dress drew in around her waist and had long, flowing sleeves extending all the way to her fingertips. She fixed her hair, put on the hat, adjusted the veil and peeked one more time in the mirror. A light cloak went over the dress. She slipped on light riding pants under the dress and threw the bag holding her golden bow and arrow over her shoulder. It seemed strange to strap the sword to such an outfit. She would let Jack carry it and the shield.

She stepped into the hall where Jack was waiting with his arms crossed. He ran his eyes over her. "I suppose that's ok." Anna blushed as he stopped to study her again. "I'd rather see you in servants' attire." He paused, making up his mind. "Just keep your cloak on and your veil, too."

"Sure." Anna couldn't help rolling her eyes. "My servant clothes are still wet. This is what your mother gave me."

He stopped in his tracks.

"Why didn't you tell me?" she asked.

He shrugged. "I just couldn't."

She put her hand on his arm. "I've told you everything about me. I want to know you more, too."

His muscles tensed under her touch. "Let's just get you home."

They walked to the stables without further speech. Anna was tired and could tell Jack wasn't in the mood for any more questions. They traveled lightly this time, as they should be to the castle before sunset. Jack had packed a meal and water, leaving their mats and other supplies behind. Her new sword fit easily on Jack's belt. They then covered the jeweled shield in canvas and strapped it to Avery's saddle. Anna's bow and arrows remained in the sack, out of sight. Servants were never armed.

The early morning sky hinted at gray as Anna swung up on Star. The stars were disappearing into the deepest gray-blue, yielding one by one to the coming sun. Anna wrapped her cloak tight around her shoulders to keep out the chilly air. They would meet the river in a few hours and follow it all the way to the castle.

"Ready?" Jack asked.

"I'll follow you," Anna answered.

Jack nodded to the guard as they rode through the gate. Anna turned her face away from him as she passed.

They walked the horses until it was bright enough to see. They were traveling due west, following the river as it wiggled at the base of the mountain range. Deer and other wildlife scurried away as they approached, even though for the most part Jack and Anna were silent.

Soon the sun peeked its way up behind them, slowly burning off the mist rising from the earth. With it came warmth and to Anna, hope. Each time they stopped a new wave of anticipation flowed through her as she thought of facing her father. Would he be angry? Would he believe she hadn't run away? Would she conceal her new weapons or wear them in? Darting through her mind as well was the fact her father would certainly offer Jack her hand in marriage. Jack had not spoken about it at all. Anna was desperate to discuss it. She wasn't sure either of them was ready for marriage, but her chest ached at the thought of losing Jack.

On they rode, neither speaking.

Her eyes followed Jack's back while Avery forged ahead on the path. Waves of indecision rolled off him. She longed for a light-hearted jest or another brush of those fingers against her hand. His shoulders were rigid. Something had changed.

As the light increased, they trotted their horses off and on and cantered a little. Before long, they rounded a river bend and found several horsemen above them on a small hill. The men waved and moved down to greet them.

"Get behind me!" Jack said, "and be ready to ride fast."

Anna hurried Star behind the larger Avery.

The horses came to a quick stop as the three knights looked them over. Anna kept her eyes down and tilted her head away from the knights.

"Who goes there?" asked the knight in the center, apparently the eldest of the three.

"I am Sir John William of Hemmington," Jack said, bowing his head. "And you are?"

"Knights of the good king, sir. I am Aric and these are Jamin and Badri," he said, gesturing to the other two.

"Out on a mission?" asked Jack.

"Haven't you heard?" asked Aric, the eldest of the knights. Anna guessed him to be in his late thirties. He would have seen her before. "We are again searching for Princess Anna. The first one who finds her will have her hand."

Anna's heart pounded in her ears. She was glad for muddy brown hair.

Jack laughed. "Well, certainly she cannot be divided into three! What if you all find her at once?"

Aric expression grew serious. "It is no laughing matter, sir. Do you not know our king will die of grief if she is not returned soon?"

Jack's face dropped. "No, I've just returned from a long journey."

"If we all find her, we will draw for her hand."

Anna's face heated. *How dare they?*

The knight glanced up with sudden interest as Star tugged a little at the reins. "And who might this be?" He pointed to Anna.

"She is a slave girl I rescued from a cruel master," Jack said. "Lady Avigail is giving her to the king as a maid to Princess Saira."

Anna was thankful for the veil as she moved her face away from the knight. She appreciated Jack's quick thinking. A maid to a princess could easily be wearing these clothes. Aric circled his horse around them. Anna held her breath as she waited for him to finish his circle.

"She's the right size, but the hair is wrong. Look at me…"

Hair rose on the back of her neck. She kept her eyes down but saw Jack's hand creep toward his sword.

She would never want one of her father's knights hurt over her. Her heart thudded.

"Have you heard the news?" Jack interrupted. "Great armies are assembling to our south. I am in a hurry to warn the King, so if you don't mind, we'll be on our way." Jack took Star's bridle and nudged Avery with his knee, turning the horses away. *Smart. A slave girl wouldn't be able to ride well, and Anna was known for her riding.*

"No, I hadn't heard."

"Well, don't ride far from Karfin," Jack called over his shoulder. "King Vilipp will need you soon enough."

"We'll keep that in mind. The chances of finding the princess at this point are small, indeed," Aric said.

Blood rushed to Anna's cheeks. Perhaps he had recognized her but was chivalrous enough to submit to the fact Jack found her first. Anna glanced over her shoulder. The eldest knight was watching them, but the other two had already lost interest. Jack let go of Star's bridle and clucked Avery into a canter.

"Let's put some miles between us and those knights," Jack said. Anna was happy to do so.

"That was a little too close," she replied. "I'm sure Aric knows me. Do you think he will track us?"

"No, I think he's an honorable man."

"Just not my idea of marriage material," Anna mumbled.

He raised his eyebrows. "Of course not." The corners of his mouth twitched up, and he squared his shoulders. A sense of safety fell over Anna.

As they rode, Anna's thoughts shifted from anticipation to anxiety to dread. Her heart raced at the thought of seeing the castle again soon. Then just as quickly, it would drop as she pictured her father's face after hearing the truth.

After a short rest by the river, Anna took a deep breath. *No matter what happens,* she told herself, *I'll behave truthfully and to the best of every ability I have.* That's all she could ask of herself. Her heart felt lighter and almost giddy as she realized home was only a few hours away. They remounted their horses, and Jack set the pace at a steady trot. After they splashed through a small brook, Anna kicked Star into a canter, pulling close to Avery. Just as she passed him, she yelled, "Yah!" and smacked Avery on the hindquarters.

The horse burst forward, slowing again as Jack pulled him up. Anna pushed Star by, shouting, "Catch me, old man, if you can!" By now Star was galloping, although Anna knew, nowhere near top speed. With each pounding hoof beat drawing her closer home, a lightness entered her soul. She let Star pull the reins through her hands. They were going to make it. She glanced back at Jack, who was moving Avery up. She laughed at the annoyed expression on his face.

"Anna!"

Anna couldn't help herself.

"Go, Star, go!" she called to the mare and squeezed her legs harder against her sides. The little mare stretched out farther. Anna glanced back and saw the distance between Star and Avery widen again. Anna laughed and pulled Star up as she saw another creek approach. Soon both horses were puffing together as they splashed through the water.

Jack wiped lather off Avery's neck. "What in the world?"

"I just can't wait to get there."

He scowled. "We still have a long way to go today. We need to pace our horses."

"You worry too much. We're nearly there, and you have to admit, I've behaved myself most of the way." Anna pushed her lips into a deliberate pout.

"Yes, but don't turn into an idiot just because we're a few hours from home. Stay with me." He walked Avery past Star. "We've had our share of bad luck. We don't know what could be stalking us."

Anna's face burned as if he'd slapped her. Of course, he was right. She must be calculated, reserved. No mistakes. She felt a pang of regret. *He thinks I'm an idiot? Probably.* She splashed through the water after him. Jack's back was straight, his shoulders set.

After another hour, the river twisted suddenly. They followed it north for perhaps a mile until turning to the west again. Anna glanced at Jack. She was still wondering whether her father would offer him her hand in marriage. *Would he say nothing?* Jack glanced back. His face was all business. They topped a hill. Jack stopped, staring at the scene. Anna pulled Star up next to him and caught her breath. The sky opened up before them full of oranges and reds. The sun was dropping below distant wisps of clouds which diffused the last light into bright yellows and pinks. The clouds were lined in deep indigo. The large, red sun was falling before their eyes. Anna was transfixed.

Jack's face reflected the warm tones. She supposed hers did as well. "We're close," he said. "When we get in, follow my lead. I'm sure I can get an audience with your father."

The words she'd been dying to say all day tumbled out. "I shouldn't say anything, but I was wondering what you think Father will do for you when you've brought me back?" Anna asked, stumbling over her words. This scene was calling her home, yet her eagerness to get there subsided. She had to take in the beauty a moment longer. She wanted him to appreciate it with her.

"I've already told you, he'll be thrilled. He loves you, and though we'll be preparing for war—"

"No, I mean, about, well, other matters, involving you." Anna knew her face was flaming by now and not just from the sunset.

Jack's shoulders relaxed a bit. "Don't worry about that. He won't force anything on you." His lips contracted as he studied her. "The thing we need to think of first is saving your people. That is what your father will focus on."

But what do you want, Jack?

She swallowed a lump in her throat. "By the way, if I don't have a chance later, I wanted to thank you for all you've done for me. We made it home, and I would never be here without you."

Jack's eyes moved over her with a pained expression. His fingers twitched on the reins as if he wanted to reach for her. He opened his mouth as if to speak and closed it again. He set his jaw and looked to the west. "We're not there yet." He squeezed Avery forward.

Their path soon broke into pasture lands. They pushed

their horses back into a trot, occasionally cantering and jumping over white stone fences. Anna's heart pounded as she was reminded of racing Farley over sod much like this. How long ago it seemed. She was on the final turn toward home. She longed to push Star faster, to just get there, for the waiting to be over.

They entered the forest surrounding the castle—to the east of where Anna had fallen off Farley so long ago. The trees opened to peasants' fields, and Anna raised her eyes to spot the turrets of Karfin rising out of the horizon backed to the white cliffs. Her hands sweat as butterflies filled her stomach. The sun, low in the sky, was shining its last rays on the castle's peaks.

She was finally home.

Chapter 18

They clucked their horses forward, covering the final miles at a trot and then a walk until they met the outer stone wall of the castle grounds, climbing fifteen feet into the air. Jack requested admittance at the gate.

The guards were gracious and opened the gate without asking any questions, although Anna heard coarse whispering as she passed. She kept her head and eyes down. She could not afford to look anyone in the eyes. Not yet.

They walked through the grounds and dismounted at the drawbridge. A guard with a graying beard approached them.

"Who requests admittance to the king's palace?" he asked.

"Sir John William, a knight in the king's service," Jack said, bowing. "I bear news and a great gift for his majesty."

The guard stepped aside. "The king might not see you until the morning. He's been sick lately and retires early."

"Thank you," Jack said. "Please find someone to attend to our horses." He grabbed the bag with the bow and arrows in it and handed it to Anna, keeping the sword and shield himself.

Anna's steps were cautious as she followed Jack over the heavy wooden bridge. She was home. Her heart pulsed in her ears as she picked up her skirts to climb the steps to the giant doors, which more guards opened. Happy and horrible memories collided in her mind. They turned down the hall and stopped before the doors leading to the throne room. Two guards stood watch. Anna closed her eyes briefly and took a deep breath in an attempt to slow her pounding heart.

"My name is Sir John William, and I have brought urgent news for the king," Jack said to the guards. "And also a great gift. Please allow me an audience with him."

"The king will have retired by now, my lord," one guard said. "I dare not disturb him."

"I promise no harm will come to you. Tell him my gift is priceless and will heal his wounds."

The guard glanced over Jack's shoulder and raised his eyebrows. He disappeared and returned a few minutes later.

"His majesty will see you now," he said.

"Thank you," Jack said.

Anna peeked around Jack to see her father slouching to his throne chair. He eased himself down in it, coughing as he went. Anna had never seen him look so old, thin and tired. She cast her eyes down under the veil which still guarded her face. Her long cloak swept the stone floor behind her as they made their way to the throne.

A side door opened, and Anna's heart jumped as a tall man strode to King Vilipp. His dark eyes narrowed upon them. *Seamus.*

They stopped before the throne and bowed low. Anna peered up. Her father's graying hair fell around his face and across his drooping shoulders. He was unshaven.

"Why are you disturbing the king at such an hour?" demanded Seamus. "Have you no manners?"

Jack squared his shoulders and straightened up.

"If it were not an urgent matter, I would not have traveled so far and fast to bow before his Highness. This cannot wait, sir." Jack's tone was curt. He was not backing down.

King Vilipp raised his hand to Seamus. "Peace, Seamus."

He glanced down at Jack's taut face. "Sir John. What news do you have from the south?"

"I have much news, Sire, but first I must return someone most valuable to you." Jack stepped to the side, leaving Anna still low in a curtsy. She was shaking all over. The moment had come.

She straightened up, tore off her veil, and rushed three steps forward. "It's me, Father, Anna." She gestured toward Jack. "This man has saved me from many cruel deaths and risked everything to bring me back."

King Vilipp leapt from his throne and gasped, clutching his chest.

"My God, Anna. Is it truly you?" His eyes took her in and settled on her hair.

"Yes, Father," said Anna, choking back tears. "I'm so sorry, I didn't run away. I got hurt and some men found me and…"

"Shh—shh-I'll hear all about it later," he said, throwing his arms around her and stroking her hair. He finally pulled back to look at her again. "I cannot believe I'm seeing you! I thought you were lost forever." He wiped his own tears. "I missed you so much."

"And I missed you, Father." It was true.

Jack stepped back. The king waved him up. "You have saved my life, young man. Mine and my daughter's, of course. I was beginning to die of grief. I cannot thank you enough."

Jack bowed. "It was my pleasure, Sire."

Seamus took a step forward. He bowed before Anna. "Your Highness," he said, taking her hand. "May I be the first of your loyal subjects to welcome you home?" He bent to kiss her hand. She snatched it back, and Seamus straightened uneasily.

Jack's jaw tightened. Anna could sense waves of bridled fury radiating off Jack.

"Seamus, as happy as I am to see you again, I would truly treasure this moment if I could be alone with Father. You wouldn't mind, of course, giving us a few minutes?" Anna forced a fake smile and stared at him until he dropped his eyes.

"You may not understand, my dear, your father depends on me greatly now." His voice dripped like syrup. "I am at his side constantly to serve him. Unfortunately, He is in much pain."

"Seamus!" said the king. "I don't need a nursemaid! Anna will have what she wants tonight."

Seamus didn't move.

"Please," said Anna. "Sir John and I can surely watch his health for a few minutes."

"I thought you wanted to be alone?" He nodded to Jack. "He can leave."

"No, Jack stays." Her voice did not waver. She would not be afraid. Seamus took one step backward. His eyes traveled over her and to her hair.

"Where have you been all this time?" he asked with sudden alarm. His eyes flicked to Jack and grew wider. "Were you in the desert, with him?"

Anna stole a quick glance at Jack. His teeth were clenched.

"Leave her be," Jack said with quiet intensity.

Seamus glared at them both and backed through the open door.

"Father, there's no time to lose," Anna said. "We rushed to warn you. An attack is coming from Anwar."

"Tell him from the beginning, Anna," said Jack.

She nodded, put her arm around her father and led him back to his chair. Anna quickly told him her story, from the moment she left with Farley, to the moment she returned.

"But Father," she said in a hushed tone. "There is one other thing. When I was locked in the closet in Kasdod, I knew the man who visited Anwar." She took a deep breath and looked directly into her father's blue eyes. "It was Seamus," she whispered. "He is setting up armies and turning people against you. He aims to take over your throne and kill us all!"

"Seamus, you're sure?" he asked. Anna glanced at Jack. He nodded encouragement.

Then Anna, through many tears, told her father about the day Seamus came into her room and all his threats and behavior since. She got up and paced with her arms folded in front of her. "Father, so many times I wanted to tell you, but I was so afraid." Now the tears were flowing steadily down her cheeks. "I'm so, so sorry," Anna stammered. "I should not have been afraid of him. If I'd only exposed him for what he was, none of this would have happened." She waited for a response. She saw shock, pain, and disbelief on her father's face. He ran his hands over his forehead. She ran to him and sat at his feet, not meeting his gaze. "Do you believe me, Father? I promise, it is all true."

Her father did not respond for a moment. He bent down and touched her cheek.

"What I don't believe is my own blindness. Why didn't I see this? Right under my nose!" He gripped the chair with his hands, turning his knuckles white. He nodded at Jack.

"How many men were gathered?"

"Perhaps five thousand."

"I don't even know where my armies are." There was devastation in the king's voice. "I've let Seamus do so much while I mourned for my daughter." His pale face flushed red as energy surged through his body. "But here she is, back from the dead. And so am I."

King Vilipp leapt from his throne and grabbed his sword. "Guards! Guards!" he yelled. "Bring Seamus to me!" He turned to Anna. "He will account for what he has done."

The guards spread the word to search for Seamus. After a time, they returned, declaring he could not be found.

"Sire," Jack ventured. "It is quite possible he sensed something was wrong when Anna asked him to leave the room. He may have deserted."

As soon as he said these words everyone in the room knew

them to be true. A check to the stables found his horse missing, and the guard at the gate reported Seamus galloping out minutes earlier.

Her father paced through the throne room. "Stefan is in great danger. Seamus will go to him and kill him. He is the heir."

"I will ride after him," Jack volunteered.

"No. You guard Anna in case he's still here. Get Geoffrey!" The king's captain of the guard bustled in.

"At your service, Sire," he said.

"Geoffrey," said the king. "Where are my armies right now?"

"Sir Seamus sent orders to move Stefan further south and the rest to the west. They could not be further from you right now."

"Listen," the king said intently. "Send your fastest riders. Ride night and day and find our armies and bring them back here. If Seamus tries to stop you, kill him. He is a traitor. I don't care if you shoot him from behind. Am I clear?"

"Yes, Sire," he bowed.

The king explained to him they could be attacked any day from the east. Geoffrey's face paled.

"How did we not see?" he asked.

King Vilipp closed his eyes and turned away. "How? My most trusted friend. My daughter's godfather. Plotting against me. Taking advantage of my daughter, taking advantage of my grief." He stopped pacing. "Anna." He placed his large hands on her shoulders. "I love you, no matter what. You know you needn't fear me."

"I know that now," Anna whispered.

"Tell me everything you know."

King Vilipp asked her many questions about Seamus, his activities, the conversation with Anwar, the gems, and the soldiers they found in the forest. She hadn't told him about

Nicholas's gifts yet, but how could she hide them from her father?

"There is one other thing." Anna glanced at Jack and then back at her father. "The priest gave me some gifts—a sword and a bow. He said he saw me wielding them."

"Yes?"

"Well." She swallowed hard. "They were from his great-grandfather, and they have gems of power in them."

"Bring them to me," he said.

Jack retrieved the weapons and presented them to the king.

"I could not use them without your consent, Father," Anna said, simply.

"How dare he keep such things?"

"He says it's not the tool, but the heart of the person using the tool that makes it good or evil," Anna said. "And he does not live within the borders of Sunderland."

He grunted and examined them closely. He checked the sword's balance.

"And you wish to keep them?"

"Yes, Father. They were a priceless gift."

"Very well. I will not hold you to the law considering the urgency of the moment. Please, Anna—use them only as a last resort in your own protection. I have no desire to see you in battle."

"Of course, Father." She bowed her head. "And thank you."

Great humility poured through her as she felt her father's love. She glanced up at his shining eyes. He held his arms open. She stepped forward and welcomed his embrace.

"When do you think they will strike?" he asked Jack over the top of Anna's head.

"I don't know," Jack answered. "Seamus's plans will certainly change. He might strike sooner—or even call it off and go into hiding."

The king's face lit up. "Even with war on our doorstep, I will sleep better tonight than I have in many months."

Anna returned his grin and caught herself yawning.

"Why don't we call Mary and let you rest after you've had a good meal?" said the king. "It's late."

"Jack, I can find you a room," Anna said.

Jack shook his head with a small smile.

"Our servants will take good care of him," said King Vilipp. "I want him in the room next to yours. It should be empty."

"Oh—of course, and Father?" asked Anna.

"Yes, my dear."

She leaned close to his ear and whispered, "Father, Jack—I mean Sir John William bought me a horse, food and many supplies. He needs to be repaid."

The king chuckled. "He can have half the kingdom if he wants it. Don't worry, my dear, he will be rewarded—soon."

Anna's eyes met Jack's for a moment. She hadn't taken ten steps toward her room when Mary burst through the door. She nearly squeezed her to death in a warm embrace. She led Anna to her room, fussing all the while about getting her something hot to eat.

Anna's thoughts drifted back to the throne room.

"Mary—whatever you fix for me, please make sure Jack receives double portions. He's with Father."

Chapter 19

The next day all was quiet in the castle. Riders had ridden out the night before to bring the army back. The guard put a few fighting men on watch. The rest were resting and waiting, except for servants who were bustling about, preparing and storing food in the castle cellars. Huge quantities of salted meat, dried fruit and potatoes were set aside for the armies that would hopefully come the next week. In addition, servants were busy preparing a feast to welcome Anna home that evening. It would be a bit more subdued under the circumstances, but the king wanted to honor his daughter's return.

As Anna walked through the grounds, people fell over themselves to bow to her. It was starting to get embarrassing. Anna crossed the garden and entered the stables. She took a deep breath and inhaled the smell of horses, hay and feed. It helped her deal with her rising nerves. Armies were on their way to conquer Sunderland. Her chest tightened at the thought.

What if they kill us all?

One of the dogs greeted her with licks and wagging tail.

Anna kneeled down and buried her chin in the soft fur around his neck as she patted his side. He pushed up against her, drinking in her affection. Tension slid out of her with every stroke. The dog stared up at her with warm, honey brown eyes. *So trusting.* She gave him a final pat, and he followed her to Farley's stall. It was empty. She had a sickening thought. Maybe they had gotten rid of him for what had happened to her.

"Farley's out in the far pasture, if you're looking for him, Your Highness," said a familiar voice.

"Bart!" She threw her arms around his neck, laughing. "How are you? I hope you didn't get into too much trouble on account of me."

Bart turned bright red as she lowered her arms. "No, no one blamed me. I felt terrible, of course. I'm so glad you're back." He nodded to the empty stall. "I hope you don't mind, but he's actually letting me ride him now."

"That's great! Can you please bring him in for me?" She bounced on her toes. "I can ride him tomorrow. I see you are all healed up from our last venture."

"Yes." He rubbed his arm. "There's no fear of that again. Besides, now that Sir John William has returned, I will continue in my duty as squire." He beamed.

"He is a good teacher. You will learn well under him." Anna winked.

"I'll get Farley now."

"Thank you."

Anna's heart filled as she watched him go, grabbing some grain and a stable mate to help. Sunderland would make it. *It must.*

She needed to return to the castle to get ready for the evening feast. As her shoes clicked down the stone floors, Mary bustled toward her.

"Come, dear, come!" Her tone was sharp. "We've been

searching everywhere for you. Almost thought we'd lost you again."

"What's the fuss?" asked Anna. "I was only checking on Farley."

"That horse!" she exclaimed. "Isn't he what got you into all that trouble?"

Anna didn't answer. *No, it was Seamus.*

"We must get your dress ready for tonight." Mary tugged her in front of the long mirror in her room. Anna saw several choices hanging up and a tailor standing by to offer alterations on the spot. Frances was here to help as well. She avoided Anna's eyes.

"Let's just choose one and be done with it," Anna said. All the dresses were lovely.

"This will be a special night for you," Mary said. "You will be the center of attention and your dress needs to be exceptional. Besides, you know at some point your father will offer your hand to the knight."

"But after the battle, don't you think?" Her throat tightened a little.

"Perhaps."

The tailor left so Anna could undress. Frances gasped from behind. Anna whipped her back to the mirror where long, ugly red scars reflected on her thin back.

"By the gods, child," Mary said. "What happened to you?"

"It's too much to explain." Anna blinked at her reflection. She remembered wanting to have Frances whipped after the race. Whipped for having fun playing dress up. She bit her lip. "Pick a dress that will cover my back."

"Of course."

They eventually settled on a pale pink silk dress designed to fit snugly around her waist. The tailor would have to take it in as she was still a little thin. The arms of the dress were long and flowing. The skirt of the dress was full without overwhelming Anna's small frame. The neckline was lower than Anna was used to wearing without being immodest. Mary placed a chain of jewels around her neck. The dress was perfect, but its beauty didn't calm her nerves.

She caught Frances by the arm.

"I hope there are no hard feelings between us?"

The girl shook her head. "I felt terrible about that night—truly I am sorry."

Anna stepped forward and embraced her. "All is forgiven. I'm sure I did not always treat you as well as I should have."

Frances's eyes lit up. Anna felt a new friendship forming.

As Mary and the tailor worked to fit the dress, Mary prattled. Anna stared straight ahead. The mirror reflected uncertainty in her eyes.

"I'm happy for you." Mary chattered. "Though he can't make you a queen, he comes from the finest of families. He's handsome, brave, and must be in love with you from all the time you've been together."

Anna's stomach dropped. She wasn't convinced.

"You'll dazzle him tonight," she said. Anna coughed as she pulled the sash tighter around her waist. "You couldn't have chosen a better man if you'd searched the whole world over."

Anna wished she would stop talking. She knew what Jack cared about right now was the coming war, and that's all she should be thinking about as well. Finally, the dress was ready. The maids helped her carefully remove it and hang it by the window. She washed her face and frowned. For someone supposedly in love with her, why hadn't Jack even tried to see her one time since they'd been back? Was he preparing for the battle? She thought of the weapons stowed under her bed. *It's what I should be doing.*

"I'll be back two hours before feast time to prepare your hair," Mary said. "Now, don't wander off."

Anna promised not to but did see her father for a small request. A guard let her into his private quarters.

"Father?"

"Yes, come in." His whole face lit up and his eyes sparkled as Anna entered. He appeared ten years younger than the night before. His face was shaven, and his hair cut.

"I haven't discussed one detail with you."

"Which is?"

"Do you remember how I got out of the castle using Mother's hairbrush that Mary gave me? It must have gems of power in it."

He frowned.

"Could I use it one time again and grow out this muddy hair of mine so it could be back to what it used to be? Mary is fussing to get me ready for this evening." With one glance at his face Anna could see how foolish she had been to worry that her own father would execute her for using a hairbrush. But would he let her use it again?

"That hair rope you set on fire didn't burn all the way. We never figured out how all that hair was hanging out your window," said the king. "It's one thing to ask forgiveness—of course you are forgiven, quite another to ask permission." He frowned again. "There's that law."

"I know," said Anna. "I understand. I just thought I'd ask." She leaned up and kissed her father's cheek. "It's so good to be home." She turned to go.

"Wait, Anna." Her father shook her head. "Despite the fact this goes against my better judgment, I'll let you use the brush this one time. Just don't tell anyone, for heaven's sake." He held out his arms, and she dove into them.

"Thank you, Father."

Anna returned to her room and took the hairbrush from the dresser drawer. She pulled the brush through her hair and softly sang her mother's lullaby. Nothing happened. She squinted at her reflection. She had a small stripe of gold hair on her scalp, but it didn't seem any longer.

She sang again and again, and no new hair grew. Anna

frowned. She'd just have to live with her muddy hair. She stared at the brush for several minutes, thinking of the last time she'd used it. She'd needed help. Mary said the brush brought luck. She thought of her mother and wished she could figure out the mystery of the hairbrush. Someday she would.

Mary knocked at the door and Anna tucked the brush in the back of a drawer.

"Are you ready to dress, Your Highness?"

"Yes. Sorry about my hair."

"No matter. We'll wash it again, and you'll be beautiful."

Mary prepared her favorite bath. *Yes, the castle has its benefits.* Anna smiled to herself. She took a deep breath and sank into the warm, scented water. Mary scrubbed her hair with soaps and oils, humming as she worked. Anna's thoughts returned to Jack. Mary was right. She wouldn't find anyone better if she searched the world over, but there was something about Jack she couldn't quite figure out. It was almost like riding a horse that couldn't decide whether to go forward or back when you kicked it.

Mary braided Anna's hair into a circle on her crown, tucking small jewels in the folds of the braid. She fussed and tucked and pulled. Anna tried to be grateful. Jewels decorated Anna's neckline and ears. Anna glimpsed herself in the mirror and hardly recognized the girl staring back. She lined her eyes and touched them with sparkling shadow. Mary stained her lips a light pink. Finally, she was ready.

One of her father's guards escorted Anna to the meal. Her dress floated down the stairs behind her. As she entered the dining room, everyone stood and bowed as she passed. Anna smiled kindly to each person. She had done nothing to deserve such a welcome.

Anna sat at her father's right, next to Saira. She scanned the room for Jack among the lords and ladies present. There were at least eighty people in the room, but she didn't see him.

"Anna," her father whispered. "Welcome our guests."

Anna stood. "Thank you all for coming this evening." Anna smiled. "This is a night for rejoicing, yet also solemn preparation. A night to be thankful for the food, friends and family we have and to prepare to fight to keep our loved ones safe."

People cried out with several rounds of "Here yeas!"

Anna continued, "So, please, enjoy this meal together. If I have learned anything from my journey, it's that we don't know what the future may hold. Relish this moment and live each one hereafter to the fullest. Love your families and care for your friends while they are with us. When you have the chance, choose to dance. Anna raised her glass. "Let the feast begin!"

Her father beamed as she took her seat.

She finally spotted Jack at the back of the room. Their eyes met briefly. He nodded and glanced away. She struggled to take her eyes off of him.

As the eating and the toasts came to a close, the king stood and tapped his gold cup. All eyes fell on him.

"As you know, in my most desperate attempt to have my daughter returned to this good kingdom, I issued a decree, not knowing Anna was already almost to my doorstep. I declared that whatever knight would bring her back could have her hand in marriage." He motioned for Anna to stand, which she did slowly. Her stomach dropped to her feet.

"And so," continued her father. "To be true to my word, tonight I offer my daughter's hand to the one man who saw her safely returned home to me, Sir John William."

Anna forced her eyes to lock on Jack, who was walking smoothly to the front. He bowed to the king and crossed to Anna, bowing before her and taking her hand. He kissed it and leaned over to whisper in her ear.

"You look so beautiful tonight." His words rushed out. "Absolutely perfect."

Anna shrugged. "Mary," was all she said, as if that

explained everything about her appearance. Her eyes filled with tears. She squeezed his hand for balance.

Jack dipped his chin, released her hand and turned to King Vilipp.

"Your Majesty," he began. "Although I deeply appreciate the offer of the hand of the most precious jewel in your kingdom, my conscience cannot accept it in this way. I only have one request, that Anna would marry the man of her choice. So though it greatly pains me, I must decline your most fine offer."

Gasps erupted through the crowd. Jack bowed before the king.

King Vilipp's eyebrows shot up. He reached forward to touch Jack on the shoulder.

"You do know her well. So be it. Anna shall marry the man of her choice whenever it pleases her!" he proclaimed through the hall.

Jack glanced once more at Anna before making his way toward the door.

Anna stood paralyzed. *Has Jack just turned me down in front of all these people? Didn't he know I was fine with marrying him?* She glanced around the room and met Lady Arissa's eyes. Her stomach clenched, and the old insecurities crept in. She saw the smirks on the court ladies' faces and the appreciative glances at Jack, officially back on the market. Anna forced a bright smile and returned to her seat. *Look as if this is what you've always wanted. And in a way, it is.* She glanced at the door where Jack had retreated. She'd never wanted to bolt out of a room more in her life. As the guests started to retire, she thanked her father again and told him it was time for her to turn in. Her hands shook terribly as she fumbled with the doorknob to her room.

She pulled the jewels out of her hair and kicked off her shoes before collapsing on the bed. *What had happened?* Anna reconsidered Jack's words. He wanted her to have the man of her choice. Did he want her at all? She didn't know. Moments later, Mary burst through the door.

"My dear, are you all right?" she asked, stroking her back.

"Tell me what happened down there." Anna said in a dull tone.

"Sir John William believes you should make the choice, and your father agreed."

"That's what I've always wanted."

"So why the glum face?" Mary asked.

Anna thought she was going to be sick.

"If he wanted to be with me, wouldn't he have just accepted me today?" A pang filled her chest. "We've been together every day for weeks," Anna said. "Maybe that was enough." *I miss him already.*

"Time will tell the answer," Mary said. "But now you have the chance to make that decision for yourself."

"Just leave me, Mary. I need to rest."

Mary gave her one last pat. "Ring the bell if you need me."

"Of course."

The old nurse left, quietly shutting the door. Anna could hear her busily shooing people away in the corridor.

Anna lay down again and stared at the wall. Silent tears slipped from her eyes and slid down her nose. *It is what I have always wanted. Then why do I feel so rotten?* Doubt swirled through her mind as she remembered a few of his harsher words. He'd even said she was acting like an idiot yesterday. *Of course, he must see himself with someone else.* A rush of shame washed over her. *Everyone in the castle must realize that. He had to have known how this was going to sting. He's from a noble family as well and probably would just as soon not marry an idiot like me.*

She pulled her dress off and let it fall to the floor. The room was chilly, so she slipped on her nightclothes and wandered to the window. The moon sparkled its reflection on the river as it continued on its journey, as if nothing had happened. Its beauty was lost on Anna as she stared back at the nearly full moon. *Seamus would strike soon.* She needed to forget Jack and turn her mind to helping her father win the battle. The wind shifted, and a cool breeze filled her room. *Would Stefan make it back in time? Seamus was out there, somewhere.*

"Please, protect my brother," she whispered to the Most High.

Chapter 20

The next day Anna awoke early and snuck down to the stables. She found Farley in his stall and went to work brushing his matted coat and picking burrs out of his mane and tail. She took him outside the stable to graze as she sat in the rising sun, thinking. She occasionally glanced to the west, hoping to see Stefan leading the army home.

Anna moved to sit with her back against a tree. Farley didn't appreciate having to move from the tender grass. He shook his head and pulled on the lead rope.

"Oh, come on, Farley. It won't kill you to come with me!" She had grown used to the sweet, compliant mare. The big horse followed her slowly, grabbing a few more bites as he walked.

As the midday meal approached, Anna returned Farley to his stall with grain and hay. She gave him one final pat and checked his water. She paused at Star's stall. The little mare nickered and thrust her head over the stall door. Anna scratched her behind the ears and on the throat. Tension drained from Anna as she stared into Star's bright eyes and breathed in her sweet, familiar scent. The mare rested her head against Anna's chest. Her heart warmed. *Thank goodness she survived.*

Anna crept back to her room before too many people were up. She couldn't bear to face Jack. She wasn't hungry anyway.

Anna washed her hands and thumbed through a favorite old book. She alternatively sat by the window or paced her room most of the day. Before long, someone knocked at the door. Saira.

"Hello, Anna." Her boots clicked on the stone floor as she entered. "I was just checking on you, making sure you weren't ill. We missed you at meals today."

Saira hugged her. *Affection from my usually distant older sister?*

"You are going to be all right," Saira whispered. "No one thinks badly of you. It was a noble thing Jack did. He turned down position for your freedom to choose."

Anna nodded. "But why would he have bothered if he'd wanted to be with me? He must not. It's like I somehow lost him."

"Well, life doesn't always turn out the way we expect—or want it to." Saira raised her eyebrows in a way that made Anna wonder if there was something Saira was keeping from her.

She couldn't argue with her point, however.

"Did you not talk about it?" Saira asked.

"Believe me, I wanted to, but he avoided the conversation."

Saira frowned. "Have you considered that it might not be about you, but him?"

"Yes, but I'm not sure what that means," said Anna.

"He was in bad shape when he first came here," Saira said. "He was in shock. I remember because Father had me look after him for a while as he is close to my age."

"What happened? I only know his family was killed, and he fled here."

"One day the whole family was together—it was Jack's fourteenth birthday. One minute everyone was celebrating, the next minute armed men ran in with swords and started slaughtering the family. Jack's father and brothers fought to the death, giving Jack and his mother time to escape. His father told Jack to flee with his mother—to get her to safety. He told me he glanced back and saw his brother dying and his father run through with the sword. He grabbed his mother and kept going."

Anna's heart wrenched to think of what he went through on that day.

Saira continued. "Jack wanted to stay and fight, but the king knew their only chance was to flee. There were too many of them. People in their own castle had turned against them. Jack escaped on a single horse, carrying his mother to safety."

"Jack may have his own reasons which have nothing to do with you," Saira said, her tone soothing. "He didn't mean to hurt you."

"I'm sure you are right, but I can't stop feeling I must have read him wrong. I thought he cared for me. What's worse is Arissa and her ilk in the court. I'm sure they can't wait to get their paws all over him. He's fresh meat now."

"Ignore those girls. They are nothing to you," Saira said.

"Gavriella isn't so bad, I suppose."

"She's the one from Durham?" Saira asked thoughtfully.

"Yes. I think I could be friends with her."

"That's a start," said Saira. "But you need to remember you are a daughter of the king. Now act like it."

Anna shook her hair down and pulled her shoulders back. "You're right. What have I been thinking?" She steeled herself and shoved the embarrassment and confusion away.

"Come down and have some dessert." Saira laughed.

Anna couldn't argue with that. Anna dressed properly and followed Saira downstairs. She held her chin high as she entered the dining room. The few people left at the table rose as she entered. She held up her hand to signal for them to be seated. She wanted no attention. She and Saira shared cake and tea. She even laughed a little. Saira was right. Most people were not at all concerned with her. They were worried about the coming battle.

A blast of heat hit Anna as she and Saira walked through the armory after dessert. Blacksmiths worked night and day, sharpening swords, pounding hot metal into shields, spears and armor for men and horses. Anna's heart swelled at the thought of protecting the people. Yes, their lives were what mattered now, even though a part of her worried about running into Jack at every turn.

The rattle of chain link armor made Anna glance up. Bart strode toward her, wielding a new sword.

"Bart!" Anna exclaimed. "It suits you perfectly."

He bowed before her. "I am happy to defend the castle, Your Highness."

"You will serve the king well in battle, as always."

His eyes glistened. "Thank you, Your Highness," he said. "I'm thrilled to fight at my master's side."

Anna's eyes narrowed. "Promise me you will stay close to Jack during the battle."

"Of course. He might need me, after all." He grinned and bounced a little from foot to foot.

She only hoped Jack could keep him safe.

———

THE NEXT DAY Anna decided to walk around the gardens for some air around noon. The place was deathly quiet, like the stillness before a great storm. Even the wind had ceased. She wasn't in the mood to chat with a great number of people, so when she saw a group of ladies approaching, Anna ducked into the hedge maze in the middle of the garden. While mazes were confusing to most, Anna knew this one well. She often had used its ten-foot-high walls for cover when sneaking to the stables.

She walked along one side and without paying attention

where she was going, turned at the first right. She turned at the next left and took two more turns as she followed the maze around. But here, to her surprise, it came to a dead-end. *They must have changed it!* She ran back to where she thought she'd begun but couldn't find the entrance. *Oh, great.* She took yet another wrong turn. Then she heard voices. *I must be close to the gazebo.* She could shout through the hedge and ask for help if she absolutely had to. Anna walked along until she heard the voices clearly. She was about to call out when she recognized Saira's voice. Anna hesitated.

"I think you've upset my sister's pride a bit," Anna heard Saira saying.

Anna's faced burned. *Oh, no.*

He laughed, "I can't imagine!" *Jack.* "She's not your typical girl."

Anna couldn't speak.

"No," said Saira, "but she still has feelings. Remember, she's only sixteen."

"Soon to be seventeen, but I know. She's young." His voiced softened. "It was never my intention to hurt her."

Anna trudged in the other direction, struggling to get out of the maze. After fifteen minutes, she found she again was within earshot of their conversation. Giving up, she plopped to the ground and listened.

"We'll see," Jack laughed. "You will have made me the happiest man alive. I never knew you were so sensible."

"That's me. The sensible, boring one. Not like someone else." Her voice was low.

"I'll never forget the time we spent together when I first came here. It meant everything to me," Jack said. "I was broken."

"You were young and in shock. Anyone would have befriended you," Saira said.

"No. Not the way you did. Whoever catches you will be a lucky man," he said. There was a long pause. *What could they be*

doing? Anna's cheeks burned. And what history do they have together?
"But all I can think about right now is the battle. Anna will be fine," Jack said. "Please make sure she stays out of trouble."

"Talk to her now, while there is time," Saira said. "She should hear from you."

"I'm not sure what to say," Jack said.

"You'll think of something."

Anna couldn't sit still any longer. She stumbled around the maze until she finally found the exit that led down to the stables. Dirty and sweaty, she ran to Farley's stall. Her heart pounded in her ears. Hands shaking, she brushed Farley quickly and then saddled him.

She hadn't ridden him since she'd returned. Anna would never admit it to anyone, but she had been a little nervous about getting on him again after her last ride. Now, she no longer cared. Recklessness pulsed through her. She wanted out of the castle, even for a few minutes. Just a quick ride through the village, out of this suffocating place. Jack had been right. Everything had changed between them. Ignoring thoughts of caution, she tightened his girth and grabbed his bridle.

"Anna!"

Anna jumped. "Jack!" She glared. "You should know better than to sneak up on people—especially me!"

"I'm sorry," he said, taken aback. "I thought I might find you here." His voice was kind, his face confused.

"Well, what do you want?" Anna lashed out.

He frowned. "Are you taking Farley out?"

"That's what it looks like."

"I don't think that's a good idea."

"Oh, please, don't parent me. I can ride my own horse. After all, I am sixteen—or is that too young for you?"

"What?"

Anna rolled her eyes.

"I overheard you and Saira talking while I was trying to

find my way out of that wretched maze," she said. "You don't have to try to make me feel better. I'm fine."

She went back to brushing Farley's neck with vigorous strokes. The big horse jumped. He didn't like rough brushing.

Jack came up behind her and placed his hand over hers on the brush.

"I don't think you understand." Anna's heart leaped into her throat. She bit her lip. *What does he want?*

She glanced up at him. His face contorted as if in pain.

"I don't know what you heard me say to Saira but let me explain." Anna stared at his Adam's apple as he struggled to swallow. He took a deep breath. "I care for you, Anna, a lot. I mean, your father and I, we had spoken, but I didn't expect him to offer your hand yet. I was caught off guard, so I said what I thought would make you happy—having your own choice."

Anna's heart raced as she processed his words. He still hadn't answered the main question. *Does he want to be with me?*

Almost in answer, Jack cupped his hand gently under her hair. She raised her chin. He hesitated before bending close, stopping an inch before her lips, his eyes holding a question.

"The truth is, I miss you. Every minute," he whispered. "But I don't know why you'd ever want to be with someone like me." She realized he was going to kiss her a second before their lips met. Her heart pounded against her ribs. When he tried to deepen the kiss, she pulled back in surprise. His arms immediately dropped to hold her hands. He tilted his chin slightly to the side. Anna blushed. She opened her mouth, but no words would come out. She couldn't meet his eyes.

Jack tucked a hair behind her ear. "You've never been kissed?"

Anna shook her head in mortification. Her face was blazing now, but he seemed to like the idea of this being her first kiss.

"It's ok. You must know I don't want to be with anyone but

you," he said, placing two more small kisses on her lips. She didn't understand how someone could be so strong and lethal and yet be so gentle with her. He pulled her to his chest. "So many times, I've wanted to do that," he whispered just above her ear as he held her.

"You did?" Anna croaked. "But you don't want to marry me?"

"It wouldn't be fair to you. There is so much you don't know about me." He pulled her back to look her in the eye. "And I do want it to be your choice. I would never force you to do something you didn't want. Never. And I don't want to be with someone who was forced to be with me, either, no matter how beautiful she is." His eyes sparkled. "You are young, and I want you to be sure. If you didn't love me, you'd grow bored and bitter, or worse, eventually fall in love with someone else." He dropped his arms from her waist and shuffled back a step. "I would just rather take this slow. We've only known each other a few weeks, after all."

Anna's mouth burst into a smile. "You had me a long time ago."

"Oh, yeah, when?"

Her eyes flashed. "I think it was the day you shaved that scraggly beard off."

He laughed. "That bad, huh?"

"Bad."

He chuckled. "You had me when you walked into the tavern carrying that tray with too many drinks on it."

"That's hard to believe. I was looking pretty rough."

"It wasn't your beauty that won me. It was what the other servants whispered about you. Never had a servant in Anwar's court traded herself for a friend. That prince wanted you, but you let her go in your place. He could have saved you, but you took her whipping instead. They said Kumud strung you up to a door." He shuddered. "Kumud is lucky I didn't have time to deal with him. When I heard what had happened, I had to get you out of there."

She reached for his hand and laced her fingers with his. "Never has anyone treated me with the respect you have. But you're right. We should be certain." Her lips pulled up nervously. "I was never sure how you felt. I'm new to this."

"I wanted to act honorably toward you in every way, especially knowing what Seamus did to you," Jack said. "And I did have to get you back to your father to warn him. I tried my best to keep my head on the mission, but you can be a distraction." He smirked.

She thought back to sleeping in his arms. He had respected her completely.

"I can't read your mind," she said.

"Thankfully." He blushed. "My thoughts aren't always so honorable…"

Anna punched him lightly and turned back to Farley, embarrassed.

"There's no one I trust more," Anna said.

"Only because you don't know everything about me." He came up behind her and gently drew her to his chest. She hooked her arms on his.

"I know some things. Saira told me about your family. I'm so sorry." She paused for a moment. "Why didn't you tell me?"

He was silent. Seething with awkwardness, Anna went back to brushing Farley's neck.

"You have to understand, I can never give you a kingdom. I'll be forever living off your father. Sometimes I just wish I—"

"You wish you'd stayed and fought with your father?" Anna saw it in his face.

He grimaced. "I saw him die," he said. "It would have been an honorable death for me, fighting for my father and my people. Instead, I ran to safety."

"Your mother would have died, too." Anna said.

"There are worse things than dying with honor."

"You worry too much about honor. You are obviously brave. That day you obeyed your father, the king. You did the right thing," said Anna.

Jack shook his head and scoffed. "I've done a lot of things—things during my training in the desert you know nothing about. You deserve better." He looked down.

"I'm far from perfect. And if you'd died fighting for your father, who would have saved me?" Anna asked. "That has to count for something."

"It counts for everything." He frowned. "But remember what the priest said, that you were supposed to be a queen someday. I can never give you that. I'm beneath you."

"You are my superior in every way," Anna whispered. "And I don't care about being queen. I care about you."

"And of course I care about you." He brushed her cheek with his fingertips and kissed her again. Her heart hammered against her chest and her knees wobbled as he tentatively deepened the kiss. This time Anna was ready. She grabbed his shirt for balance and lost herself in his embrace. Her hands seemed small as she gripped his muscled arms. She wanted this moment to last forever.

He pulled back and gave her that lopsided smile. "Anna, I can't imagine—

A great bell rung. He dropped his hands from her waist.

"Did you hear that?" he asked.

Anna shrugged. It was the chapel bell. She tugged his hand back to her. *What was he going to say?* "What?" She felt like she was in a dream.

Jack gently pushed her back and tilted his head, listening. "That ringing. There it goes again."

Anna blinked. A great bell was ringing haphazardly, instead of in a rhythm or a melody. Anna had never heard it ring like that.

"That's the warning bell!" Jack raced to the window and

peered up at the castle. "There's fighting." He spun, reaching for his sword. "I need a horse."

"We'll take Farley," said Anna. She threw his bridle on and led the great horse out into the aisle. Without a thought, she threw her foot into the stirrup and leaped on. "Come on, behind me!" As Jack swung up, Farley sprung forward, crashing into the barn door on the way out.

"Easy, boy!" Anna called. "Hang on!" she shouted as the horse raced up the incline toward the castle. She had forgotten how fast he was. He spent so much of his stride suspended in the air he was difficult to steer. Anna pulled him hard to the left. The drawbridge was still down, but the gatekeepers were fighting for their lives. Two Sunderland men fell into the river. Slowly, the bridge began to ascend. She pulled Farley to a sliding halt in front of the bridge.

"No!" shouted Anna. Without another thought, she swung her left leg over Farley's head and jumped to the ground. Farley reared and threw Jack off balance. He lunged for the reins while Anna ran for the bridge. She had to make it to her father. *They can't find the weapons.*

"Anna, stop!" yelled Jack.

"Come on!" she yelled back as she ran. She could sense him behind her. The bridge surged upward. Anna jumped. Her fingers barely caught the end of the bridge as it sprung up higher. She felt Jack's fingers brush her heel and heard him yelling for her to drop, but something deep inside drove her to hang on. *Jack hadn't made it.* She hesitated one second and then heaved herself over and slid down the steep descent on the other side. He couldn't follow. She'd left him.

Chapter 21

Right as Anna hit the ground an arrow whizzed by her ear and stuck in the bridge behind her head. She bolted, dashing away from the bridge to a stairwell leading up to her room where her jeweled weapons were hidden. She made it to the top of the stairs and heard screaming. Several women shrieked as they fled hooded men with swords. One man shoved a woman down the stairs and ran another direction with the others following. *Arissa.* Anna pulled her up by the arm.

"With me, now!" The path looked clear as they raced back up the stairs—right into an enemy soldier.

"You!" He lurched for her. "Lead us to the king!"

Anna's mind raced. A knife handle flashed in his belt. She snatched it and struck him in the neck as hard as she could. His eyes widened in surprise before he dropped. Arissa screamed. Anna grabbed his sword and ran down the stairs with other soldiers close behind. Anna's blood roared in her ears. *Did I just kill a man?*

Anna darted through the castle's labyrinth halls, tugging Arissa behind her. The stench of death pushed her to run faster. The men were close behind, but they didn't know the castle like she did. She ducked into a narrow passageway which dumped out into screaming crowds of servants, pulling Arissa with her. The weeping girl was slowing her down, but where would she be safe? Anna could almost smell her fear. The grunts and roars of the battle pounded in her ears and drowned out her pounding heart and rasping breath. The other staircase was close. She raced up and cut back through the corridor to her room, jerking Arissa along behind her. She threw the door open and tossed the soldier's sword on the bed.

"Take this!" she spat at Arissa.

She pulled the gemmed sword out of hiding and strapped it to her side. Her fingers shook as she strung the bow and swung the quiver over her shoulder.

"What are you doing?" Arissa screeched.

"Hush! Either hide somewhere or stay with me. But you have to keep up. I'm going to the throne room." She thought about what her father had said about the use of these weapons. Well, if this weren't dire need, she didn't know what was. They were looking for the king. She ducked down as she heard soldiers running through the hall.

"To the throne room!"

Seamus.

She glanced back at Arissa. She couldn't just leave her. Seamus would send someone to search her room.

"Arissa! They will find you here. You need to come with me." The girl nodded through her tears. Anna paused for precious seconds. "Take a deep breath. You can do this. Stay behind me." She glanced at her dress. "And pick up your skirt when you run." With a sudden burst of anger, Anna sprinted out the door. *Time to see how these gems work.* She would protect her father. Two brut enemy soldiers charged down the hall toward them.

"We have the princess!" That was the last word one of them spoke, as a golden arrow pierced his chest. The other soldier lunged for her and also was met with an arrow at close range. He sank to the floor. Anna retrieved her arrows and bolted down the hall. Arissa whimpered behind her. They ducked into a drawing room. The soldiers passed by.

"They've bolted the throne room door!" They shouted. "Get the battering ram!"

Anna realized she could not make it in with her father now. *We need help.*

At once, she remembered the beacons. Light the beacons, and Prince Lewis from the north would give them aid. That was the treaty. His kingdom was known for its swift horses, but once notified, it would still take him at least two days to arrive.

If Father is killed and Anwar's troops attack, it might be our only chance.

Anna had to try.

The beacons were on the roof of the west side of the castle. She had no way of knowing whether the beacon guards were alive.

They ducked down a passage into another room and hurried up a dark, narrow, winding staircase. It was a treacherous climb. One missed step and they'd tumble to the bottom of the dungeons.

They finally reached the top.

"Stay here and keep quiet," Anna whispered to Arissa. "If I don't come back, stay here until the castle is still." She pointed to a tiny cubby below the crack of a window.

I'll be right back.

The small, wooden door creaked open into a tiny room at the top of the west tower. She only had to slip outside and travel down a covered stone hall to get to the beacon. Anna knew it hadn't been lit for a lifetime. She hoped the oil was prepared.

She crept a short way toward the beacon and stopped to listen. Her heart pounded in her ears, drowning out the sounds of clashing metal from the fighting below. She put her sword in its sheath and snatched a torch off the wall. The beacon was perhaps forty steps away. She could surely make it now. She hunched down below the banister so she could not be seen from below, blinking as the heat from the torch reached her face. The beacon sat atop a large stone platform with a huge metal bowl of oil inside. On she crept toward the goal. Suddenly a man jumped from beside the beacon and drew his sword.

"Intruder!" he shouted.

Anna fought the desire to run. Dropping the torch, she drew a golden arrow from her quiver. She released quickly, and the man fell in his tracks. She pulled the bloody arrow from his chest and sent it flying into the next enemy. She paused for a second, hand on another arrow. Biting her lip, she grabbed the torch again and dashed for the beacon. At the last second, she saw a form leap from the side of the platform—right at her. Anna just had time to dart to the other side, his sword slashing across one of her thighs. Pain flashed through her as she fell to the ground, and her fingers closed around the burning torch. She lunged forward and tossed it into the beacon. *Whoosh!* The fire was ablaze. The man paused and then bore down on Anna in full fury. A beacon on top of the mountain above answered. Within minutes, the northern kingdoms would know of their peril.

"No!" the man yelled, raising his sword. Anna rolled to the side. Then, without thinking, she leapt to the wall surrounding the beacon. Her leg throbbed with every step, but she pushed on. Looking down, she saw a small ledge. As he charged again, she dropped off the side, landing on the ledge. Anna breathed a prayer of thanks as she saw an open window. She was about to dash through it when the sound of a great horn stopped her in her tracks. She looked up, but the man wasn't following.

The horn sounded again. A huge army was galloping through the far gates into the grounds. Stefan! She caught a brief glimpse of Farley, so Jack must be safe. The drawbridge was still up, blocking the army from coming to their aid.

Hovering outside the window, she saw many of Seamus's men surrounding the drawbridge. Two guarded the chains which raised and lowered the bridge—one on each side. Balancing herself carefully, she put an arrow to the string. She put all her weight on her good leg. Her balance wavered, but she didn't dare look down.

No, it's crazy. Those men are much too far away. Anyway, someone else would run up and stop the bridge from lowering. Anna frowned and took a deep breath. She had to try, even if it did waste an arrow. The armies must get in.

Stefan approached the drawbridge. "Open at once and fight like men!" he yelled, raising his sword. "What honor have you, sneaking in to capture our people with no battle?"

A great man yelled back, "Soon your father will be dead, and these lands will be ours!"

"We will stay and fight whether he is alive or not!" Stefan yelled back. He signaled to his soldiers. "We will wait until you rot in there or come to face us. The day you leave will be your last!" As he said this, he lowered his arm. Showers of arrows fell, landing just on the other side of the bridge. Enemies dropped, while others dashed to shelter. Anna glanced down again to see one of the gatekeepers fall. His side of the gate wavered as chaos ensued. As she peered down, the other man seemed to be tightening the chains on his side with a rope. His body blocked the rope, but then he left his post to run to the other side. Anna drew her arrow again, pointing directly at the rope. "Please, let this arrow be true," she said out loud. She aimed as best she could and released. She could hardly watch, but by some miracle, the arrow landed on the rope, splitting it in two. That side of the bridge lurched forward.

At just that moment the gatekeeper reached the other side and tried to tighten the chains. The lurch pulled the rope through his hands, throwing him toward the giant gears. He released his grip and the bridge fell to the ground with an enormous thud. Stefan's army charged into the castle with wild cheers. Somewhere in that crushing crowd of men was Jack, fighting to defend her people.

Anna limped through the window. She found herself a few stories above the main level of the castle. She thought of Arissa. *She can wait.* She had to get down to make it to the throne room. She was sure her father would open the doors and fight now. She crept into a spare bedroom and ripped up a sheet to bandage her leg. The wound wasn't deep and was already clotting.

She waited in the room as she heard invaders rush by to meet Stefan's army. When the hall seemed quiet, she ran into a small room used for maid's quarters. Her leg throbbed with each step. A few scared servant girls were cowering under their beds.

"Shh!" said Anna. "Keep still, and I'm sure you won't be found. Do not come out."

She knew this room. She had played hide-and-seek here as a child. She pulled a huge mirror back and found the secret latch. A second door opened inward, and she pulled the mirror behind her as she entered the dark passageway.

Mice and who-knows-what scampered around her feet as she rushed along with her right hand following the wall. A ramp led her gradually downward, spiraling so that she lost all sense of direction. She gulped the stale air. Luckily, the passageway was narrow, and her hand could guide her all the way. The other side occasionally opened up to a larger expanse. Anna shuddered to think about what was hiding in the dark. Just when she was beginning to doubt, she rounded a corner and spied a small door with light around the edges. Anna felt around it, cringing as spider webs covered her fingers. Finding it had no latch, she realized it had to be opened from the other side. She listened for a moment before knocking. There were no sounds of fighting, only earnest discussion. She knocked as loud as she could. There was no response. *Please, open the door, before someone else finds the passageway!*

"It's me, Anna! Please open the door!"

The door flung open and Anna threw herself through the small opening, landing on her hands and knees. She blinked in the bright light. Two of her father's guards held their swords above her neck.

"Stop!" yelled the king. "It's Anna!"

"Father!" Anna ran to him while guards barred the door.

He held her in his arms. "Are you all right?"

"Yes. Stefan's come through the drawbridge. We can fight them now. How did they get in?"

"We think through the dungeons."

"What?" she said. The river surrounded the castle on three sides. The rear of the castle was set into a mountain rising up hundreds of feet to a great cliff. It was impossible to come through the mountain.

"I never told you, but our ancestors dug an escape tunnel from the dungeons in case the castle was overcome by invaders. Only a few members of the guard and the royal family know."

Anna's mouth fell open.

"You never told me because you thought I'd sneak out," Anna said.

Her father shrugged.

"You were right. I probably would have," Anna said under her breath. "Seamus knew?"

The king nodded. "Instead of attacking from the south as planned, he led the traitors through the mountains to the tunnel."

"What is the plan?"

"Our men are dying. It's time to fight."

Chapter 22

The king paced in front of the guards with a presence and purpose Anna had never seen. "Take courage!" he shouted. "We will throw back these doors, and fight to the last man. Are you with me?"

"Yeah!" The small band of about twenty men shouted.

"Then let us defeat them!"

"Yeah!" They called again.

Anna heard metal clashing metal as men battled outside the room. A man posted high at the window shouted down. "The men are leaving the door, my lord!"

King Vilipp drew his sword. "Let us drive our enemies out!"

He was answered with another battle cry from the men in the throne room. "Anna, stay here. Don't fight but to save your life. Open the doors!" he yelled and led the charge out of the room.

Anna wasn't sure what to do. She climbed the rough stones up to the high window that overlooked the front of the castle grounds. Horses were running wild. Men lay everywhere, and the ones still up were madly fighting. The battle was a mass of bloody confusion. A noise behind her made her turn. She saw a man dragging a woman into the throne room.

Saira!

"Go, tell the king I have his daughter and unless he turns this castle over to me, I'll cut her throat!" hissed the man to his cohort. Seamus held Saira with a knife to her neck. The other man ran out of the room.

Seamus hadn't seen Anna yet. She still had her quiver on her back, but she couldn't balance and retrieve an arrow. She hovered above him. Two quick steps and a jump and she'd be down, but all he had to do to spot her was to look up. Her throat went dry.

Saira screamed and fought as he dragged her along the floor toward the throne. The noise of her echoing cries covered the sound of Anna's quick footsteps for a moment. She scrambled down and dropped to the floor.

Anna put an arrow on the string. Seamus' head snapped up.

"Coward!" Anna yelled as she drew her arrow. "You let her go, or I swear, I'll pierce you through."

Seamus threw his head back and laughed. "You! Anna! Why don't you try if you don't mind killing your sister!" He pulled Saira closer so Anna could only see his eyes and forehead over her shoulder. "Go ahead, give it your best shot. You know Saira's your father's favorite. What will he say when you've killed her? I think a little more than losing your Farley privileges, eh?"

Sweat trickled down Anna's back as adrenaline shot through her. Her eyes ached in concentration. Every muscle was ready to spring. The battle's roar quieted. All she could hear was her heart pulsing blood through her ears.

"Let her go and fight me like a man!" she roared. "You always hated me. Kill me instead. Just let her go!"

"Can't do that, so sorry," Seamus said. "I know how much worse it will be for your father to lose this one."

"Anna! Just shoot him! Don't worry about me!" yelled Saira. Seamus yanked her head back by her hair, exposing her throat.

"That's enough out of you," he said to her.

Anna's arm trembled. Pulling the tight bowstring back so long was sapping her strength. "Seamus, Stefan's army is through the bridge. Your men are dying. You cannot win. Let her go!" Anna clenched her jaw and hoped Seamus didn't notice her shaking arm. She tried to settle it down. Her shot had to be true. "Quit hiding behind a woman, coward. Come fight one!"

"You are weak. Soon your shot will be meaningless," Seamus taunted.

Anna took three steps toward him.

"Uh-uh," Seamus said thrusting his knife again under her throat. "Not too close. I don't want to do this before your father arrives."

Anna's arm was now visibly trembling. She would either have to shoot or lower her bow. She could not shoot her sister. He heard the priest's voice in her head telling her the arrows don't miss. *But what if they go through Saira to get to him? If he would only move.* At once she heard the quiet sound of an arrow releasing. Her arm felt numb. *Oh, no, had she released her arrow accidentally?* Anna's heart skipped as she watched Seamus drop to the ground, carrying Saira with him.

"*No!*" yelled Anna as she ran toward them. Saira flung herself away from him.

She's alive!

Anna glanced down at her bow. She hadn't released her arrow, yet Seamus lay gasping on the floor with Saira sprawled next to him. Behind him approached her father, bow in hand. She flew to Saira's side.

"Are you hurt?"

"No. I'm fine."

As King Vilipp embraced them, Anna heard a rasping voice behind him.

"Anna!"

Seamus was calling her.

"He doesn't deserve a word from you," her father said.

Seamus's face contorted.

"Just give me a minute. He won't hurt me," Anna said.

Her father nodded. Anna dropped to her knees beside him, keeping aware of his hands that clutched his side. She made sure no sword or knife was near. He was trying to speak. She leaned forward as he gasped. The bloodied arrow protruded out of his side.

"I—shouldn't have done—so many things," he paused, panting. "Your father was weak. I only wanted Sunderland to rise." His breathing grew ragged. "The gems. They would have made Sunderland the most prosperous, powerful kingdom ever. And then…" His eyes glazed. "I would have stopped Anwar. None of this should have happened."

Anna couldn't speak as blood pooled behind him. Her stomach turned.

He grimaced. "I should have been a father to you." His eyes pleaded with her. "It's what she would have wanted. I—am—sorry." His face blanched as his eyes closed.

"I forgive you," she whispered.

His eyes sprung open. He reached for her.

"You are like your mother after all."

His hand dropped to the floor as his head tipped to the side.

Anna stumbled back. Her chest ached at the sight of the dead man and the memory of all the terrible choices he'd made. It could have been so different.

How many will die because of it?

She stood to find her father and Saira standing behind her. The king pulled her into his arms.

"He was a tortured soul," said Saira.

Anna nodded in shock.

"I would gladly kill him a thousand times before I'd let him hurt either of you," King Vilipp said. "If only I hadn't been so blind. Thank heaven you're safe!"

"We're safe for the moment," said Anna, "but how is the battle going?" Her thoughts jolted to Stefan and Jack.

"Victory will be ours soon." He ran to get a couple men to help with Seamus' body. They strung it over the side of the castle and blew a great horn. Most of the fighting stopped as the men watched Seamus' body flop over the castle wall.

"Followers of Seamus!" yelled the king. "Look, traitors, your leader is dead! Surrender, and I might have mercy on you. Keep fighting, and you will surely die. You are outnumbered!"

A few men jumped into the river and swam downstream. A volley of arrows followed them. The remaining men surrendered. They would be marched to the dungeons.

Just then a horn blew.

"Sentry coming, sentry coming!" shouted a guard from the outer wall.

The king rushed to the castle stairs to meet the rider. Saira and Anna hurried after him.

"Thank you for not shooting me," Saira whispered. She smiled and bit her bottom lip.

"At first I thought I had." Anna held her sister close. "I was so afraid."

"So was I." Color was just beginning to creep back into her blanched face.

The rider galloped right across the drawbridge, jumping dead bodies as he went. He slid to a stop as King Vilipp burst through the castle doors.

"Sire, Anwar's next wave of armies has been spotted," shouted the rider, who jumped off his heaving, lathered horse. "They are not two days behind me."

Chapter 23

Anna's heart skipped a beat. Anwar still marched toward them. Seamus must have thought he could take the castle before Stefan arrived so her brother would gallop home to find his father dead and thousands of soldiers waiting for him to surrender. But Seamus' failure had given them the gift of time. She hoped it was enough.

Commotion burst through the castle as King Vilipp ordered battle preparations made. Oil was primed for throwing over the walls on the enemies. Soldiers were fitted in the armories and the wounded tended to.

Anna retrieved Arissa from the tower, though her wounded leg ached with every step. She found the young woman calm, quiet and more than relieved at the news that for the time being, King Vilipp had the castle in hand.

"He should send word to my father," Arissa said. "He has a large standing army."

"I'm sure that's already been done," Anna said.

Arissa nodded as they walked toward their rooms to get cleaned up. "Thank you, Anna." Her voice shook. She took a deep breath. "And, I am sorry for how we all treated you in court." Her gaze held Anna's for a moment before dropping to the floor. She was pale.

"All is forgiven." Anna gave her hand a squeeze. "Truly."

Arissa smiled. "Thank you again for saving me."

"You're welcome, of course." They stopped outside Arissa's door.

"Can I ask you a question?" Anna asked. Arissa was so perceptive.

"Anything."

"What do you think of Jack?" Anna's face flushed. "I struggle to read him sometimes."

Arissa smiled. "He's a fool for turning you down, but I suppose that's what makes him mysterious. He's obviously got eyes for you only, if that's what you are worried about."

"How do you know?"

She shrugged. "Trust me. I know." Her eyes held a twinkle of mischief. She turned the doorknob to her room. "I don't know about you, but I'm calling for a bath."

Anna shook her head. The servants would have little time for scented baths with everything else going on in the castle. A mild hum of murmurs and activity rose from the servants and soldiers alike. All were filled with urgency and anticipation. They were commanded to rest, but how many could sleep? Anna greeted the troops, offering words of encouragement.

Where was Jack?

As night fell, everyone ate a cold supper and retired to their quarters. Anna slept fitfully and paced the castle until late in the next day. Another horn sounded. Hundreds of soldiers on horseback appeared on the horizon. White turbans littered the landscape like a snowstorm moving toward them. Thousands more were on foot. Anna ran upstairs to get a better look. Teams of horses pulled catapults. Anna drew in her breath when she realized there must be hundreds of them. Laboring horses pulled wagons filled with large stones for hurling at the outer wall. It wouldn't withstand that assault for long.

Anna raced down the stairs to find her father. On the way to the throne room, she caught up with Stefan.

"Stefan, have you seen it?"

"They are at our door," he answered as he strode along. "Don't worry. We can hold them off for some time." He stopped and gently took her by the arm. "Jack told me how Seamus treated you all those years. You know you could have told me. If I thought he had tried to lay one finger on you, I would have…"

"I know," Anna interrupted, shrugging a little. "I should have told you. I was foolish to be so afraid. It seems ridiculous now, looking back."

"It wasn't your fault," said Stefan, hugging her with one arm. "Go now and rest while you can. There will be many keeping watch."

"No. I'll stay with you," she answered. "And Jack—he made it all right, then? I haven't seen him since…"

"He's fine, and Anna—" he glanced at her again. "He's an honorable man."

Her stomach leapt. "I know."

Stefan hesitated at the throne room doors as Anna stuck to his side. "Well, you might as well come along then." His brow furrowed with worry.

They walked in together and bowed before the king, who was pacing.

His gaze met Anna's. "You have brought the fury of the desert with you, I'm afraid." He reached forward and touched her shoulder. "I promise if we are granted more days together, life will be better for you here."

"It is already."

"So, Anwar comes at last," King Vilipp said to himself. "He perhaps does not know Seamus has failed. He may be surprised." He paced back across the room. "War brings grief, and I hate putting our people through it. With every man who falls, someone loses a son, a husband, a father. Many have fallen already."

Several more knights entered including, Einar, Hadrian and Nadir. Anna bit her lip when she recognized Aric, the knight they had met leaving Hemmington and drew in her breath when she realized Jack had slipped in behind him. He tipped his chin to her but didn't cross the room. Anna restrained herself from running to Jack, but she couldn't take her eyes from him. He didn't appear injured from the battle.

Other knights came in as well, but Anna didn't pay them any attention. She was reliving those last moments with Jack in the stable. Her heartbeat quickened just thinking about his touch.

"You might want to get your battle-face on, Princess," a voice said next to her, shaking her out of her daze. *Stefan.* "You're looking a little lovesick." He smirked.

Anna felt the blood rush to her face, and her stomach flipped as she snuck a last look at Jack. He was holding back a laugh.

She focused back on her father, who ordered the women and children to move underground to the back of the castle. The battle would surely be fought inside the outer wall. Men left to carry out his orders.

He then motioned all remaining in the room to a table, including Anna and Saira, who had just run in. Anna saw some narrowed eyes among the men as she found her seat.

The king began. "Men, and princesses," he said turning to Anna and Saira. "Anwar has us greatly outnumbered. What is our strategy?"

"No one has ever taken this castle down," said Einar. "No number of men can go against us here, as long as they don't come through the mountain," he quickly added.

"Yes, well, the mountain escape is closed," said the king. "We will have no more visitors from that door. If necessary, our women and children will use it for escape."

"Anna?" His eyes traveled over the glimmering sword, shield and bow.

"Yes, Father?"

"If it comes to that, you will lead them through the mountain, north into southern Durham. King Edward will welcome you, if he and Prince Lewis don't come in response to the beacons."

"We have food stores for many months here," Einar added. "We could hold them out."

"Did you see those catapults?" asked Hadrian. "He hasn't come all this way to leave us standing. He'll fight to the death."

Anna silently agreed. The proud Anwar wouldn't just give up once he discovered Seamus had failed.

"I say we fight head-on." Stefan stood. "We can't have this king ransacking the countryside and killing our peasants while we stay here. Besides, Prince Lewis will come."

"I know he will come," said Saira carefully. "He has told us many times to light the beacons at the first sign of trouble. Even now I bet he is through most of the mountains."

Stefan nodded. "My sister is right. The beacons were lit yesterday around what time, does anyone know? We'd like to know when we can expect Lewis."

It seemed no one quite remembered, as most of the men were with Stefan when it happened.

"Does no one know?" asked Stefan. "Father, when did you give the order?"

Everyone knew the king was the only one who could give permission to light the beacons. King Vilipp cleared his throat, but Anna interrupted.

"It was within the first couple of hours after Seamus arrived," Anna said.

"How do you know, Your Highness?" asked Sir Einar, looking down his nose at her. Everyone turned.

"Because I lit the first one myself."

"What?" Her father gasped. "It would have been guarded."

243

"Anna is an excellent shot," said Jack.

"But without your father's permission?" stormed Einar. "How dare you?"

"I beg your pardon." Anna sat up straighter. "At that point, we had no army, our people were dying, and the king was locked in the throne room. We needed help."

"That wasn't your call to make!" Einar's face grew red.

"Peace, Einar. Let's not quarrel over things that don't matter now." The king winked at Anna. "I applaud Anna's courage," he said. "I could have been dead or captured for all she knew, and the crown prince wasn't here to take charge. She did what she thought was best."

Anna couldn't believe her father was sticking up for her. Her eyes locked on his.

"So," he continued, "we can conclude Prince Lewis will be here sometime this evening or perhaps tomorrow, depending on how long it took him to gather his troops. In any case, we must again prepare to fight. We will wait for them to strike first."

Jack spoke up. "Anwar must have a weakness," he said. "We must discover it if we're to defeat him."

"His weakness is his arrogance," said Anna.

"Then we draw him in and trap him," said Stefan. "Let him come through the wall. Let him see us retreat. Then we'll attack from this side as Prince Lewis surrounds from behind. He can't know Lewis is coming."

THE TIRED MEN WAITED. They sharpened their swords and cleaned their armor. Wounded knights and men filled almost every room of the castle. Women and children huddled together, sipping small bowls of broth or porridge. Anna had her leg properly cared for.

And the enemy gathered outside the wall.

Night fell, and still there was no attack. Everyone in the castle braced for the horn, the battle cry or the first rock to strike the castle wall. *Anwar must not know that the longer he waits, the closer Prince Lewis comes.* Every eye was on the enemy, gathering its strength. Soon hundreds of fires ignited just outside the wall, and the rising smoke cast eerie shadows from the huge numbers of attackers camped so near.

Anna returned to caring for the wounded. As she finished wrapping a man's wounded arm, she felt a tap on the shoulder. Jack. She jumped up into his arms. He caught her and gently pushed her hands down.

"I was so anxious to see you," Anna locked her hands behind her.

"I came to tell you about Farley," Jack said. "I lost track of him. He bolted during the battle. But he's smart. He'll find his way back to the barn."

Anna bit her lip. She hoped he wasn't hurt, but compared to the dying men, she knew she shouldn't worry about the horse. She pictured him in the barn aisle now.

"He'll take care of himself. I wondered how you two got along. You rode him all the way to Stefan?"

"Yes. Once I saw I couldn't reach you, I wanted to let Stefan know what was going on in the castle. I think Farley finally had his fill of galloping. You run him for four hours straight, and he settles right down." Jack chuckled. "Maybe when this is all over, I can help you work with him a bit." He looked at her cautiously. "He needs a couple months of hard work. He's a fast horse and all, but wow, Anna, he's, he's—"

"Undisciplined?"

"To say the least."

Anna nodded. "If that horse ever shows up again you can train him however you want. But he is hot-blooded."

"Well, I'm not that great at taming wild things." His voice had an edge to it.

Anna raised her eyebrows in question and followed him to a quiet corner.

Jack ran his fingers through his hair. "How could you do that to me?" His words were clipped as he scowled at her.

Her stomach dropped. She instantly knew what he was referring to. "I thought you were with me," Anna lied.

His face grew red. "You did no such thing!" he spat. He took a step back. Anna sensed he was intentionally keeping a safe distance from her.

"I just wanted to get to Father. It was my first reaction."

"Noble, but it's a miracle you weren't killed. I can't keep you safe if you're not with me."

"So, you get to charge off into battle, but I'm always to stay behind?" Anna's voice rose. "No." She crossed her arms. "It isn't your job to keep me safe."

He waited a long moment. "It ripped my heart out. That's all." She had to strain to hear his words. "And it will always be my job to keep you safe. Seeing you go over that bridge—it killed me."

The words socked her in the stomach. She hadn't considered that. She reached for his hand.

"I'm sorry, but I came all this way to warn Father. I had to get to those weapons and help somehow. Please understand." His jaw relaxed. "And I was safe."

"You were lucky." He sighed through his nose. "But I understand. I would have done the same."

"No. You would never have left me. I am sorry." Anna stepped closer to him.

"I could never stay angry with you. All is forgiven," he said. "Just don't do it again."

"I can't help it. I'm impulsive. Plus, I had gems of power in my weapons. It was amazing," she whispered. "Those arrows don't miss."

Light flicked through his eyes. "Tell me."

They found an empty room and sat on a couch together.

She recounted her use of the bow. She hadn't used the sword yet but trusted it would be powerful in battle. Jack held her hand and grazed her knuckles with his thumb.

"Just promise me you won't go into battle." He squeezed her hand.

"I'm not planning to."

"That's not a promise."

"I have no desire to be on that bloody field." It was the truth and as good an answer as she could give.

They whispered into the night until Anna's eyes drooped. Her chin nodded into her chest.

"Come here. Rest." He stretched out his arm, and Anna curled into it. Jack leaned his head back and closed his eyes.

Anna slowly relaxed as her head rested against his warm chest. Soon she heard his soft snore. She closed her eyes and drifted off.

It was dark when she jolted awake as Jack sat up.

"I need to get to the barracks. I've been here too long." He stood.

Still sleepy, Anna grabbed a fistful of his shirt.

"Stay." She wasn't ready.

He shook his head. "I wish I could." He pulled her up and cupped his hands around the nape of her neck. His thumbs grazed her cheekbones. He ran his fingers through her hair and tilted her face toward his. Those ice-blue eyes penetrated into her soul.

Anna's mouth dropped open as he drew near. He paused as their noses touched. She closed her eyes as his lips met hers. He kissed her like it was their last kiss, pouring his feelings into her like there wasn't a certainty of more kisses to come. She leaned into him and gasped for air when they pulled apart. Yet still she clung to him.

"Save your arrows until you are at your greatest need," Jack whispered into her hair. His hands trembled on her back. "There's no guarantee our army will stand. You may have to lead the women and children through the dungeon and into the mountain. If Lewis doesn't come…"

Anna shivered. "If Lewis doesn't come, you will fight to the death. I can't bear to think of it."

"Be brave. You are stronger than you think." He took a step back and she released him.

"Be careful," was all she could manage.

He touched the end of her nose with his finger. "I'll find you when it's over."

He disappeared into the darkness, and Anna wandered to her room, but more sleep did not come. She went to the armory and found some light armor small enough for her. She might as well be prepared.

After some time, a great rumble shot Anna to her feet. She stumbled to the window. Hundreds of bouncing torches flickered in the night. With the small amount of light and confusing shadows, catapults unleashed and hurled great stones at the outer wall. The battle had begun.

Chapter 24

Again and again the terrible thuds sounded as stone crumbled. Anna watched Stefan's scant thousand men move into position. Soon arrows came flying from behind the catapults and Stefan's men put up large shields to defend themselves. Their arrows volleyed back on Anwar's men, but there was no way to tell if any hit its mark. The darkness made the battle confusing to watch. *How long until dawn?*

Suddenly a cry went out from the invaders as Stefan's men repositioned closer to the wall and took out some of those running the catapults.

Perhaps the cloak of darkness could work for our advantage. If there is a way to outsmart them, Stefan will do it.

Anna knew her father was in command with Stefan directing the men. It was a team that had worked flawlessly in the past. They had never fought together this close to home, however, and never against an enemy so strong. Anna found a clock and realized it was only an hour or so until dawn.

Time seemed suspended. Anna put her back to the wall and slid down to the floor. She heard the constant catapults, the endless whir of arrows flying and men screaming. And all she could do was sit and wait for it to end. The fighting continued as the sky turned from black to gray. Anna anxiously awaited the sun, but when it finally dawned, there were no golden rays to cheer her. Thick, gray clouds muted the light. No rain fell, but the clouds descended onto the castle, the bleak mist hiding its highest towers. Even in the gloom, Anna's spirits lifted a little, knowing every passing hour drew Prince Lewis' army closer. She could only hope.

She jumped as a great crash brought down a large section of the outer wall. Anna peeked out the window to see men with swords running over the rubble straight toward Stefan's men. The clash of metal rose and fell with the voices in the distance. They were drawing nearer to the river. Catapults continued pounding on other sections, which wouldn't last much longer. Stefan's men fought bravely but were falling, one by one. The stream of enemy through the wall was endless. *There are too many!* A great horn sounded, and the drawbridge crashed down.

"Retreat! Retreat!" rang the voice of the king. "Into the castle."

Anna touched her sword as men swarmed to the bridge. A few were shot by enemy arrows and dragged in by their comrades. Anna closed her eyes. *Where was Jack?*

As all the troops entered the castle, they quickly drew the drawbridge back up before it, too, was overwhelmed by the enemy. With the bridge doubly secured, Anna felt safe for the moment. She hoped they had done enough damage to the enemy to make up for the lives they had lost.

She left her window and ran to help any needing medical care. A few men were carried upstairs where Anna helped servants attend to their wounds. Anna scanned their faces. A part of her hoped one of them was Jack. *At least he wouldn't have been killed.*

With the army inside the castle, there was hardly room to move. Every window facing the drawbridge was covered with archers. Anna peeked outside to see if Prince Lewis had made it yet. She couldn't see far through the mist. It clung to the ground, covering the men's feet, giving the fighters the eerie appearance of floating over the earth as they moved.

Anwar's men took their time clearing away enough rubble so their horses could pull the catapults through the outer wall. Several hours passed as the enemy regrouped. Men with axes chopped through hedge rows and destroyed castle gardens. Nervous horses pulled the catapults through the debris. The catapults lined up across the river from the castle. Anna heard the jingle of the harnesses and the cracks of the whips as the horses worked to pull the enormous killing machines into position. There would be no escape once they sent those large pieces of stone sailing through the air into the castle walls. Anna had a feeling they wouldn't get far even through the mountain pass.

The castle had its own smaller catapults which were ready to be released at her father's word. Anna thought he probably wanted to drag this out as long as possible to give Lewis more time. Anna closed her eyes and prayed he was coming.

Her father would want her down with the women and children by now, but she was frozen where she was. She touched the sword fastened on her hip and glanced at the shield, bow and arrows lying close. Her weapons. With gems of power. She strapped the quiver to her back and settled in to stay a little longer. If needed, she could race downstairs fast enough.

Anwar seemed to be taking his time. A hush came over the castle. In the silence, Anna's heart pounded away the seconds. Then she heard it. The command to strike!

The first stone hit with a sickening blow. Then rock after rock flew through the air, knocking out stone and mortar. The castle shook as the larger missiles found their mark. Dust showered down from the windows. Arrows rained down on the enemy, some laced with burning oil to set the catapults on fire.

"Release!" Anna heard her father's voice ring out as they

answered with their smaller catapults. He was a balcony above her window. Anna peered out. Several of the enemy's catapults lay in pieces, but more soon moved into their place. Anna couldn't believe the size of this army.

"Release!" her father's voice rang out again, and again the enemy suffered losses. They returned fire with arrows and large stones. The castle shook at every blast. *How long will it stand against this onslaught?* Perhaps she should go to the women and try to comfort them. But Saira was there.

The moments crawled by as Anna could do nothing but watch her home get destroyed. The beautiful palace, full of gardens, fragrant fruit trees and manicured shrubs, all ruined. Of course, once the walls fell, the enemy would still have to swim the river to get the drawbridge down—no easy task, laden with armor. But the river was neither swift nor overly deep. Anwar might lose troops in the process, but if there were a large enough breech in the castle's walls, men could storm across the river and get in with ropes or ladders. Parts of the castle were beginning to crumble, and Anna stifled her panic. Anwar would keep coming and kill—or worse, enslave them all.

Anna sank to her knees and closed her eyes for a moment. *Don't despair,* she kept telling herself. A huge stone hurled through the window above her head, taking large chunks of walls with it. Dust sprayed over her. Just as she rose to flee to the dungeons, Anna heard a faint horn blow in the distance. She strained her ears and a few moments later heard it again, now more clearly and along with thundering hooves. Anna dared to peek.

Out of the dismal fog came riders on swift, armored horses of every color. At least a thousand. The lead rider carried a flag emblazoned with a red horse over a lightning bolt. The men's heads were covered with metal helmets, and they carried large shields on their arms. Many were drawing swords while others held spears. Anna presumed archers would be coming in the rear of the group. More than the sight of the men was the sound—pounding, rumbling power was headed their way.

Prince Lewis had come.

A huge cheer rang through the castle as Anwar's men turned to meet this new attack. Many dropped by a shower of arrows Stefan directed over the castle wall. Anwar's men scattered in confusion for a moment as horsemen crashed into them, mowing a path through the ground troops.

The king shouted for the drawbridge to lower and Stefan's men ran out to battle with renewed fervor. The enemy took heavy casualties. Anna sensed victory, thanks to Lewis. She heard a loud trumpet sound from Anwar's line. She grabbed her bow, trotted down the staircase and cautiously opened the front door of the castle. She saw across the drawbridge that Anwar's men had stopped fighting altogether and were in full retreat, running hard back behind the outer wall. Relief gushed through Anna.

It only lasted a second.

From behind the outer wall came a black fog, covering the horizon and now rising toward them. Fear shot up Anna's spine as she caught a foul stench like something that had been dead a long time. As she covered her nose, a gigantic black bird, twice the size of any eagle Anna had ever seen, shot straight out of the fog and high into the air. It cried a piercing bone-chilling shriek. Men cowered and covered their ears as if in pain. Anna crouched back toward the door as it shrieked again. Its cry pierced through her and at once those evil red eyes were on her. She crumpled to the ground. The bird now circled in the sky and dove toward the fallen men, crying out as it came.

Then she saw Farley. He was running right at Stefan's troops, whinnying shrilly, almost as fast as the bird flew. The black fog would catch him though he was not slowing down. He would crash right into Stefan's men. Anna had to stop him. She burst forward, darting down the castle stairs and across the drawbridge. She yelled to Farley, waving her hands in the air as he hurtled forward. Farley shifted course straight for her. He whinnied again. He was still half a minute ahead of the bird when he slid to a stop. Anna grabbed his bridle. Her shield was on her back, and now she thought to place it over the horse's ears to block the sights and sounds. She pulled his head down and covered both their heads with the shield just as the shrieking bird flew overhead. Anna wrapped her fingers through his mane and kept the shield over his head. He threw his head up, taking Anna with it. She held on as he dropped his head again. Her feet slammed into the ground.

The black fog followed the bird, swallowing the air right behind it. But it went around Anna and Farley like it had hit a giant glass bowl. Anna looked behind her, and anyone and anything that had been standing in the bird's path was now stunned or dead. Men and horses lay sprawled on the ground, silent and unmoving. In confusion, she glanced up at the bird which had flown straight up in the air. Now it circled and came in for another pass. It dove on the far side of the troops, knocking down a strip of men flat, suffocated in black mist.

"Spread out!" came Stefan's voice. "The bird is evil, find cover! Find cover!"

The panicked men rushed for the castle. Farley reared in the confusion. Anna grabbed the reins. Now the bird was aiming straight for the drawbridge, where most of the men were retreating. Prince Lewis's men were jumping off their horses and running for the castle as well.

Anna looped Farley's reins around her shoulder and drew an arrow.

Please don't kill me, Farley.

She breathed a prayer to the Most High and fired. She fired another before she was sure the first had struck and saw a red flare in the air. The bird spiraled down. But no sooner had it fallen than two more shot up from behind Anwar's line. They too streaked across the sky, and Anna shot down another one.

She was now down to one arrow. The second bird shrieked to her left, and Anna dropped it as well. Regretfully, she dropped the bow, grabbed Farley again and swung up into the saddle. *I have to stop whatever evil thing is sending these birds!* She knotted her reins in front so they wouldn't slip and sent Farley forward, holding the reins in her shield hand and drawing her sword. She'd never used it before, but it felt like an old friend.

"Go, Farley, *go!*" Her legs and voice sent the crazed horse toward the enemy. In a flash, he was at the outer wall, leaping over broken stone and rock. It would be a miracle if he didn't break a leg. The sword glowed bluish white through the black mist as Anna thrust it out over Farley's neck.

A shrieking black bird swung right at them, but Anna's shield deflected it. Farley swerved, nearly unseating Anna as they crashed forward into the black fog. Arrows bounced off the shield's invisible bubble of protection which was now projected in front of them.

Farley pinned his ears against his head. He leaned hard against the bit as he surged through the line of troops. They tried to strike them, but both the force of the horse and the strength of the shield were too strong. A few more strides and Anna saw a perfect circle of stones with Anwar chanting loudly in the middle. Men with arms dripping blood circled Anwar. She turned Farley straight for him.

Anwar was in a trance, surrounded by statues with gems for eyes, glowing blue, red and green. Black smoke came out of the statues' mouths as Anwar wailed on and on. Both his palms were cut, and blood poured from his wounds. Common ravens and crows were coming in droves from the trees, entering the smoke and shooting out as large winged devils, with red eyes shrieking and spewing a foul stench as they flew toward Stefan and King Vilipp's men. And her home.

Farley flew right into the circle, and Anna raised her sword. Before she could even jump off, fire spewed out of her sword, slicing the statues in half and setting them ablaze. Farley reared in terror, and Anna nearly set his neck on fire as it bumped the sword.

Anna jumped off, and Farley bolted to the side. Anwar jerked out of his trance, facing her with cruel, black eyes.

"You! I've seen you in my mind's eye! Kill her! Kill her!" he screamed.

But it was too late.

As Anwar's men rushed forward to attack, Anna swung her sword in an arc and blue-white fire flew out of the tip, carving a semi-circle of safety around her.

"Kill her!" Anwar's scream grew desperate. He had no weapon and had lost connection with the statues. He darted to the closest one and snatched the gems. He frantically mumbled some words, and before Anna took a step, his eyes turned blood red, even while his skin paled. His mouth opened and a black fog erupted with his words.

"I will not be denied my rightful power!" His breath came at her in a rush of dizzying stench. She pulled her shield up just in time to deflect it.

Anna tightened her grip on her sword. Her mouth was too dry to swallow.

"You will not destroy my home," she said through clenched teeth. "Go back to the desert and take your evil brood with you!"

Anwar's lips stretched into an unnatural grin.

"The gems will be mine, and the world will bow before me, starting with you—" He lifted the gems above him.

At once, Anna's knees buckled. She had an overwhelming desire to give up and bow before Anwar. She swayed, and the sword felt heavy in her hands. She glanced at the shield as it fell to the ground. What did she need that for again?

She heard voices laughing, mocking, taunting. Anwar's red eyes penetrated her mind, her body, her soul.

So glad you came.

Can't wait to maim.

Her blood's so sweet.
What a treat!

Black spots pierced her vision, and her heart thrashed in her ears. Anwar approached with a smile straight from the abyss. He drew a long dagger. Anna froze.

Please, she prayed. *Help me, Most High.*

Farley screamed behind her. The sound jolted her awake. She leapt up and raised the sword with both hands straight at Anwar.

"I will not bow before evil! This is Sunderland, you devil, ruled by King Vilipp by the will of the Most High. He will defend his own."

As she said the final words a shot of power surged through her arms. A blaze of fire billowed out of the sword, burning a hole through Anwar's torso. His face contorted into a murderous glare. He screamed in fury. A dense black cloud charged into her and then disappeared. A look of utter confusion crossed Anwar's face as he fell. His eyes closed as he hit the ground.

Anna's head swam.

Anna thrust her sword at the men watching. They slowly backed away. Then one yelled, "Grab the jewels!"

Anna backed toward the jewels and Anwar's body and again swirled the sword around her, forming a ring of protective fire. She scooped the shield up from the ground. It kept the flames at bay from her and stopped the fighters from striking her down. Anna was terrified at the numbers surrounding her. *I might not make it out of this, sword or no.* Three men charged through the flames at her. She pointed the sword at them. As they crossed the circle, they were consumed by flames erupting from the sword's tip. The other men backed off as the three shrieked to their fiery deaths. The putrid smell of burning flesh choked her. Her stomach heaved.

At once, Anna heard a hiss and raised her shield just in time to block an arrow. Soon arrows were raining on her.

How long could she last?

Then she heard a great cry from her own men. The black mist had lifted, and men were waking up. They were coming.

The arrows stopped as her enemies scrambled. Anna hid behind her shield as men fought around the fire. Within minutes, the enemies fled. Those on horseback pursued them, while the soldiers on foot routed any remaining enemies.

Stefan himself rode up on his battle charger. The ring of fire had burned low, and Anna jumped over it. He held her bow in his hand.

"By all that is holy, Anna! What do you have there?" Stefan asked, swinging down out of the saddle. Others were drawing close, curious. "I saw fire come out of it!" Anna looked down at her hand, black from heat and soot. It was still holding the sword. She looked over her shoulder at the dead men.

"It consumed them with fire." She loosened her fingers a bit and felt the tension leave her forearm. She glanced to the charred body of Anwar.

"It's just a sword, Stefan." Her voice was barely above a whisper. "A sword with gems of power. It was a gift, along with the bow."

His eyes were wide.

"Father knows and let me keep it, for just this sort of thing."

Stefan stared. "You are still full of surprises, little sister."

Anna wiped the sword on the grass and slid it into its sheath. Stefan handed her the bow.

"This is yours, too, then."

"It all happened so fast," she said, swooning, overcome by exhaustion, heat and stress. Stefan held her up. "Don't let anyone take these from me. It's important the right person owns them, or they can be used for evil."

She stumbled to where Anwar lay and scooped up the other gems.

"Anwar used these for evil. They should be destroyed." She swayed again as she stood, her body drained of energy.

"I don't understand them, nor do I want them." Stefan picked her up. "Still light as a feather, even with this armor."

"Where's Farley?"

"We'll find him."

He helped her on his horse and swung up behind her. They were met with cheers as they approached the castle.

"Is Father all right? And Jack?" she asked.

"Yes, and yes," he said. "I can't believe it, but you saved us all."

"I can't believe it either."

Chapter 25

Anna treated herself to a quick bath to rid herself of the smell of fire and death. She couldn't get the image of burning men out of her mind, and she didn't want the smell of it to be a constant reminder.

She crashed on clean sheets for a few hours and then rose to help tend the wounded along with those who were skilled in medicine. Many other women and servants were busy cleaning and wrapping wounds, preparing food and making beds for soldiers. Anna worked feverishly trying to save some and make others more comfortable. Many, she knew, would die.

Hours went by and the cries of the wounded mingled with the cries of the women as they found their loved ones wounded or worse. Anna went from room to room, bringing water, wound dressings and kind words. The parlor, library and great hall were filled with men—some lying on nothing more than a blanket on the floor. One man was sitting up as a maid wrapped his trunk with a bandage. He glanced up as she approached.

"Your Highness." His voice was quiet. He reached for her.

"Bart!" Anna gasped and kneeled next to him. "How bad is it?" The maid revealed a deep wound to his abdomen. Anna's heart stopped for a moment as she realized Bart might not live. He looked so pale as he lay back down. Anna gave him her hand.

"You are going to be fine," Anna told him, trying to sound sure of herself as tears threatened to overflow. "You are going to get through this and serve my father for many years as a royal knight."

His mouth raised into a smile as he closed his eyes.

At once Anna remembered the healing herbs the woodsman had given them for Star. Didn't they have some left over? She let Bart rest and instructed the maid to give him extra care. She left the room and searched for Jack in a panic. He would know where the herbs were. She headed for the throne room, where someone might have remembered seeing him. On the way, some men carried a wounded man across her path. She stopped to offer assistance when someone came through the door.

Jack! She raced to him and threw her arms around his neck.

"Are you all right?"

A corner of his mouth came up. "I'm fine, fine," Jack whispered into her hair.

"Thank goodness." A wave of exhaustion swept over Anna. She didn't want to do anything but lean into his chest. "There are so many wounded. So many are still dying. I can't stand it."

"Those men did not die in vain," he said. "They gave their lives to protect their people. With honor."

Anna saw blood smeared down Jack's neck onto his shoulder. "You're wounded!"

"It's not bad." He grimaced as he moved.

"I hope I didn't hurt you," Anna said.

"It was worth it." He smirked.

He took off his shirt and let Anna dress his wound. Although not overly large, his chest was solid muscle and covered with scattered scars. He was right, the wound wasn't bad, but just a few inches more toward his neck, and it could have been fatal.

Anna shook the thought from her mind. Jack didn't seem fazed.

"Are you all right?" Jack asked as he gingerly put his shirt back on.

"Just a little tired."

Jack put his arm around her. "I would think so. When I saw you ride out on Farley, I thought I'd never see you alive again." He shook his head. "You will be the death of me. You know that?"

"It wasn't me. It was like the sword did it through me," she said, a little embarrassed. "But Bart, your squire, is terribly wounded!"

Jack's face dropped. "No! Where is he? I lost track of him out there."

"I'll show you, but first, did you bring any of those healing herbs from the Black Woods?" she asked.

Jack's face lit up. "Yes. I'll go find them and show the healers how to use them."

Anna followed Jack to his room where he had packed away several pounds of the plants. Anna took the plants and boiled them into a special broth, as Jack instructed. She notified the nurses and maids and showed them how to apply the broth. For the next several hours, Anna administered the healing broth to the wounded, starting with Bart. She could only hope it would save some of the injured, especially Bart.

Later, when she raised her tired eyes to glance out the window, Anna couldn't believe the sun was beginning its descent over the castle. Her stomach growled. She had not eaten at all that day. She finally threw herself down on a sofa in a spare room, not sure she could climb the stairs to her room. Her arms, neck, back and legs all screamed for a break. She rested her head back and knew she could be asleep in minutes.

Jack followed her in, easing down next to her.

"By the way," he said quietly. "I'm proud of you."

Anna shrugged. "It wasn't me. The bow and arrows don't miss, and the sword, well, the sword had a mind of its own. I didn't strike a single man. As it turns out, I didn't need all that practice after all."

"I'm glad. I never wanted you to fight. How did you know to ride for Anwar?"

"I just knew I had to stop those birds."

"You were—no *are* amazing."

"Stop it. Anyone would have done the same in my place. You more than anyone know the real me. You had to put up with me all the way home."

"Pure torture, that was."

She punched him, and he doubled over in mock pain.

"Oh—I'm so sorry—" she began and rubbed his arm where she'd punched. He sat up and swiveled his back to her.

"Ouch—oh, now to the side—no, higher a bit."

Anna shoved him lightly. "What is wrong with you?"

He chuckled. "I thought I'd let you see the real me," he said. "Bad behavior and all. You need to know what you are in for."

"I can handle it."

"I hope so." He sat still for a moment and reached for her hand. "Because I'm not planning on letting you go, if you'll have me."

"Of course I'll have you." She squeezed his hand. She never wanted to let it go.

They talked quietly for some minutes while they shared a small meal. Anna sensed her body slowly relaxing. She felt so natural, so comfortable just sitting with Jack. His presence alone was reassurance that everything would be all right. Fatigue soon overwhelmed them both and Anna dozed against his good shoulder.

Dawn broke gray a few hours later. Anna woke up with a start, not quite remembering where she was. Jack was gone.

She quickly washed and went downstairs. All seemed quiet. Many servants who had worked all night caring for wounded soldiers were sleeping. Anna checked on a few patients and found some with dire needs. Others, however, were up and walking, or limping around.

"Did you get some rest?" said a voice behind her.

"Father!"

"I hate to admit this but thank goodness the priest gave you those weapons." He placed his hand on her shoulder. "I panicked when I saw you ride for Anwar. I thought I'd lose you all over again, but you did well, Anna."

"It was my place to do it. Nicholas said those weapons were meant for me. I was scared, but for the first time, I feel like my life makes sense. If I'd never been lost, or chased by wolves, or captured by the people in Nicholas's forest, or given the weapons in time, we'd all be dead, and Anwar would be ruling our people."

"I am so proud of you." He pulled her into an embrace.

Anna glanced up at her father, beaming down at her.

"Thanks," she said, smiling. "And I'm sorry I haven't been the perfect daughter."

"All is forgiven and forgotten. But do you know what the best part of all this has been?"

"What, Father?"

"Simply having you back."

He hugged her.

"I'm so glad to be back."

"Great thanks, of course goes to Lewis," said her father. "I don't know what would have happened if he hadn't shown up when he did."

Chapter 26

Great relief filled Anna's heart in the next days. At last, her family and people were safe. At the same time, her heart tore in two at the wails of the widows as they discovered their husbands were among the lost. Worse were the mothers.

Caring for the wounded kept her spirits up as the herbs healed many. She just wished they had more. Bart was making slow improvement, and Anna hoped against hope he would survive.

Jack thought he would. He had taken a position in Stefan's personal guard, something Anna appreciated because he would remain close to home, or at least close to Stefan. She saw Jack at meals, where he was welcomed at the royal table. Every night after dinner, Jack would invite Anna on a moonlit walk through the rubble. Though her father had assigned a few guards as escorts, they kept a polite distance behind them. She would lace her fingers through his and simply drink in being near him. His presence alone somehow steadied her. She still had nightmares about the battle.

"Do you ever forget?" Anna asked Jack one night.

He cocked his head to the side.

"Their faces." Anna gestured to her face. "Of the men I killed. I see them every night. I hear their screams in my dreams."

Jack pulled her close to his chest. She could hear his beating heart. "I see them sometimes." His voice was quiet. "But it gets easier over time." He kissed the edge of her forehead.

She inhaled his leather and saddle soap scent. She could bury herself in his arms. She would be lost without Jack.

SHE ALSO FREQUENTED the chapel these days, where the priest told her he'd never seen the flame of the Most High burn brighter. Indeed, the light from the flame on the throne seemed to fill the room. She gave her weapons to the priest for safe keeping. They were put on display behind the altar. King Vilipp saw they were bolted and locked but opened the chapel to peasant and nobleman alike. Many came to see the weapons.

Anna spoke often to Priest Tobias, asking many questions about the Most High.

"If his light means love, how can it also be a flame that kills?" she asked one day. The men she'd killed still troubled her.

"How can love be pure if it allows evil?" Tobias replied. "Ah, that is the question of the ages. The great sages answer this question by saying there cannot be love without justice."

"But he allows some evil to exist." She wrinkled her brow.

"Yes, he is ever patient with his justice. Sometimes too much so, for our taste. But if he weren't patient with the evil, he couldn't be patient with any of us. For none of us is perfect."

"But someday, everything will be made right?"

"That is our hope and belief."

Anwar's gems were even more troubling for Anna. Neither the priest nor King Vilipp wanted them in the kingdom as they had been used for such grievous evil. They proved difficult to destroy, even by burning.

In the end, Anna and Jack rode out in secret one day to dispose of them in a great lake at the edge of the kingdom. They paid a fisherman to take them to the middle of the lake. They mixed the gems in with several leather pouches of gravel and dropped them into the deep. Hopefully no one would ever find them.

Anna felt a little afraid as she watched them sink.

"Remember," Jack whispered. "It's not the gem, it's the one who uses them."

But these gems were evil. She knew it.

The next weeks ran together for Anna. The castle bustled again with people preparing food for all the soldiers, beginning repairs on the castle, and caring for the wounded.

Anna had never been happier with her family. She and Saira worked side-by-side nursing the wounded and bringing the castle kitchen back to order. Stefan didn't miss an opportunity to tease her about Jack. One day at breakfast, he pounced.

"You never cease to entertain me, sister," he said with a smile and raised eyebrows.

"Is that so?" she answered.

"The castle is wild with talk that you have found yourself a man—the same one who turned you down before."

"I don't see how this concerns you, brother." Anna took a long sip of tea to keep from smiling.

"As the future king, everything around here concerns me."

"Oh?" Anna said in mock formality. "I should think the future king should mind his own affairs and find himself a suitable future queen."

He laughed. "Why would I do that when it's so much more fun to watch you two in the courting business?" He turned to their sister. "Saira, do you know if Prince Lewis has a sister?"

"No, I don't believe he does," she answered.

"Such a pity. Now that would have been a good match." He winked.

Saira's cheeks flushed. She glared at Stefan.

"Come, on, Saira. I think the toast is a bit stale this morning." Anna stood. "Let's go."

Stefan leaned back in his chair with a satisfied grin.

"He can be insufferable!" Saira fumed.

"He's just bored," Anna said. "The battle is over. Now he can only entertain himself with teasing us." She didn't mind the teasing. Stefan would always be there for her.

The King tapped the girls to plan a victory celebration for everyone in a few days. Anna was relieved Saira took the lead and had many cattle slaughtered and huge pots of stew made in advance. Bakers prepared cakes and special breads and saved them in the cellars, along with apple pies and fresh cream. Anna became so consumed with the preparations she hardly saw Jack outside of meals, where he was uncharacteristically thoughtful. She so looked forward to the celebration where she'd be in his arms all evening.

The gardens were cleared, and tents were set up there for those who couldn't fit in the castle. The king's banners flew at every corner of the castle and flags flapped from long ropes running from the castle to the riverbank. Anna wanted every single soldier to feel special, especially those from Durham who had come so far from home to defend their country.

Finally, the feast came. Servants set up tables, opened bottles of wine and barrels of mead. Women fussed over what they would wear. Good nurse Mary took Anna by the hand and made her try on a certain light blue silk gown. Anna loved the feel of it around her shoulders and how it gathered at her waist. It fit perfectly.

"It's beautiful," she said to Mary. "Where did you find it?"

"It was your mother's," she whispered. "She would have wanted you to wear it."

Anna smiled tentatively at her reflection in the mirror.

The tailor examined the dress and decided it needed no altering. "You fill it out beautifully, my dear," he said, smiling.

That evening, the food was set on a long table in the center of the dining room, with chairs throughout the castle open for seating. The king drew as many as possible into the ballroom for an announcement before the meal began.

"Thank you all for preparing this victory celebration tonight," he began. "Our people have been preserved once more. In gratitude, we toast those who gave their lives so we might live here tonight." Everyone raised a cup with him and toasted those who were no longer among them. "We will always remember them and the sacrifice they made that we might live freely on this land."

Cheers erupted through the crowd, and King Vilipp continued.

"We also want to especially thank Prince Lewis and all his men for coming so quickly to our aid. If it had not been for him, we would certainly not be here tonight." Louder cheers roared through the castle. "Where is Lewis?" yelled the king to the crowd. He was bustled to the front where he bowed before King Vilipp. "Prince Lewis, do not bow to me, for tonight, we bow to you." The king lowered himself to one knee and the whole crowd followed.

"King Vilipp, you know it is our honor to join with you in protecting the northern kingdoms," Lewis said.

The king rose to his feet.

"Lewis, for your great deeds in aiding us, please name a gift you might take back with you." The king bowed again.

"There is only one thing I might ask for," he said. "It is the greatest jewel of your kingdom, the brightest gem, the costliest pearl," he paused.

"Name it, Lewis and it shall be yours." The king paled for a moment.

Not a gem of power?

"The treasure I would take home is nothing other than the hand of your daughter, dear king, that we may be joined more than by friendship, but by family as well."

"Ahh," said King Vilipp with a twinkle in his eye. "I have learned that the best way to accomplish that is to ask the girl yourself."

Prince Lewis looked a bit surprised. His eyes darted to Anna and then to Saira, standing next to her. Now he was walking toward them and seemed to be looking right at Anna. She scanned the crowd for Jack. *Where was he?* Not finding him, Anna glanced quickly at Saira and noticed she was glowing, no, blushing a deep pink. The crowd backed away, and so Anna retreated as well. The prince glanced at her and back to Saira with a hint of a smile. He took Saira's hand.

"Princess Saira of Sunderland," he began. The crowd was completely silent as if everyone had inhaled, waiting for the rest to come. "Many days I have longed to ask this of you. You are the light of my eyes, and tonight, I humbly ask you to join me as my wife, our princess, and someday the Queen of Durham. Will you marry me?"

Anna's heart swelled. Through welling tears, Saira choked out her answer.

"Yes!"

The happy couple embraced. Cheers roared through the ballroom. Lewis and Saira met the king on the stairs, where he embraced both of them. Lewis was most welcome as a new son-in-law. Saira couldn't have looked happier as she hugged her father. Anna couldn't wait to congratulate them. The king turned to the crowd again.

"Let the celebration begin!" he boomed. It was time to eat.

A better party had never been thrown, thought Anna as she walked through the crowds of happy, feasting people, nobility and commoners together. Later string musicians played merry dancing tunes in the main room and on the castle grounds for all those who didn't fit into the castle.

Dancing began, led by the new couple. Anna scanned the crowd for Jack to no avail. *Where was he?* She stood at the side, truly enjoying this moment for Saira, until she was tapped on the shoulder for a dance.

She laughed when she found Stefan there. He scooped her up and tossed her on one broad shoulder and ran next to his father.

"Stefan! Stop!" Anna shrieked, holding on to his head. The music paused as everyone turned to watch the sibling spectacle.

"Ouch! Mind the hair, Anna!" he said under his breath. "Don't forget Anna!" he shouted to the crowd. "My sister, Anna, slayer of Anwar, with more courage than ten men! Cheers to Anna!"

The crowd roared, "*Cheers!*" in answer three times.

"Come, everyone, dance!" he shouted as he whirled his sister down to the dance floor. When the first dance was over, another knight tapped her for a dance. She appreciated his kindness, but spent the entire dance looking over his shoulder for Jack.

Where was he? She bit her bottom lip. She had envisioned dancing the night away with Jack. *Just Jack.* Her stomach clenched, and she shoved the disappointment down.

She spun away from a young knight and spotted Jack whispering to her father.

Ahh. He's not getting out of dancing now. But she lost him again in the crowd, and when the dance was over, she decided to get some air on the small balcony overlooking what once was the garden. Her face felt flushed and her heart was heavy.

Hundreds of lights scattered out through the grounds where people were eating, drinking and dancing. *What a difference from just a few days ago!* She heard footsteps behind her.

"Anna, do you know how beautiful you are?" He swept her into his arms and kissed her lightly.

Her face warmed, and her irritation melted away. He was with her now. "You look handsome tonight." It was true.

Wearing a sharp black tunic, he was clean-shaven and smelled of soap. "Where have you been all night?"

Jack tapped his fingers against her back. "I've been here, just didn't want to be the center of attention."

She wriggled free of his arms. "What's wrong?" she asked. "I've danced with every man here except you," she added with a sly smile.

"I'm going to have to put a stop to that," he said, pulling her close again.

"Then dance with me. Please?" She pursed her lips. "Please?"

"I don't feel like dancing." He rubbed the back of his neck.

"Is your neck healing all right?"

"Oh, it isn't that." His words were rushed. "I've never been much of a dancer." He pressed his lips together.

She waited for a better explanation. Even as a young prince, he would have been schooled in the art of dancing. "I think you're going to have to prove it." She grabbed his hand and dragged him toward the floor. She knew once people started noticing them, he would have a harder time declining her.

"All right," he said under his breath. "But you are doing this at your own risk."

Anna laughed. "You're usually such a good liar. Besides, every other man here wants to dance with me," she teased, "why not you?"

"I guarantee every other man here would prefer to have you alone on the balcony."

Anna blushed a little as he put his hand on her waist and took her hand in his. He wasn't truthful when he said he wasn't much of a dancer. She'd never danced with anyone better. Smooth and graceful, he guided her with a touch on her back or a squeeze of her hand. She felt like an ice skater—spinning, twirling and gliding across the floor. He even seemed to be enjoying himself.

Finally they returned to the balcony. Jack exhaled deeply and leaned against the stone archway. She glanced up at the quarter moon just rising above the trees. The glow of the fires in the garden filled the balcony with a soft radiance. The early autumn air was still warm.

"I could dance all night long," Anna said.

"I noticed." He rolled his eyes.

"I knew you were lying. No man here can dance like you."

"Only for you."

Anna beamed. "Even with the sadness of losing so many men, this turned out to be an amazing night."

"You think?"

"Yes. I love parties as much as any other woman—the dresses, the dancing, the music—everything."

"But you're no ordinary girl."

"I'm not a boy."

"I concur with that." The corners of his mouth pulled up. He ran a hand through his hair.

"Did you even know Prince Lewis proposed to Saira?"

He nodded. "I'm sure they will be happy."

"I'll be sad to see her go. We were becoming friends," Anna said.

"You'll have time with her before the wedding," he said.

"And I've never been to Durham," she mused. "They say it's beautiful."

Jack grew quiet at the mention of Saira's engagement and an awkward silence settled between them. Anna tried to break the tension.

"Look at all those people," she said. "How different things could have been."

He stepped close to her, brushing her hand. "We made it just in time."

"You may not have been able to save your own family," she paused as she looked over the hundreds of people, "but you've saved mine and my people as well."

"They are my people now, too." His voice turned low and serious. "And besides, you were the important one."

"If you hadn't led us back here in time, all those people would have certainly died," she said.

"And if you hadn't lit the beacons, taken down the drawbridge, and oh—destroyed Anwar single-handedly, things would have been different."

"I had a good teacher."

He shook his head and chuckled.

"Are you teasing me?" Anna frowned.

"Of course not." His lips tugged up just at the corners.

"Then why the smirk?"

"I'm not smirking. I just think it's amazing how the same girl who rushes to face danger without a second thought also loves gowns and dancing." He gestured to the party.

She shrugged. "I'm odd."

"You're perfect." His voice softened. "I have something for you."

Anna looked down and saw a white gold ring in his trembling hand. It was on a chain.

"It's beautiful!" Her throat tightened. The stone, surrounded by tiny white diamonds, shone the deepest blue in the subdued light.

"This ring is the promise of our future. Wear it if you want to keep yourself for me."

Anna gasped as she absorbed its beauty. The blue stone reflected his eyes, and the diamonds shown like tiny ice crystals. *Was he proposing?*

He read the question in her eyes.

"I could marry you tomorrow and be the happiest man on earth, but we don't need to rush it. I want to make sure it's what you truly want. If you like, wear it over your heart."

Anna fingered the jewel and the chain. Her head swam as she tried to understand his words.

"It's a promise ring. I promise to save my heart for you—it's just short of engagement. And if you wear it, you'll be saved for me."

"But why not get engaged?" she asked.

"I want to make it easier on you if you change your mind about me."

"I won't. I can't imagine ever being with anyone but you." She slipped it over her head. The ring fell just level with her heart. She clasped her hand around the ring.

"Every time you feel it near your heart, you'll think of me."

Her hands went to his chest, and she slowly worked them up around his neck. Her eyes never left his.

"Thank you."

His hands slipped to her waist, and he pulled her close. She trembled as his lips brushed hers, soft at first, and then deep and intense. Anna's head spun as his lips moved to her neck. A thrill shot through her along with sensations she couldn't explain. She'd never been kissed there. Her fingers found his chest, and she pushed lightly against him. As if sensing she was about to faint, he pulled back and quickly kissed her nose. He grinned as his finger trailed down her jaw to the chain around her neck, lifting the ring off her chest. Anna glanced down and imagined it on her finger.

"It's so beautiful," Anna said again.

"It was my mother's."

"When did you get it from her?" Anna asked.

"The morning we left her castle." His lips curved upwards in that lopsided way.

"That long?" Anna laughed.

Jack grew serious. "I hope you understand about my family. You will never have what Saira is getting."

"As I've told you," said Anna. "None of that matters. Only you."

He pulled her into a close embrace again and leaned his cheek on the side of her head. "Neither of us quite fit in here, but we make a good team."

"We do."

"More dancing?" He rubbed his thumb across her knuckles.

"No, I'd rather stay here with you." She melted into him. Her heart pounded, her cheeks were flushed, and her legs wobbled beneath her. She couldn't imagine dancing right now. But she could imagine spending the rest of her life with him. She could live with this feeling—this calm, close security —forever.

His chest swelled, and she felt his exhale in her hair. "I'd like for you to ride back to my mother's with me in a few days —or when you might be ready."

"I'd like nothing more. But of course, you'd have to ask Father. He may not be keen on me leaving so soon."

"Earlier this evening I had a long discussion with your father," Jack said. "I wouldn't have given you the ring without asking him first."

"He was pleased?"

"I believe so."

"I'm more than pleased."

"Me too." He pulled her close.

"I'll never forget this night," she said, leaning against him.

Anna slipped her arm around his back. They stared at the moon together.

Anna smiled. She closed her eyes and rested her head against his shoulder. She was home.

IF YOU LOVED Gems of Fire, Check out the whole series on Amazon or keep reading for an excerpt from the next book.

Afterword

Thank you so much for reading this book! I hope you enjoyed this world and had as much fun diving into it as I did creating it. If you'd like to know more about me you can sign up for my newsletter at:

https://mailchi.mp/737d6fa20356/authordianesamson

Subscribers get a monthly newsletter that includes author news, updates on my writing world, books I recommend and often deals and fun giveaways to enter.

Also, reviews are super important for authors and future readers. If you have a minute, please leave a review at Amazon, Goodreads, Bookbub, or any other site. It's not book report, so don't sweat it, just a rating and quick sentence or comparing the book to another in its genre can be super helpful. Thank you in advance!

Anna's story has just begun. The Gems of Fire series continues with **Valley of Bones** and **Mountain of Flame**. Companion novel, **Shadow of Death**, will be available Fall

2022. Find out more at https://www.dianesamsonauthor.com or check out the series on Amazon HERE

Keep reading for a preview of *Valley of Bones!*

Left alone to rule Sunderland, Princess Anna forges an unlikely alliance and trains gem-wielding warriors to fight the coming horror and rescue Sunderland's army—if they are even alive. But first she must survive the treachery brewing in her own court.

Excerpt from Valley of Bones

The cold, round stones numbed the old man's palm as he rolled them in his right hand. He'd painstakingly selected each one, as the correct combinations were crucial. Power pulsed through his wrinkled hand as the gems bumped into one another. He opened his fingers. The garnet hummed next to the dramatic red ruby. Orange dravite sparked as it knocked against the peridot, itself a potent gem. The peridot's green hue contained life and growth, ready to remake, renew, and regrow. Deep blue sapphires flashed as if in warning.

The black jade he kept apart from the rest. Its presence was a solid weight in his pocket. Its deep, ancient darkness swirled with a hint of green. It could attach to the others, absorbing and warping their very essence into dark life. He had many black jade stones.

His hand shuddered as he rolled his thumb over the treasure that had come from the depths of the ocean, locked in a small box his grandfather had caught all those years ago in his fishing net. The colored gems caught the light and sparkled with brilliance and deep secrets, as he let them fall from one hand to another, the jewels thrumming with life. The black jade pulsed, as if slithering to reach the others.

He touched his pocket and eased his aching body onto the balcony. He stepped into the mist rising from the unusually warm sea. Cool air from the mountains behind pressed toward it, enclosing the city in a dank cloud. His gray hair hung slack against his head. He sniffed. The damp, still air kept the foul odors from drifting away. He couldn't escape the smell of the reeking, unwashed humans spilling out from the taverns, some not making it far before they vomited or relieved themselves on the way home. He turned up his nose, eyeing one man curled up at the entrance of an alley. Even his watchtower wasn't high enough to shield him from this filth. How had his city come to this?

Long ago, when he was a boy, his great city on the shores of the North Sea had shone like a star leading a weary sailor home. His people sang, danced, and feasted to the gods and goddesses of old. Those blessed days were a mere memory of the aged, along with those gods.

His eyes moved to the waves beyond the harbor as he leaned against the polished stone railing, slick with moisture. The warm currents had driven the fish too far north, and the boats came back half-full. Some fishermen risked the dangerous northern waters. A few boats never returned, including the one his son had been on.

Other fisherman had turned into pure savages and abandoned their nets for swords as they rowed out of the harbor. They'd taken to pilfering the islands surrounding them, slaughtering peaceful men and coming home with sheep, food, and women. Too many women. Young mothers took to the streets with their children and scrambled to provide for them, some selling their own bodies to survive as they wandered the streets with vacant eyes. When winter came, where would they shelter? The taverns?

The old man's hand closed around the purple sapphire.

"Give me sight, Elin, goddess of plenty. Make us strong," he called into the mist as he squeezed his eyes shut. He saw a land where the women dressed in finery. The mountains opened up to bountiful farmland. Grain and hay filled their barns, and horses raced for pleasure. Rich soil produced apples, plums, and cherries all summer. Cattle grazed and milk flowed. All kinds of cheese graced their tables, complete with grapes and crisp bread. Children drank foamy mugs of milk while their parents sipped wine.

His eyes snapped open. Here people scrounged for scraps. Even the clams were gone—every day as the tide went out, a few hopeful children would dig in the sand for a rare clam or crab and fight off a gull if they happened to find one. Sometimes, they were so hungry, they'd eat them raw.

He touched the purple stone around his neck. His eyes clouded, and he saw ships, full of beasts of men sailing for distant shores. A tear rolled down his face. The black stone called to him. If the gods of the sea had betrayed them for their lack of worship, he would save his people, by any means necessary. It was time.

He opened his closet door and brushed dust off the ancient statues. He carried them to his veranda and set them on the stone floor in a circle. Two red rubies went into the eye sockets of the god fashioned into a silver ox. Power and strength would come from him. Next, two white sapphires served as the eyes of the wolf. Swiftness and the ability to track resided there. The old man's hands shook as he lifted the next one, a small iron statue that looked like something from his nightmares. The god of war and vengeance.

"Grandfather? They've arrived." His grandson lifted his chin and met his gaze. He was not afraid.

Waiting men scuffed their feet in the hall.

"Hurry up, old man. We don't have all day." The brute pounding on his door would be his first convert.

He'd found the worst marauders and gave them the proposition of becoming an army. Instead of plundering their island neighbors, they could invade the wealthy peoples to the south. Their prosperity called to him. It was his people's time to enjoy full stomachs and lands of green.

"Come in." His keen eyes assessed the group of men and chose three. "That is all. The rest of you, come back tomorrow."

"I thought you said you wanted an army."

"I said I'd make you into an army no man can conquer. Your sons and daughters will populate the lands to the south."

"When?" The burliest man curled his lip at him. "I'm not getting any younger."

"You can be the first. Come, the rest of you wait outside."

The man's eyes widened at the sight of the statues on the veranda.

The old man lit the fire in the hearth. "This is your last chance. In exchange for your blood, the powers here will remake you into an unstoppable warrior. Faster. Stronger. Fiercer. What do you say?"

The man grinned. "Do it."

The old man sliced his arm with a flash of an old fishing knife. He dipped his finger in the blood and drew a wide circle on the floor. He motioned for the man to lie down in the center. With a toss of powdered herbs and resins in the fire, the flame bloomed into blue and purple. A sweet, calming scent floated out of the fire. The old man filled his lungs with the incense as he called to the gods of old.

Chapter 1

A jolt of power shot through Princess Anna's hand as she pulled the jeweled brush through her hair. She dropped it on her dresser like it stung. Sapphires, chrysolite, and beryl sparkled up at her, used for clear vision, good fortune, and seeing truth. She hesitated a few heartbeats until the tingling left her fingertips. The brush had been quiet all these months since the night she'd escaped Karfin. She wondered at its sudden pulse of power, but she couldn't delay.

She scooped up Saira's gift, a necklace centered with a single golden topaz, which would fill the wearer with compassion and wisdom. Sparkling common sapphires surrounded the gem of power. She'd designed it for her sister herself. Anna tightened the bow on the red velvet box as she hurried back to the reception. Halfway through dinner she remembered that she'd left the gift in her room.

Anna slipped back into the ballroom, placing her gift on top of the mound of presents on the receiving table. Music from stringed instruments drifted from the front and dancers swept around the room.

Jack arched an eyebrow her way as she slid into her seat next to him and popped a piece of cheese into her mouth. It lodged in her throat a second later when Jack asked the question. She stretched for her water glass as he patted her back. Jack wouldn't let her choke to death.

"That shocking?" His eyes sparkled like the diamonds in her sister Saira's wedding tiara. She glanced over his shoulder at the newly wedded couple waltzing in one another's arms.

"Y-you hate dancing," she coughed the words out.

"But you love it." He brushed her fingertips with his. "Come on."

Anna couldn't keep the grin from her lips as she gripped his hand. Heads turned as they moved through the crowd, still dense after watching the Landseer Cup horse race earlier that day. Anna ignored their stares. All she cared about was Jack. His touch at the small of her back was as light as an evening breeze. She stopped short at the edge of the dance floor, just to feel his warm hand push into her back for a moment. She leaned into him for a second longer before he nudged her forward.

"Anything for you," he whispered into her temple, as he pulled her against his chest.

She closed her eyes and rested her chin against his collarbone, inhaling the scent of soap mixed with lingering oiled leather. A saddle was never far from Jack. She draped her left arm around his neck and slid it down his shoulder into place. They joined hands and merged with the dance on the next beat.

His shoulder was solid beneath her fingers. Jack had always been a wiry sort of strong but exercising with the castle guard every day was filling him out with an extra layer of muscle. Jack's feet never missed a beat as they glided around the room, which wasn't surprising as he was trained to be light on his feet.

"You know you grow more beautiful every day?" he whispered before spinning her.

Anna squeezed his hand. She was seventeen now. Her birthday came last fall in an explosion of fanfare. She had stayed fit by training her young horse, Farley, for the Cup these past two months, sparring with a few of the men, and constant training with Jack. He'd taught her ways to move and strike that took advantage of her light weight, not only with her sword, but also with the dagger. She was usually drenched in sweat by the end of it. All with the blessing of her father.

"If you're going to be Sunderland's Defender, you might as well train for it." Her father had said. "You might not always have those gems around." His confidence in her was empowering. Her life was finally coming together. She couldn't resist smiling up at Jack.

Jack reeled her in. "Let me know when you've had enough."

Anna raised an eyebrow. "Not even close."

She glanced over Jack's shoulder and caught Bart dancing with Gavriella.

"I didn't know Bart danced." The former stable boy and squire was a guard now.

They spun around, and Jack glanced his way. "He's doing well."

"Did you teach him that, too?"

Jack laughed. "Hardly. I left that to Gavriella."

Gavriella contrasted Bart's hulking frame and sharp focus with her petite body and light laughter. His large hands encircled her waist.

"How is Bart doing in your training?"

"He's a quick learner."

"The guards are training him, too."

Jack's lips were just above her ear. "If he's going to be your guard, he'll know what I know."

"But I'm always safe with you." Unless Anna's father sent him on a mission, either as a spy or an assassin. She wanted him officially transferred to other duties.

Jack spun her another turn. They floated around the dance floor while their feet skipped in time with the music. She was breathless at the feel of his touch—light and firm all at once. He leaned near her lips as the corner of his mouth pulled up into mischief. Anna's heart thumped. Jack drew back at the last second, twirling her in a long, slow movement as the last notes of the song lingered in the air.

When the musicians took a break, Anna and Jack followed the other dancers out to the balcony to catch the cool evening breeze. It had been just more than a year since the fateful day Anna was taken by traders.

Jack kissed her temple and left to get drinks. Anna ran her fingers through her hair to smooth it as the breeze tousled her locks. Her heart skipped a beat as her fingers tingled. Did her hair still hold a whisper of power from the brush? She touched the cool stone balcony. She felt nothing unusual. Perhaps her hands were just throbbing from getting bruised at the race earlier.

The music had started up again by the time Jack returned with two glasses of punch. The other dancers flocked back to the floor while Jack and Anna sauntered to the far end of the balcony. Jack downed his drink in one long gulp and leaned with his back to the railing, watching her.

Anna set her glass down and fell into his chest, half-closing her eyes. "The look on Father's face when we won the Cup. It shouldn't have mattered compared to everything else we've been through, but it still meant the world to me."

This year, King Vilipp had allowed Anna to ride in the Cup. Farley ran faster than the year before, winning by ten lengths. "I didn't even let him all the way out." Anna looked at her palms where the reins had cut into them.

"I'm proud of you." He reached down and massaged her hand, frowning at the red marks. "You should have worn gloves."

"I did." Farley had jerked the reins through her hands at the last turn like she wasn't even there. She'd pulled back all the way to the finish. No horse was even close.

"Have you thought about what's next?"

She shrugged. "A little."

"You could retire Farley and set up a farm. People would pay a fortune to breed their mares to him."

"No. Not yet, anyway." Someday, that would be perfect. She wasn't ready to give up racing him yet.

"Then why don't we take him to other kingdoms' races? Durham's festival is next month. We could make it there and back, and you could see your sister settled. Then we'd head to the west coast and south to Puledor. You wouldn't believe how beautiful it is there. Beaches, mountains, green pastures, and fast horses." The corner of his mouth quivered as he searched for her reaction.

He knew exactly how to make her happy. She grabbed his collar and pulled his mouth to hers.

When he pulled away, laughter danced in his eyes. "I take it that's a yes."

"But don't you have responsibilities here? What will Father say?"

"He'll let us go with a guard escort. And you'll have to bring a maid with you. She'd sleep in your tent and do whatever maids do."

Anna made a face. She wanted nights under the stars with Jack.

He brushed the wrinkles on her forehead with the side of his thumb. "It can't be like when we traveled together before. People would assume the worst." He smiled. "And this time, they might not be far off."

Her eyes drifted to his lips. He pulled her close and kissed her playfully.

As she kissed him back his embrace tightened, and his kiss deepened. Her hand slid to his chest. His heart knocked against his ribs beneath her fingers. Someone could walk out and find them, but he was intoxicating.

He broke off the kiss after a long moment more. "Sorry. Anyone could come out here."

"I don't care," she breathed against his neck.

Jack's eyes battled passion and duty. He glanced back toward the reception. "We should go back before we're missed."

It was the last thing Anna wanted. "One more minute." She stepped to the railing and looked out into the dark sky where faint stars twinkled. Now that Saira was married, it followed it would be their turn. A shiver of doubt crept down her back. She wanted every part of marriage with Jack except one—motherhood. She just wasn't ready, and she'd never heard of a sure way to prevent it.

These stolen moments were rare as Anna's father had assigned guards to escort the couple when they spent time alone together. He claimed it was for her reputation, and though she hated it, she admitted he was right. She should at least *appear* respectable, she supposed, even if her father had already given her permission to choose her own husband. She wanted Jack. But until she was formally betrothed, her father was guarding against all contingencies, as well as from vicious court gossip.

Jack came up behind her, trailing his lips along her jaw and just below her ear.

She closed her eyes and leaned back into him. By the gods, it was hard to be alone with him. And hard not to be.

A guard coughed and boots scuffed on the stone floor.

"We should go." Anna reached for Jack's hand at her shoulder.

Another song started up and Jack led Anna back into the ballroom.

Lady Avigail meandered across the room as Stefan, Anna's older brother and crown prince, motioned Jack over to a group of guards and soldiers.

"You look lovely tonight." Anna bobbed into a quick curtsy.

Though Anna outranked her, Lady Avigail was Jack's mother, former queen of Oclen and the kindest woman Anna knew. And she did look beautiful dressed in deep blue silk with her brunette hair piled high and sparkling diamonds in her ears. The wedding had drawn her to Karfin from Hemmington Castle on the eastern border. "How long are you staying after the wedding?"

Avigail shook her head. "That depends on whether I can get John William to come visit." She always called Jack by his proper name. "If I can't, I'll stay here a few more weeks, but I was hoping to head back soon." They watched Jack laughing with the guards.

"I'll talk to him," Anna said. "Not that he always listens."

Avigail's eyes lit up. "He listens to you the most."

She watched Jack from across the room as a group of three young ladies approached Stefan and curtsied before him, batting their eyes. *Shameless*. Jack caught Anna's gaze and winked.

"I'll speak to father," she said to Avigail. "A trip to Hemmington is just what we need."

Chapter 2

A week later, Farley's hooves sank in the soft sod as he cantered away from Hemmington Castle. Jack had indeed decided on a quick getaway to visit his mother with Anna. They'd snuck out before dawn and mounted just as the sun's first rays peaked over the horizon. Cool, crisp air rushed at Anna's cheeks as they slipped away.

"What will happen when the guards figure out we lost them?" Anna asked as they dropped down below a hill. Jack hadn't said where they were going.

"Nothing." He cocked an eyebrow. "Trust me."

Anna grinned and let Farley lengthen his stride. He tugged on the bit, sensing her excitement. She loved Karfin, but getting out of the stuffy court and away from the guards was exhilarating. Farley's muscled neck stretched forward as he galloped, snorting with every stride. He could go on like this for miles. Anna checked him again. His ears flicked back as he dropped his nose in submission.

"Easy, boy. Poor old Avery is getting run to death." Her calves burned as she kept steady pressure against Farley's side so she wouldn't get pulled forward.

Avery, Jack's chestnut mount, puffed near Anna's knee.

"Sorry!" Anna called to Jack. "He's strong this morning."

"We're close." Jack motioned to a clump of trees to the south. "Pull up over there."

Aiming for the trees, Anna slowed the horse to a trot as they reached the edge of a small wood. Her arms ached from Farley tugging on her. She would have to work with him more —or give up and just let him be a racehorse.

"Follow me."

Farley tossed his head as he trailed Avery in the cool shade along a wooded path lined with freshly cut timber and brush. Fragrant pine scent flooded the air. Farley snorted and clamped on the bit.

"How long has this trail been here?" Anna asked, her curiosity piqued.

Jack shrugged. "Not long." His shoulders were stiff.

Butterflies buzzed in Anna's stomach. Just being alone with Jack was making her crazy. And now this surprise. Farley's walk bounced into a prance. She checked him back for the hundredth time that day.

"Easy, boy." She had to calm down, at least for Farley's sake. Her every emotion transferred down the reins to the sensitive horse.

After a hundred yards, the path opened up into a small clearing of violet, yellow and white wildflowers dotting the green grass. A clear, bubbling stream flowed down from one of the small mountains bordering Sunderland on the southeast. Distant, immense white-capped mountains seemed to watch over them.

A picnic basket held down the corner of a light brown, soft-looking blanket, strewn with red rose petals. A bottle of wine bobbed in the cool stream, tied to a tree root. Anna's fingers trembled as she shoved her hair behind her ears. He'd done this for her. Anna sat still on Farley, dumbstruck.

When had he managed all this?

Jack swung down from Avery. "Come on." He reached for her with a grin.

Anna swung a leg over Farley's head and landed in Jack's arms, the reins still hanging over her shoulder.

Farley pulled back, causing both of them to stumble.

Jack laughed. "Let's get the horses watered and tied up."

Anna felt like she was in a dream as she tied Farley's rope. She floated behind Jack as he led her to the blanket where they slipped their boots off. They stared at the mountains in the distance with the light, sweet scent of roses swirling around them.

"It seems like yesterday that we came over those mountains." Anna leaned against his shoulder, her heart near bursting. Touching him without a guard in sight made her giddy. She closed her eyes in an attempt to control the rush of feelings inside her. The one thought she'd tried to keep in check entered her mind. She held onto his shirt. The rough cotton assured her this was real.

Will he propose?

Her hands broke out in a sweat just thinking of it, but as Jack pulled her close, all rational thought left her mind. His lips were on hers, and every feeling she'd tried to contain burst into that kiss. Something inside of her cracked open as they lay down, lips never parting. She had no idea how many minutes passed, but it was more than a few.

He pulled her on top of him. A tiny warning bell sounded in her mind, but she ignored it as his arms drew her closer and then rolled her over on her back. A louder bell went off as his chest pressed against hers. She pushed her palms against him.

"Jack," she whispered between kisses. "Jack, please." They should stop, but she couldn't even say the words. He pulled back.

"I don't want to—"

"Don't worry," he interrupted. "I'm in complete control." His eyes bathed her in adoration. She ran her fingers over his solid back muscles as he kissed her neck. Anna could lose herself in the security of him. He was thinking of her, always in control even while she was at his mercy.

He propped himself up on an elbow and trailed a finger down the edge of her face. "You're so beautiful."

She furrowed her eyebrows, and he touched the wrinkles between her eyes.

"What's the frown for?" he whispered.

"How can you be in such control when I'm obviously not?" Her face warmed.

He chuckled and rolled to his back. "I learned discipline in the desert."

"Oh?" *With a girl?*

"When I first arrived, I was so eager and proud of my skill with the sword and dagger. My master was not impressed." Jack sat up and stared into the mountain range.

"What happened?"

"I spent the first three months learning humility, calmness, patience. My master believed no one has any business learning what he was about to teach without exceptional self-control." He squeezed her hand. "Trust me. I learned the hard way. It's just part of me now."

Anna sat up. "Did he teach you to bury your feelings?"

"Not bury them, but to recognize, 'yes, I'm angry, but anger will not control my next action.' I control my actions. Always. Not my emotions." His jaw muscle tightened. "It means keeping calm while someone goads you to anger or refusing to panic when your best friend is in peril. It wasn't easy."

"But you do feel deeply?" Her feelings for Jack were so strong she couldn't see straight. She'd never been drunk, but this might be what it felt like. She was a little out of her mind. *Was he?*

Jack's attention snapped back to her. "I love you. Don't ever doubt it." He took her hand and kissed her knuckles. "But I'm also starving."

The mention of food sent her stomach rumbling. They shared sandwiches, apples, small cakes and drank a little of the white wine. He'd also brought a canteen for Anna as she preferred water.

After breakfast Anna lavished in the feel of him holding her close, leaning back against his chest. She closed her eyes.

"Hey." He shook her shoulder a bit. "Don't fall asleep on me."

Anna smiled. She wouldn't waste a moment of this by sleeping. "Don't tell me we have to go back." She slid into his lap and looked up at him. He played with her hair, slipping his fingers through piece by piece.

"No."

"Good." She could stay here all day with him. Her fingers brushed his shirt.

His eyes crinkled at the corners as he stared down at her. Then, in one easy motion, he took her hand and pulled her to her feet. "I want to show you something." He pointed to the mountains in the distance. "What do you think of this spot?" His lips were close to her ear. The view was breathtaking. The white-topped, tree-covered mountains rose from a green valley dotted with wildflowers and blue springs.

"It's gorgeous," she breathed.

"What would you think if we built a cottage right here? With a balcony stretching over the water. It would be small, just for you and me. No servants. We could pack all we needed and get away here when all the politics and gossip from the Karfin court gets you down."

Tears filled Anna's eyes. "It would be wonderful." *But that would mean—*

"Your brother offered me the position of Captain of the Guard."

Anna's pulse quickened. She grabbed his hands and spun to face him.

"That's wonderful! No more missions." She squeezed his hands.

Jack dropped his chin and gave her a lop-sided smile. "He did it for you as much for me. Keeping me at Karfin."

"You'll always have a place here with me." Her hand went to her necklace. He covered the ring with his hand.

"I'm counting on that." He cupped her chin. His lips fell open slightly.

She arched back and tugged on his arms.

He ran his hand along the chain holding her ring, the one he'd given her. Her throat tightened and her heart hammered like it would burst through her chest.

"Anna." His eyes sparkled.

He is proposing.

Farley snorted and pulled back on his line, whinnying when he hit the end of it. He reared and pulled.

"Farley!" they yelled in unison.

Don't ruin this, Farley.

He settled for a moment before locking his legs and snorting. Now Avery startled as well. Hoof beats approached.

Anna's heart sank.

Before she could clear her clouded head, Jack flashed his dagger out and thrust her behind him. A horse and rider appeared on the path, just a guard. They relaxed. Waves of irritation flowed off Jack that matched her own frustration.

"I apologize for interrupting, but a horse approaches from upstream." The guard, Finn, looked down as he gestured to the stream.

"How did you find us?" Anna asked.

"I let them know where we'd be in case of an emergency," Jack said.

They were keeping a safe perimeter. They probably helped him set all this up.

Faint, faltering splashes of an unsteady horse sounded. Anna and Jack tugged on their boots as a putrid smell filled the air. A horse stumbled into view with a man slumped over its neck. The bay staggered toward them, head down, wandering in its gait on swollen knees. It gave a low, strained nicker. Anna ran toward the heaving horse, right into the stream. Jack splashed in behind her. The poor thing's girth had rubbed its skin raw.

But the man was much worse. He had deep wounds running down his back as if a giant claw had swiped him head to tail. The stench of rotting flesh overwhelmed Anna's nose. The man had tied his hands into the horse's mane and then dropped out of consciousness. She gagged into her collar.

Jack gritted his teeth and checked the man, who was mumbling. Jack and Finn cut the man free and hauled him up on Finn's horse. The man's back was shredded. What could have done that?

"What did he say?" Anna asked Jack as Finn started leading the horse back to the castle, the stench dissipating as he went. The man's poor horse groaned. Anna thought it might collapse. "And where in the world did he come from?"

"Oclen. I'd recognize that uniform anywhere." Jack kicked a loose rock into the creek. "He said something about beasts and war." Jack's face fell for a moment as his eyes swept over what remained of their picnic. He kissed her forehead. "I'll make it up to you, I promise." He tucked a hair behind her ear. "We should head back."

Anna's heart tumbled. Their moment was gone. She knew exactly what she would have said. *Yes.*

ORDER ***VALLEY OF BONES*** HERE
https:/www.amazon.com/dp/B08WLGFDNW

About the Author

Diane E. Samson is the author of ***Gems of Fire***, ***Valley of Bones*** and ***Mountain of Flame***. She was lucky enough to grow up on acreage just north of Kansas City, Missouri, with horses and dogs in the backyard. When she wasn't dreaming of Narnia, she was outside riding her horse, training her dog or spending time swimming at the lake. Her love of words led her to earn a degree in magazine journalism from the University of Missouri-Columbia. She subsequently worked as a reporter, editor and in public relations. After moving around the country, she has returned to the Kansas City area where she lives with her husband, children and dog. She will never be without a golden retriever.

www.dianesamsonauthor.com

www.ingramcontent.com/pod-product-compliance
Lightning Source LLC
LaVergne TN
LVHW041621060526
838200LV00040B/1384